WHITE DARKNESS

DOCTOR WHO – THE NEW ADVENTURES

Also available:

THE NEW

Doctor

WHO

ADVENTURES

WHITE DARKNESS

David A. McIntee

First published in Great Britain in 1993 by
Doctor Who Books
an imprint of Virgin Publishing Ltd
332 Ladbroke Grove
London W10 5AH

ISBN 0 426 20395 X

Cover illustration by Peter Elson
Phototypeset by Intype, London
Printed and bound in Great Britain by
Cox & Wyman Ltd, Reading, Berks

Author's Notes

Yes, I know most of you aren't reading this, but I might as well try to get value for money out of my word processor.

As a mostly historical story, this book required a lot of research, since I set out with the intention of giving Haiti and *vodoun* society a fairer representation than is usual in fiction. Since the historicals were always supposed to be educational, therefore, I thought I'd best mention a few of those sources, should any of you be further interested in the subject. The first and main reference was Wade Davis's *Serpent And The Rainbow* (forget the film of the same name). Also useful was 'Bare Feet and Burros of Haiti' in the 1944 collection of *National Geographic* (single volume), and another feature in Volume 2 of the two-part 1934 collection in October. Minor details were also gleaned from the Encyclopaedia Americana, and the BBC Chronicle programme 'Black Napoleon', which was conveniently repeated one afternoon while I was writing this book.

Although this research has been done, in order to fit the timescale of the story and prevent the TARDIS crew from having to remain in Haiti for weeks, some facts about the actual timing and strategy of the revolution and American landing have been tweaked, adjusted, or thrown out the window altogether in the name of dramatic licence . . .

This brings us on to a small matter of spelling. Throughout the book, you might notice Voodoo usually spelled as *vodoun*, and zombie usually spelled as *zombi*. This is because these are the correct Haitian spellings, and so have been used in the narrative or when the words are spoken by someone who knows this fact, such as the

Doctor. When referred to by one who doesn't know the difference, the more common spelling is used.

Acknowledgements now, and thanks are due to the following: Peter Darvill-Evans for commissioning the thing in the first place, and being so useful throughout its creation; Kerri Sharp at Virgin for also being so useful throughout the writing process; Peter Elson for doing such a neat cover; anyone else at Virgin whose name I've forgotten or don't know, but who was involved in the book's production; and the staff at Stirling Central Library, who let me dig through all those ancient *National Geographics* dating back to the thirties.

Finally, I've been warned that I'd better mention Derek, Andrew, Richard, wee Gary, and the rest of the Falkirk & Stirling Federation, who all wanted to be written into the book. Sorry guys, but this mention's the closest you're going to get.

Cities lay in ruins, smothered in acrid smoke which was a kiss of death to any who ventured into its softly enveloping embrace. Between the great mountainous cities, flashes of light and peals of rolling thunder marked the creation of new and terrible valleys.

None ventured out into those wastes, lest the rebellious servants who had been driven there should attack. While the last remnants of civilization fretted behind their metallically-glazed walls, the slave caste were the ever-multiplying rulers of the wastelands between. Little else lived out there – the reptile men had long since departed from the face of the world. The Star People had been the first to feel the wrath of their genetically engineered servitors, most of the others had returned to the stars – no one knew what had become of them. Even the augmented apes had taken any chance to bury themselves in the deepest caves they could find.

Only the Great Ones were left, virtually under siege from the unarmed predators who hunted with one huge fang and the touch of decay.

The Great Ones had held out for centuries in their war, but the destructive power of the weapons used had affected the very bones of the planet. They could tell that earthquake, fire and flood would soon follow. The only recourse that could be seen was a retreat to the deepest, darkest places in the heart of the world. As the time drew near, the parts of the great multi-lobed brains which could sleep gently drifted into a state of suspended animation. Those parts of the mind which could follow the magnetic fields of the world, soar along the solar winds, and even travel the Time Winds themselves, did so.

At the last suitable conjunction of these intangible forces of time and space, the Great Ones left their former lives, drifting through the vortex to seek new experiences as they waited until the time when they could return to their true forms. But the return could not simply be whenever the planet's biosphere had recovered. For one thing, they would need assistance after being gone so long.

Secondly, they could only return when the stars were right.

Aeons passed . . .

Prologue: 1750

On a small backwater world amidst an infinity of stars, a child's eyes stared in trepidation at a small gap in the wood that had been his sky for weeks. Oblivious to the stench and the peculiar metallic rattle that surrounded his people, their dark skins blending into the shadows of the unlit hold, little Nkome – rechristened Gilles by those who couldn't pronounce his given name, and who were too aware of its barbaric nature to try – stared out at the thin strip of cloudy sky he could see. The darkest of clouds roiled there, harbingers of a terrible storm. Some part of his consciousness knew that the others could sense it also, though they couldn't see the approaching dark.

At the first sickening drop in the uneven ocean, a collective sound of cry and moan swelled the air. Nkome – Gilles – could sense, however, a sort of area of silence, something he couldn't have explained how he recognized. Turning briefly from the storm, he looked across the rat-infested hold, and saw a single figure sitting as calmly as any herder watching his beasts. A notably aging stick-figure, he was known to Gilles only as the *Egbo-Obong* – the Leopard Chief. The others had kept away from him, but – though he had no idea what a Leopard Chief was, or what he was getting into – Gilles had occasionally listened to this strangely disconcerting man as he told Gilles stories of the ancients, and taught him . . . things. Peculiarly, Gilles couldn't remember what they were, but put it down to the distraction of the storm. As if aware of Gilles's observation and thoughts, the *Egbo-Obong* glanced at him, and smiled reassuringly.

Outside, the small fleet of wide-hulled ships lurched and fell sickeningly as if on some eternal rollercoaster.

3

The sea had developed a huge swell, driven on by almost solid winds and stinging rain. Thunder echoed above like the roaring of the gods, and lightning blazed momentarily across the seething sky.

Several of the pasty-faced crew were hurled into the heaving waves, which crashed down on to the decks with enough weight and force to stun, or break ill-positioned limbs. Despite all efforts, this one ship, upon which Gilles was travelling, began to slip off course. The crew estimated that they were close to their destination, but in such darkness and with no lights on shore, it was impossible to be certain.

This time, when the lightning flared, it was reflected, or perhaps echoed, in the seas.

The next huge wave snapped the mainmast like a twig and brought it crashing down through the deck, driving lethally into the hold. Screams rose amidst the bloody wood, but were drowned out by the thunderous roar outside. Since the others of his family had died during the journey, Gilles's first thought was for the old Leopard Chief. Even as he recognized one of the screams for his own, he was rushing to where he had last seen the old man; clambering over a mixture of things solid and sticky, he was glad it was too dark to see properly. Another wave came then, accompanied by a mocking peal of thunder. This wave blew apart the weakened edges of the wound left by the mast, and a steely wall of water blasted into the crowded hold.

The last thing Gilles's terror-widened eyes saw before he was slammed into the hull was the old man still sitting calmly, watching him with a slight smile . . .

Struck by several massive hammerblows of water, the struggling ship snapped in the water, as opposing high-pressure waves tore at its frame from several sides. Finally, the waves succeeded in ripping the fragile oak apart, hurling sections of decking far into the dark corners of the storm where the sea and sky boiled together.

In a tormenting irony, a jagged sheet of lightning illuminated the shores of Hispaniola just at the edge of vision.

When the lightning died, along with the last screams, the faintest echo of an answering luminescence became briefly visible deep in the heart of the black waters.

Chapter One

An acrid tang of rotten foodstuffs was clearly noticeable, drifting up the rusted hull plating from the spreading collection of garbage which had just been tipped over the side of the ship to speckle the glassy waters. Leutnant Katze idly tossed his half-burnt cigarette into the middle of the floating scraps and, lifting his nightglasses, turned his attention to scanning the distant island coastline. Lulled by the rhythmic thrumming of the heavy diesels deep in the ship, he assured himself that there was no sign of activity ashore.

Satisfied, he switched his attention to the mercifully calm sea, watching for a tell-tale disturbance of the gentle waves. Katze grimaced at the sensory overload he was receiving; he had a certain dislike of being a sailor, though he was careful never to let it show. It was not that he was prone to seasickness, merely that he was irritated by the constant rumblings of the engine, the endless sweltering weather, and the smell of the brine itself; not to mention the stale stench of the crew. No one knew, fortunately for him, that the only reason he had chosen to serve in the navy was to avoid being sent to the trenches, which he felt would have been intolerable for someone of his comfortable upbringing. Sighing, he wished he were back in the Black Forest, where at least it wasn't so unbearably warm at nights.

Under the unblinking stare of the moon, whose maria were particularly distinct that night – giving it the appearance of a gleaming skull glaring down on the mortals below – a battered Model T Ford ground slowly to a halt at the side of a dirt road. A few feet to either side, the undergrowth began its climb up to the low trees above. A man, his white linen suit stained by its time in the tropics, climbed out and moved to examine the engine. He was sure it must be the engine since, after all, he had just filled the tank that very day. Poking about in it, he failed to find anything wrong. Perhaps that was because it wasn't really bright enough to see . . . He didn't convince himself; the simple engine was ably illuminated by the moon. Nervously, he glanced about himself, worriedly recalling the warnings in town about travelling the country at night, especially on foot. Still, it seemed he had no choice.

Pulling a briefcase from the car and cuffing it to his wrist, he set off down the road, continuing his constant anxious glances at the surrounding countryside.

Silvery moonlight illuminated the dusty floor of a small village cemetery, bestowing upon it an appearance very similar to that of lunar soil itself. The cemetery was merely a collection of crudely fashioned wooden crosses or scratchily carved stones, all of which sprouted from the lifeless stony ground at tired angles. The moonlight cast a sharply contrasting light which made the shadows deeper and more clean-edged than they might otherwise have been. As everywhere else on the island, a constant sound of drumming pervaded the warm night air. Gradually, one particular piece of rhythm grew louder, insinuating its way through the surrounding vegetation with liquid ease and sending small lizards scampering off the stones into their hollowed lairs. A jarring yet peculiarly persuasive rhythm, it was accompanied by the appearance of a double row of eerie lights, which soon resolved themselves into flambeaux torches.

The torches were carried by perhaps a dozen shabbily dressed men and women in the midst of a larger group, some of whom carried the drums with which they beat the cadence which drove the walkers on in irregular, spasmodic movements. In the centre of the group, four men carried a coffin, on which was mounted a battered top

7

hat, with feathers sprouting jauntily from a band around it.

In a matter of minutes, they came to the stone posts and wooden arch which marked the gateway to the cemetery. Just before those bearing the coffin and torches arrived, several of the others rushed forward, chanting and scattering cornmeal and droplets of rum in a cruciform pattern across the gateway.

This done, they formed up again and entered the cemetery, followed by the rest of the group. Those bearing the torches thrust them into the ground then formed a wide circle, while the four pall-bearers put down the coffin and joined the circle along with most of the others. The drummers moved to one side and beat the drums even more insistently.

While the drums rattled out on a surprisingly shrill note quite unlike most of the background drumming, the members of the group began to dance in a strange spasmodic manner which made them seem like puppets under the control of a master other than themselves. In mere moments, several were thrusting hands into the torches, without giving any indication of feeling pain. Their skin also remained unblemished. Meanwhile, two robed priestesses had appeared and taken the arms of a youth of no more than fourteen. Accompanying them willingly, he lay down on the somewhat darker earth of the newest grave in the cemetery.

The dancers now calming slightly, though still in the grip of some internal rhythm, one man, slightly older than the rest, stepped towards the coffin, and knocked three times, then stepped back. Instantly, the coffin lid soundlessly whipped open, and a figure leapt out to dance to its own discordant rhythm. A good six-feet tall, he was solidly muscled. When he smiled at the congregation, it was the sort of smile usually associated with the bloodiest of carnivores. The grin widened on seeing the youth, at which point the figure reached back into the coffin and drew forth a machete and a calabash, which was then sliced in half and scooped out. Half of it was placed above

8

the youth's navel, while the others all danced around him, before stopping as the tall figure approached, a chicken in one hand, the machete in the other. The dancers slowed until they were swaying on the spot, while the tall figure drew back the chicken's head and slit its throat, allowing the blood to flow into the hollowed-out calabash. He then lifted the calabash, and offered it to each of the most frenzied of those present. Each of them sipped a prescribed amount.

Next, the senior of the two priestesses – in advancement, not age – left the cemetery, and the others formed an aisle along which the youth, who had stood, followed her. When they had gone, the tall figure spun delightedly over to the coffin, followed by those who had sipped at the blood. Inside the coffin were many long, sinuous forms, which could have been taken for snakes in the shifting torchlight. The tall figure drew out one for each man, and handed them over. The objects were about four-feet long and dry to the touch, while at the same time feeling oddly rubbery.

Each of the men thus equipped then ran off, scattering into the countryside, heading for all the nearby roads, while everyone else set off for their homes. In a few minutes, only the tall figure was left, emitting a low, knowing laugh. Still grinning, he turned from the gateway, and walked off into the deepest of the surrounding shadows to be swallowed up as completely as if he had sunk into a pool of ink.

Less than an hour later, a second car passed by the abandoned Ford; practically a traffic jam by Haitian standards. A few moments afterwards, it came upon a man's corpse lying in the roadside bushes. One of the two men in the car, a young man with fair hair and a broken nose, got out to examine the body. He turned it over to see the face, which was contorted abominably. Displaying no reaction to this, however, the man simply turned back to the car and called, 'It's him all right.' A few seconds were all that were required to cut the briefcase free, check its

9

contents, and return to the car, which then resumed its journey.

Inside, the young man turned to face the driver, a man in his mid-thirties, with thinning hair, thin lips, a chiselled face and hooded eyes, who was dressed in a black jacket, trousers, and a charcoal shirt. 'Major, we took an awful risk simply siphoning off his fuel and hoping for the best. It would have been better just to have ambushed him.'

'Henri said to arrange to deliver him to his people and they'd do the work. It seemed like a nice opportunity to see how effective his men are.'

' "Henri said?" Do you always do what he says?'

'When it suits me.'

Standing beside Katze, Kapitan Weber of the SMS *Raubvogel* leaned against the rail of the flying bridge, savouring the clean air now that the ship's garbage had drifted away. With them was another man, tall, ebon-skinned, and lithe. He wore a permanent smirk, which unnerved the two Germans with its peculiarly detached quality.

Weber indicated a point on the distant shoreline. 'We could have problems if our friend up there is watching this month.'

'He isn't. At your superiors' request, I have had him removed from the field.' The dark man's grin broadened.

'A shooting, Henri, or a few sticks of dynamite?' Weber asked with a faint smile of professional interest.

'Neither.' Henri tapped the side of his nose. 'The ways you *blancs* use to kill people are far too disruptive. We believe that death should always be a part of life.' The look on Weber's face at this remark was almost enough to make Henri laugh out loud, but he stopped himself, and also refrained from answering the unspoken question written on Weber's features.

Overhead, the stars wheeled.

Chapter Two

There were no stars in the space-time vortex – an imperceptible maelstrom of everything and nothing. Through it, sweeping around the minor eddies and turbulences that swirled within, came one of the few vessels capable of traversing the corridors of eternity.

The ship's captain monitored the read-outs on a large hexagonal console-unit in the centre of a large white room. His two human companions were off about their own business somewhere down in the heart of the ship, while he guided them safely through the journey. He was a short – apparently human – man in a brown jacket, checked trousers, zigzag pullover and paisley scarf. His hands gently played the controls with the finesse of a concert pianist. He smiled slightly, allowing himself some small measure of pride that he finally seemed to have got the hang of operating this antique TARDIS of his.

Satisfied, having checked the navigational read-outs, he – the Doctor – settled comfortably into an overstuffed armchair which crouched incongruously in one corner, glanced at the ormolu clock, and dug out a book to read from one pocket.

A nice tropical holiday would do them all good, he felt, and he knew just the place. He closed the book with a snap, and stood up thoughtfully. 'Tropical holiday, eh?' He glanced down at himself. 'Can't go like this, now, can I?' Smiling faintly, he disappeared through the interior door, pausing only to knock on Ace's door and call out that she'd better change as well, into something less anachronistic for the early twentieth century than her usual combat suit.

* * *

11

Lemaitre watched the stars with a kind of reserved and apprehensive eagerness. Dark, almost inky-black eyes peered up from the aged face as he searched the heavens . . . There! He saw it first from the corner of his eye, the distinctive trailing flash of a falling star.

Suddenly, another star fell with a tail of light. Then another, and another. In minutes, the whole sky above the jungle hills was filled with the flashing of falling stars, and their light was echoed in a spark that flashed in Lemaitre's dark eyes. Lowering his greying head, he turned to the French windows that led into his villa. 'Carrefour?'

'Mait,' came the respectful answer, as a tall and lean shadow detached itself from the darkness within.

'Here, take this.' He handed over a slim envelope that seemed to have appeared from nowhere. 'Give it to President Sam.'

'Yes, Mait,' the shadow answered, departing with a rich, deep chuckle. When Carrefour had gone, Lemaitre, whom his closest servants and allies were allowed to call Mait, let out a soft chuckle of his own. 'I done your bidding, Bobo,' he murmured, 'but now . . .'

The stars fell over a wide area of sea and land, visible from all over the island as they burnt up. They were seen from the overgrown mountainous country at the eastern border; by squid fishermen in Gonave Gulf; from the scrublands along the hillsides and the fields of sisal and cane nearer the coastline. They were seen by those who lurked in the jungle-like undergrowth that covered the mainland area between the capital and the northern peninsula. They were even seen by those who were sufficiently unoccupied in Port-au-Prince itself, where mansions decked in bougainvillea neighboured tin shacks.

Accompanied by the heartbeat drumming from the mist-shrouded hollows inland, the stars fell over Haiti.

They were not alone.

Vincent sat on the crate that served as a porch outside

his dilapidated house in the northern part of Port-au-Prince, pulling from a plain bottle of Clairin, the local spiced rum. No one could recall Vincent's surname, if ever he had one, not even Dumarsais Leclerc, with whom he was drinking.

They were both old men, old enough to recall times before even Lincoln's recognition of Haiti's independence. Though Vincent's home was a rough wooden shack with a leaky tin roof, sitting in a small allotment, times were such that he could afford to pay for a servant to do those elements of his work that he was no longer able to perform himself. It wasn't that Vincent was rich – far from it – but that his servant was so much poorer than even he was. He didn't feel any bitterness, mind you, since he didn't miss what he'd never experienced, and at least the well-cared-for plants added a touch of vibrant living colour which pleased him.

He passed the rum back to Dumarsais, and picked up a deck of cards, dealing them out between them. 'Been a few years since the stars fell like tonight, eh?'

'Yeah, mon. Last time was just before Lecomte blew up the palace.'

'And forgot to get out first.'

Cards moved.

'Well, he was always afeared – one card – and rightly so.'

'Ah, come on now, you going to tell me the Secte Rouge was scaring him?'

'Shh, don't say the name so loud.'

'Hey.' Vincent laid his cards face down. 'You afraid of jumbies, or what?'

'Where you been? Didn't you see that woman last year – What was that?'

'What was what?'

'That sound. Like a howling noise.'

'It's probably all that rum you've been – ' Vincent stopped. He could hear something: a sort of raucous groaning howl, which seemed to be coming – along with a blazing light – from the other side of a particularly large clump of bougainvillea. With admirable calmness, Vincent gathered up the cards and the rum. 'What say we play inside, eh?'

'Good idea.'

Nearby, amidst the brightly coloured flowers, a large blue box sat. A lamp on top flashed briefly and then went dark, while a dim light glowed behind frosted windows, set under the sign reading 'POLICE public call BOX.'

Inside the TARDIS, two women had entered the console room. Bernice Summerfield – Benny – was a tall and striking woman with cropped hair, newly released from its dreadlocks, wearing a multi-pocketed safari jacket over khaki trousers. Ace, on the other hand, was shorter, though no less striking, and wore a pair of black trousers tucked into knee-length boots and a silver waistcoat over a black silk shirt, the whole ensemble topped off with a suitably cool floor-length black duster-style coat about which several grenades could be secreted. She also wore a disgruntled expression at having had to change. A blaster was held in a low-slung holster, while a knife-handle was barely visible protruding from the top of one boot. A slim rectangle of toughened kevlar was strapped to her left forearm.

They entered to find no sign of the Doctor.

'Do you think he's gone out already?' Benny asked.

'I doubt it. We'd have heard the doors.' Ace went over to the interior door. 'Doctor,' she called, 'we've landed somewhere.'

'Be there in a minute,' came the distant shout.

The Doctor, in fact, was tugging at the sleeves of his new jacket, to try and straighten them out a bit. Satisfied, he nodded to himself in the mirror of the TARDIS's wardrobe, and turned to the door. He stopped at the umbrella stand beside the door, and examined a couple of the occupants. 'Too garish,' he muttered of a large multicoloured brolly, before twirling a small lace version. 'Victoria's, eh? I think I'll stick with the old one,' he said, returning the parasol to the stand, and hefting a black umbrella with a red question-mark-shaped handle. Before he took another step, however, his attention was caught by a weight in one of the jacket's pockets. Puzzled, he pulled out the weight, which turned out to be a small jade brooch. Finely carved from a single piece, it took the form of a serpent coiling around a beautifully finished eagle. He looked at it for several moments, recalling the graceful lady who had given it to him – since engagement rings hadn't been invented at the time. He had kept it in his pocket for a while, until after that business with the Dalek time machine, when Ian and Barbara had decided it was time to leave him and return to their own lives. Perhaps, he thought, he had been somewhat embarrassed by the whole situation, else why had he never worn it? It was all a long time ago and, after all, the brooch was intended to be worn. Perhaps, now that he had more experience and understanding of human emotions, he could accept it as the gift it was intended to be. Determinedly, he pinned it on to his left lapel. Finally ready, he left for the console room.

He was greeted by a pair of unashamedly dumbfounded stares when he entered. Ace looked him up and down, from the battered and sagging white fedora, complete with paisley hatband, to the old two-tone cream and brown brogues he always wore. Her gaze was arrested by the glistening silk shirt and green silk cravat that broke up the plain cream-coloured field of his rather wrinkly linen suit. 'Smegging hell,' she whispered stagily, 'it's our man in Havana.'

'You nearly gave me a heart attack there, Doctor,' Benny added. 'I thought Peter Lorre had just come back from the dead.'

'We're in Key West, actually,' the Doctor said, glaring at them. 'I thought we'd drop in on old Ernie and have a chat. Besides, that's fine talk coming from the twin sisters of Lee van Cleef and Allan Quatermain,' he remarked pointedly. He stepped over to the console, and began to fiddle with the scanner controls.

'What is that?' Benny asked curiously, peering at the

brooch. 'Aztec, isn't it?' she ventured a little uncertainly, as she had only seen such things in books.

'Yes,' he replied in a strange voice. The two women looked up, and noticed that he was peering up at an almost totally black scanner screen.

Benny nodded towards the screen. 'Taking a dim view of the proceedings?'

'Very droll. Usually, even in the darkest of areas, the image translator should be able to enhance the available light enough to let us see.'

'Perhaps there's none to be had?'

'Impossible. We're in a street open to the sky.'

'Maybe the image translator's burnt out,' suggested Ace.

'Not according to the diagnostics. Unless they're malfunctioning as well, of course.' He grimaced: just when he thought he'd got this old heap the way he wanted it . . . 'Still, all we have to do is step outside.'

'Unless this is the dark side of the moon or something,' Ace muttered.

'Your trust in my abilities is underwhelming. I told you, we're on Key West in Florida, in the second decade of the twentieth century. I felt we all needed a holiday after all that corporate mayhem . . .' He trailed off, examining the read-outs more closely. 'Oh, correction, we're on a Caribbean island, same time zone. Ah well, that's close enough.' Grinning, he began to pull the door lever, but suddenly stopped, pointing an almost accusing finger at Ace's blaster. 'Leave that here,' he ordered, 'and your wrist computer. There's nothing to hack into here anyway, and they'd be dangerous anachronisms.'

She acquiesced without a fuss, and the Doctor watched her with narrowed eyes, troubled by her lack of protestation, but said nothing.

Ace followed him out, sniffing the night air happily, and wondering about the Doctor's odd glance in her direction. After all, it wasn't as if she had any grenades in her pockets or anything. Well, only the odd one or two, and that hardly counted.

Even in the middle of the night, the air was filled with the pungent aroma of exotic spices and rotting fish, while a constant drumming added colour to the sounds of the night. Half-glimpsed insects buzzed about among the bushes. Glancing up, the Doctor noted the last few meteors with an odd look. In the moonlight, he could see that several hovels were built among the shrubbery, while just downslope were a number of clapboard houses, and the occasional more solid plantation house. It was an oddly unsettling thing to see such a variety of homes mixed together.

'Weird,' came Benny's voice, causing the Doctor to start. 'I've never seen anything like this before. Mansions and hovels mixing happily, I mean.'

'Anything but happily,' Ace joined in sadly, pointing in the direction of a small stand of roadside trees at a crossroads.

The others looked round, and Benny had to squint to make out the dim sagging figures among the twisted trunks. Curved, sickle-like objects lay glistening at the feet of each one. Only human corpses could form such shapes.

The Doctor strode straight towards the three bodies. He stopped a few feet away and glanced back towards the others. 'Stay there! You don't want to see this.' Hesitantly, he approached to examine the closest body, his lips tightening bloodlessly in anger. The Doctor had seen many forms of death and horror on hundreds of worlds, but he never ceased to be sickeningly surprised at how inventive humans were at that art. He wondered why he liked them so much.

The body, like both the others, was that of a black man dressed in some kind of colonial uniform, which was torn and scratched, the insignia and accessories ripped away, the front sticky with blackening blood. A number of flies left the red feasting ground on the dead face, as the Doctor drew a pocket-knife and cut through the ropes that bound the man to the tree, allowing him to fall to the ground beside the lower jaw that had been cut and torn from his face. The others were in the same condition.

A quick examination of the body showed many bruises, though death had been through trauma and loss of blood. The pockets had been stripped of any money or valuables, but each man carried identification proclaiming him to be an infantryman in the Garde d'Haiti.

Ace had spotted a glint of metal in the bushes, and uncovered three ancient French rifles that probably dated back to the Napoleonic era. There was no sign of ammunition for them, however. Benny crouched beside her. 'Perhaps the ammunition was stolen by whoever killed them?'

'Nah, that doesn't fit. If the stiffs over there are police or army, then the killers were probably some sort of rebels; in my experience, rebels are always short of weapons, so why not take the guns as well?'

'Well, the only other explanation is that they never had ammunition for them, and that's ridiculous. I mean, there's no point in arming an army if they've no ammunition, is there?'

'No, there is that.'

'For effect.' The Doctor had returned, with some stained papers. 'We're in Haiti, probably about nineteen-fourteen or fifteen. The presidents at that time, and for several years before, were paranoid about treachery and the risk of a military coup – so they didn't dare really arm the army, except for their own personal guard.'

Benny examined the IDs carefully. 'The most recent is dated nineteen-fourteen, but the earliest is a good ten years earlier. Why do you say this can only be fourteen or fifteen?'

'Because the United States Marines invaded in nineteen-fifteen and stayed until thirty-four. I don't see any signs of the Marines, and if we were later than thirty-four, those bodies would have been in more modern uniforms.' The Doctor straightened.

Ace waved in the general direction of the bodies. 'Who

could have done that to anyone? Even on the frontier worlds after the Dalek wars, there was nothing like – '

'That type of death was a trademark of the Secte Rouge. They're undoubtedly working for the leader of whichever rebellion is in progress just now, who is – oh, I wish I still had my five-hundred year diary – er, General Bobo. That's it, General Bobo. And the president is Jean Vilbrun Guillaume Sam, who gets assassinatcd in July nineteen-fifteen.'

Benny grimaced. 'Then perhaps we'd best think about heading back to the TARDIS and leaving the island, if it's in the throes of revolution. I mean, it's not what I would have called a holiday hotspot!'

'Now,' the Doctor said, instantly on the defensive, 'I hadn't planned on arriving here, you know. Considering what the TARDIS has been through, though, I don't think a mere few hundred miles off target is much of a failure. She's got to get the hang of things again, you know, sort of build up to her full strength.'

'I'd have thought that if you can cross the galaxy, then a few hundred miles – '

'Is a hairsbreadth by comparison. I must have forgotten to account for the minute changes in the calendar – the odd few seconds here and there – which can have a notice-able effect when you take into account the speed of the Earth's rotation, the galaxy's rotation . . . It isn't like dusting cro – '

'Well, let's just get back to the TARDIS then, and take a short hop to Key West.'

'I don't think we're likely to be doing that, actually,' Ace ventured.

'Why not?' Benny thought that Ace seemed to be get-ting as reckless as the Doctor.

'Because I don't think they'll let us.' Ace nodded to some point behind the others.

'What?' The Doctor spun round, to find himself face to face with a uniformed figure holding a revolver pointed at his chest. A couple of soldiers were backing him up, while another pair recovered the bodies.

The Haitian, a scar-faced mulatto in a beribboned colonial officer's uniform, grinned. 'A most interesting conversation, indeed. I'm afraid, however, I can't let you leave in your boat quite yet.' Benny realized he must mean the TARDIS. She opened her mouth to speak, but the Doctor put a restraining hand on her arm as the officer continued, 'And I assure you, our weapons *are* loaded.'

The Presidential Palace at the western end of the city, built on the ruins of the previous fortress/palace, which had been blown to bits in 1912, was a long white building, faced with marble. Two low domes topped the squared-off ends of each wing, while a larger dome and bell-tower rose from above the colonnaded entrance. A lawn separated the palace from a low wall, beyond which were several sculpted gardens in which stood statues of Toussaint L'Ouverture and a revolutionary blowing a conch-horn. Outside those were the higher walls, fences, and guard posts.

Jean Vilbrun Guillaume Sam was the fifth president to hold office in the new palace, since, as old Vincent and Dumarsais were aware, President and former General Lecomte had perished with the old fortress.

Sam knew better than to believe that Lecomte had been blown up, though, since he had seen him murdered by agents of his successor, Tancred Auguste, while crossing the Champ de Mars after having been lured by a false message sent by Auguste. He used to recall these events with a grin, though since becoming President himself, he had become much less amused by this quaint Haitian tradition. He still allowed himself a smile at the memory of Auguste having the palace, and the President's body, blown up to disguise the true cause of death – after all, an exploding palace causing three hundred deaths wasn't at all suspicious, was it? No wonder Auguste hadn't lasted long – he'd had the brains all right, but no common sense.

Sam had no intention of suffering the same fate, and did have some common sense. For these reasons, he was already having the state of the treasury assessed, lest he should have to speedily remove to Jamaica – another quaint Haitian tradition for Presidents who managed to survive much beyond their first fiscal year.

It could have been worse, mind you. There was the case of President Simon, the goat, and the *vodoun* Mambo in 1908 . . . Ordinarily, Sam would have dismissed such tales, though some deep part of him had always believed. Today, however, that part of his mind had rushed to the fore, as his chamberlain announced that a message had come from one LeMaitre, brought by his servant, Carrefour.

Even President Sam had heard of LeMaitre, whom those in the know referred to as Mait, and knew that he was rumoured to be quite possibly the most powerful *houngan*, or *vodoun* priest, on the island. Some even said that he was not just a *houngan*, but a *bocor* – a sorcerer and practitioner of the darker rites of the Petro Gods from the Congo. People had been known to whisper of dark ceremonies stumbled upon by accident, of *jumbies* and *duppies* – the *zombis*.

Those people who claimed to have witnessed such rituals were also known to turn up in mangled pieces in fishermen's nets; the lucky ones, that is.

Sam was unnerved by the appearance of Carrefour, when the chamberlain finally showed him into the office. The well-dressed figure was one of the tallest men Sam had ever seen; he was also very thin. Rather than making him look like some sort of stick insect, however, his slimness made him very lithe. He moved like a snake that had grown legs and learned to walk.

Oddly deep eyes bored into Sam's skull from the ebony skin which had creased into a very unnerving easy smile. Sam smiled weakly in return. Carrefour coiled himself into a chair. 'Good morning, sir,' he began in a soft lilt. 'I hope I have not inconvenienced you by rousing you from your bed?' It was still a couple of hours before dawn.

'Not at all,' lied Sam, who had been advised that it would not be a good idea to refuse this audience. 'I was working tonight anyway, while it's still cool enough to concentrate.'

'Ah yes, it will be very hot today. It's going to be a beautiful day, in fact.' The grin widened.

'I was informed that you were here with a message.'

'Indeed.' An envelope appeared, apparently from the air itself. 'Mait wanted you to see this.' Carrefour handed over the message, and stood expectantly as Sam hesitantly opened it, then read it. The grin spread across Carrefour's whole face as a mixture of emotions rushed across Sam's face like scudding clouds across the face of the moon. Carrefour bent towards Sam, until their faces were inches apart. 'There's no need for a reply,' he said pleasantly.

With a dancer's grace, Carrefour unfolded himself from the chair, and slipped out of the room.

Haiti was exceptionally rich in minerals. Gold, silver, antimony, copper: all were fairly abundant nearby, while bauxite was mined in the north. Several ore silos stood by the harbourside, where foreign companies, mainly American, British and French, loaded their produce for the trip home. The French section, however, was temporarily closed down, due to the war raging on her soil in Europe.

The French office, however, was manned by a skeleton crew for maintenance and essential services. On the wall, a calendar of 1915 had just been turned to the August page.

Francois Lacombe decided to allow himself to sleep, since it would be dawn in just a few minutes. He had kept watch throughout this night, as on every other for the last week, an oil lamp above the table, and a shotgun across his knees while he filled in his journal. Fear had given him the stamina to stay awake at nights. Fear, and the not-so-distant sounds of shots and screams that had counterpointed the constant drumming for these past few weeks.

Turning back the pages, he recalled the others, who had shared this responsibility with him before. Before . . .

He recalled Claude's chubby cheerfulness, even when the heat made the job of cooking over the stove almost unbearable. Claude had been the first to go, he remembered. It was he himself who had first noted Claude's disappearance, nodding to him as he left for a walk over a week ago. When he heard the scream, he had rushed out, only to find Claude's footprints in the sand along the seafront. Prints which suddenly stopped. Francois had lit a candle after mass that night, for the safe return of Claude.

When Joseph reported seeing Claude sitting dazedly in the market, Francois rejoiced that his prayer had been answered, and threatened violence if ever that fat fool got drunk on the cooking wine again. Joseph took Antoine back to the spot where he had encountered Claude.

They never returned. The trio who were left naturally reported their trouble to the authorities, but they seemed no more than contemptuous of the Frenchmen.

Earlier tonight, the remaining three had been awakened by scraping and scratching at the door, and at the skylight. It was a hard sound of claws. Jean, as supervisor, had taken the gun and stepped out, promising to blast any mangy cur that was after their dustbins. Next, they had heard him call 'Antoine!' in relief. Then there was a scream of fright, the thuds of several heavy bodies landing on wood, a shot, and finally a hoarse cry that choked off bubblingly to the accompaniment of a wet tearing sound.

Francois and Simon intended to wait until morning to venture on to the wooden landing outside the office. Simon was obviously in shock, but Francoise was still lucid, and it would be dawn any moment. They would be safe during daylight hours.

Something moved among the beams of the roof . . .

Had he survived, Francois would have liked to know that two soldiers did indeed decide to come round and visit their compound. They got no answer to their knocks, and if either of them noticed the coppery smell from behind the board door, they didn't show any inclination to investigate.

Inside, it wasn't just ink that soaked darkly into the open pages of Francois's journal.

Chapter Three

Kapitan Reise Heinrich, of medium height, lean and scruffily unshaven, had long since stopped noticing the rank smells which permeated every corner of his cramped vessel, *U–29*. Not so Professor Victor von Stein, nor Dr Ingrid Karnstein, both of whom Heinrich felt were getting uncomfortably acid-toned when speaking to him. It was only to be expected, he supposed, since they found themselves squeezed into bunks in the galley, the only free space aboard. However, their incessant irritability was beginning to rub off on him. Even now, von Stein, a tall and cadaverous figure with thinning hair, was trailing Reise from his curtained-off cabin to the control room, complaining all the way.

'Kapitan Heinrich, you were ordered to deliver us safe and well; the least you could do to aid that is to run on the surface and let some fresh air into this mobile sewer.'

'Herr Professor, my orders were to carry you in safety. Comfort was not mentioned anywhere in the wording of those orders.' Heinrich's voice was surprisingly husky for his appearance, though it couldn't disguise his Prussian arrogance.

They emerged from the cramped passage into a chamber some fifteen feet by eight, which was dominated by the steel cylinder of the periscope. Seven people were already crammed into it, virtually hiding the controls, pipes and junctions. As if that weren't enough, the glaring von Stein had to stoop to avoid banging his head on the pipes and boxes which bulged from the curved ceiling.

'Even you,' Heinrich continued, 'must surely be aware that if we surface in daylight, we risk detection by the British. Or perhaps you really would prefer to swim the rest of the way?' As they stepped in, Dietz, the junior officer manning the hydrophone, finished scribbling readings on a piece of paper, and handed it to Heinrich with a salute. Heinrich took it with an inward grimace; the brown-haired officer was a by-the-book, heel-snapping young gun with a fanatic's eyes. He was putting in for a transfer at their next stopover – he'd probably go far, Heinrich reflected sourly.

Moving to a table-like shelf in a slightly recessed alcove, Heinrich unrolled a chart, and began making course and bearing notations, occasionally glancing at Dietz's paper. 'Is the Frau Doktor not joining in this day's complaints?' Heinrich asked conversationally.

'We've decided to take turns, Kapitan.'

Ignoring the professor's sarcastic tone, Heinrich chuckled, knowing it would irk him. 'Taking a decent military approach to your attacks, eh? Introducing a duty roster so that one of you is always fresh for the next bout of verbal sparring?' He nodded to himself with a smile. 'That's more like it; we'll make a submariner out of you yet!'

Von Stein looked in mounting disbelief at what Heinrich was doing. 'Surely you can't be planning to make an attack run while carrying passengers such as us?'

Heinrich was about to glare at him and deliver a withering put-down, but . . . His first officer glanced at von Stein's back with a barely concealed smirk, something the other crewmen – with the exception of the stiff Dietz, of course – were undoubtedly also doing. Heinrich straightened with a grin. 'I also have orders to attack and sink all enemy shipping we encounter.' He didn't add that he was already aware that Dietz's hydrophone contact was certainly not an enemy vessel. He swung away from von Stein's gaping visage to his attentive first officer. 'Leutnant Klenze, make revolutions for six knots. Hydroplanes, steer course three-one-seven.'

Grinning openly, the crew set to work.

Ensuring that his men were keeping the three *blanc*

prisoners covered, Captain Eugene Petion returned to his private musings. He was, understandably, worrying about the probability of his survival should the rebels actually succeed in overthrowing President Sam. Certainly their support grew each day, as Sam pandered to the emissaries of the *blancs* who were stripping the country bare. But regardless of how Petion personally felt about Sam's actions, he would be singled out as having served under the President. He had only escaped such a fate during the last coup by virtue of having been hospitalized by a practice grenade which had turned out to be live. As usual, it had been an inferior reject which the manufacturers – a French company – had dumped on them; presumably on the grounds that they wouldn't know any better.

He was jolted out of these thoughts by an unusual sight. As well as three strange *blancs*, who admittedly seemed more personable than the typical example of the breed, standing stark against the flame-coloured floral display was a large blue box, perhaps big enough for two or three people to squeeze into. It certainly wasn't a local construction. A pair of doors was set into the front, above which ran the legend 'POLICE public call BOX'. Petion didn't remember being told about anything like this, but since a panel on the door announced that a free public telephone was inside, he decided to thank heaven for small mercies and ask no questions. It occurred to him that he could phone the garrison for transport, so, grasping the small panel-knob, he tugged firmly – but it seemed to be stuck. There were two handles on the doors themselves, though, so he tried them next, but they too were jammed solid. He shook the handles in frustration, then stopped with a frown; there was a sort of tingling, pins-and-needles sensation in his hands. He let go of the handles, and the sensation ceased immediately. Tentatively stretching out one hand towards the chipped blue paintwork, he again received the same sensation in his fingertips as soon as they made contact. Strangely, the surface felt totally smooth, though its appearance was rough, and Petion had to resist the temptation to try and

27

see for certain that he was really touching the box. He was afraid that if he did so, he would see his fingertips held back a hairsbreadth from the actual surface. Nervously, he snatched his hand back. Some other sensation was niggling at him, however. Trying to trace it, he bent his head to the door, careful to stay far enough away to avoid feeling the stinging in his ear or cheek. Sure enough, when he concentrated on ignoring all the other sounds of the town and harbour, he became certain that there was a slight humming sound emanating from the box. It sounded electrical, almost like a generator, but so quiet and smooth-running as to be unearthly. Petion felt a trickle of cold sweat run down his back.

'Is something wrong?' The polite voice was that of the man, speaking in an accent Petion couldn't identify: it wasn't quite English, nor was it American, French or German.

'I was just curious about this box. It wasn't here a few hours ago.'

'Perhaps it just appeared out of thin air.'

'Don't insult my intelligence, *blanc*.' Petion couldn't help sounding slightly sneering. 'I'm not in the mood for patronizing tales of *jumbies*. Do you have anything to do with this?'

'Well, I have a key here. If you let us try it and it fits, well . . .' The little man held up a delicate key with a faint smile. The two young women seemed to be stifling smiles. They began to edge nearer to the box as Petion snatched the key irritably from the man's hand.

'I will try the key,' he said stuffily. He inserted the key and turned, and nothing happened. He turned back to the man. 'Enough amusements.' He absently dropped the key into his uniform pocket, and the man's face briefly flushed with what might have been anxiety.

Petion gave the blue box a final puzzled glance, and gestured to his men to lead the prisoners away. It seemed they would have to walk after all.

Straddled by the vertical and horizontal step-markings

for rangefinding, the medium-sized freighter sat squarely in the picture afforded to Kapitan Heinrich by his periscope. Dr Ingrid Karnstein had squeezed into the room a few minutes earlier, heralded by a waft of cologne, with which she doused herself liberally against the stale smells which permeated the boat. When informed by von Stein of what the crew were doing, she took great pleasure in warning Heinrich of precisely what consequences he would face from the naval high command should his recklessness have any detrimental effect on their work. She didn't rage or gasp like von Stein, but simply put her threat across in steadily unvarying tones of icy calm. Heinrich thought she and Dietz seemed made for each other, if he had been of a mind to act as matchmaker.

He cocked an eyebrow at Leutnant Klenze, and slowly spoke, 'Leutnant, I think we will not waste a torpedo on this target.' Von Stein visibly relaxed, while Karnstein smiled very slightly. 'Instead we shall sink her with shellfire.' His two passengers resumed their disapproving expressions as he continued to give orders. 'Bow planes to forty degrees, blow tanks two and four . . .'

The waters were very calm, the freighter moving almost imperceptibly in a one-foot swell. Kapitan Weber scanned the waters of the Caribbean from the starboard flying bridge of the SMS *Raubvogel*, looking for the telltale spurt of white water that would betray a submarine periscope. It was several minutes before he finally saw it. Once he had noticed it, and refocused, he could make out the foot-and-a-half or so of steel which formed the exposed section of scope tubing. Moments later, the sea in that area swelled up briefly, as ninety feet of grey steel lurched unstoppably into the fresh air.

Weber instantly signalled to his crew, who were already rushing to their posts on deck, dragging hawsers and cables with them, as a swarm of uniformed figures appeared on the submarine's hull while rivers of water were still pouring off it. Several of the Kriegsmarine submariners tugged the waterproof tarpaulin off the deck gun, but swung it out away from the *Raubvogel*.

As the U-boat pulled alongside, Leutnant Katze supervised a group of sailors, who swung a gangladder out away from the side of the ship, where a pair of submariners grabbed it and tied it down.

When von Stein and Karnstein appeared together at the conning tower, von Stein appeared livid at the sight that greeted him, while the air in Karnstein's vicinity took on a palpable chill.

Heinrich crooked his mouth at them. 'Fortunately, when we surfaced, the ship turned out to be our rendezvous.'

'You knew it all the time,' protested von Stein.

'Oh? These are international waters – it would be quite possible for another vessel to have been here before the *Raubvogel* – and I couldn't take any chances; not with such distinguished and important guests on board, now could I?'

Clearly not trusting himself to speak further, von Stein clambered stiffly down to the deck, where a crewman was lifting his and Dr Karnstein's luggage from a hatch.

Karnstein gave Heinrich the cold, disinterested look she gave any man. 'This journey will be fully reported in our log.'

'And in mine.' This time Heinrich's voice was as humourless as her own. With a nod, she moved down to the deck, and followed von Stein and their erstwhile baggage handlers aboard the *Raubvogel*.

Henri had observed these exchanges from the bow of the freighter, standing in front of the peculiarly-shaped deck fittings which bulged from the superstructures. Though he was too far off to have heard their voices; and though their backs were to him, preventing him from reading their lips, Henri's broadening smile throughout the conversation gave the impression he knew what was occurring, and that it amused him. If so, the amusement failed to reach his eyes, which were as dark and unreadable as always.

As the two scientists boarded, he peeled off one card from a tarot pack for each of them. Von Stein's card brought a smile to Henri's mouth. It was The Fool. On turning Karnstein's card, however, his face assumed a more thoughtful cast, as he seemed to ponder over why she was represented by the Queen of Cups. With one final look at the cards, he put them away and turned his attention to the pair themselves.

'You will have nothing bad to report of this captain,' he murmured to himself. Nodding to himself at some unspoken decision, he stepped gracefully towards the bulkhead door which would eventually lead to his cabin.

In the light of the Cuban sun, Colonel L V Mortimer, USMC, watched one of his platoons drilling in the square below his open office window. As a career military man, he liked to see soldiers drilled like this; though it occurred to him quite often that actual experience was more important – an opinion he light-heartedly pretended to keep secret from his sergeants.

All Mortimer's male family had been in either the Army, Navy or Marines, right back to the days of the Civil War, and it had been inevitable that he would sign up as well. He had done so partly due to the tales of glory told at reunions, and partly because he would have felt guilty about not following in this family tradition, though the latter was a reason he scarcely admitted to himself, and never to others.

Returning to the large mahogany desk that was almost the only piece of furniture in the office, he reread the note which had been handed to him a few moments ago by an adjutant. It was from the office of Admiral Caperton himself, ordering his men on to stand-by readiness for overseas posting. Closing his perpetually hooded eyes, he leaned back to contemplate this news. As far as he was concerned, there was only one possible reason for the new alert – President Wilson must be planning to enter the war in Europe and, naturally, he intended to send in his elite fighting Marines. Mortimer smiled, the look of a vulture overflying a battlefield. It was satisfying to know that his men, who were as much a part of him as his right arm, had been selected for what was obviously going to be an important military operation. All Mortimer could hope was that there would be a chance, or preferably many chances, for him to lead his men by example. Mortimer had always felt that he would like to die on the bloody field of battle, covered in glory. When asked why, by those who felt that a good warrior should be more concerned with staying alive to fight future battles for his country, Mortimer had always answered that there was no real reason – it was just his way.

Something stirred deep in Mortimer's being whenever he gave that stock answer. Something that whispered 'Liar,' with malign glee.

When he got back to his lakeside villa on the shore of Lake Saumatre, Henri relaxed somewhat, glad to be back on home soil again. It wasn't that he was prone to seasickness or the like, but he tended to feel rather drained when off the island, his powers depleted. Henri's villa was one of the few former plantation houses which still stood, protected from the ravages of time and assorted slave rebellions by being constantly occupied by generations of *houngans*. The central courtyard, which once held a fountained garden, was now a dusty *hounfort*, a *vodoun* temple where Henri conducted ceremonies every other night. A couple of small lizards basked in the sun there, while the occasional buzz of some large insect swept across the area.

Henri ignored the *hounfort* for the moment, however, and made straight for his study. Earlier, he had felt a strange sensation at the back of his mind, as if his subconscious were trying to warn him of something. Determined to find out what, he went into the study, which was lined with full bookshelves and decorated with exotic prints and statuettes. He removed a small bottle and a pouch from the desk drawer. Stepping aside, he sat cross-legged in front of the fireplace and drew an odd symbol – which seemed to blur and shift in front of the eye, as if it didn't want to be recognized – in the smooth layer of grey ash below the chimney. From the pouch he took a small jar of ointment, which he put on to his face and hands in a ritual pattern. Next he withdrew a sachet of red powder, which he tossed into the centre of the ashes. Instantly, a dazzling flame sprang up in the centre of the dead hearth, hovering a few millimetres above the ashes. Finally, he drained the bottle, and with a brief wince sat perfectly still, staring into the unnatural fire.

The Doctor, Ace and Benny were escorted to the fortress which stood at the back of the Presidential Palace. There, they were led through French-style, stone-built colonial barracks to a small office, which was well-decorated with rugs and wall hangings, yet had a cold, impersonal feel. Petion knocked on the open door, and a voice called for them to enter. The guards ushered the travellers in, and Petion followed and stood to one side.

Behind a solid desk was a large black man, his hair cropped closer than most, his eyes devoid of any normal human spark of life. He looked up as Petion approached the desk. 'Yes, Captain?' His voice indicated that he neither enjoyed being interrupted while working, nor enjoyed working at this hour.

'General Etienne, I have brought back the remains of the patrol that went missing last night.' He paused to lay on the desk a handkerchief-wrapped bundle which he unwrapped to reveal one of the sticky lower jaws. 'The bodies bore all the hallmarks of murder by the Secte Rouge.'

'And these *blancs*?' His eyes dismissed the Doctor and lingered calculatingly on Ace and Benny.

'Were by the bodies, in the presence of a strange box I've never seen in that area before. They seem to have no documents registering their entry into the country.'

'Very well, Captain, you are dismissed. Wait outside.'

Petion saluted and left, the guards following and closing the door behind them. Etienne appraised Ace and Benny more closely, much to their annoyance.

Benny gestured at the door. 'Your tactics are amazing – throwing the guards out and locking yourself in with three prisoners found at the scene of a triple murder.'

Etienne looked momentarily nonplussed, but recovered quickly. 'I am armed, woman.' He indicated a holstered revolver at his hip as he stood and came round the desk towards the prisoners.

Ace snorted barely perceptibly; the revolver was an old manual model that had to be cocked by hand before being fired. She resisted the temptation to tell this arrogant fool that she could disarm, disable, or dispatch him before he could do anything to harm them. She shifted her weight, preparing to deliver a swift boot in his groin if things didn't go their way.

Benny noted Ace's movement through the corner of her eye, and decided to prove that she could hold her own. Nonchalantly, she relaxed and moved her arms to a freer position. Someone as astute as Petion would have been instantly on his guard, but Etienne had gained his rank through exuberant brutality in the service of his paymaster, and knew little of combat against a prepared opponent.

'Perhaps,' Etienne began, 'I should simply sentence you for the murder of three soldiers – three *blancs* more or less will make no difference to anyone here.'

'Your own Captain says it was the Secte Rouge who killed your men,' Ace said, leaving off the words 'whoever the Secte Rouge are.'

'The President will always take my word over my subordinate's.'

'Yes,' drawled the Doctor, 'which is just as well, isn't it, Charles Oscar?'

'How do you know my name?'

'I believe the phrase is that I have the advantage of you.'

'Really?' Etienne's expression flattened dangerously. 'Please explain further.'

'Well, I was just thinking that if I were your President – and I have some experience of such office, you know – I'd be very interested to hear you explain in your own words the, er, loss of quite a few of your Cacos.'

'What?'

'Your Cacos. You know, the ones that have been deserting in droves to General Bobo's army?'

'How do you know of this?' Etienne fingered his revolver, and Ace tensed.

'As I say, I have the advantage of you.'

Etienne wasn't amused by the Doctor's cheeky grin. 'I think I should just kill you now.'

'I wouldn't do that, if I were you.'

'Why not?'

'Because,' the Doctor said, fishing out a yellowed piece of paper from one of his cavernous pockets, 'if you do, His Majesty's government will be most annoyed with you when I fail to make my regular reports.'

Etienne's face clouded thunderously, and he snatched the paper, reading it slowly, his lips moving as he stumbled over the words. Eventually, he handed the paper back with ill-grace. 'Very well, Doctor.' He seemed puzzled that the paper had given no name other than the title; possibly he assumed it was a code name. 'Very well.' He strode to the door and flung it open. 'Petion!' When the Captain appeared, Etienne indicated the three travellers. 'We would be best to allow these *blancs*,' he said, seeming to let his true feelings spill over as he spat the words, 'to continue with their business. I would like you, however, to escort them and make sure they come to no harm.'

He took Petion aside, and added, in a whisper, 'And you will report their every word and every action to me, do you understand?'

'Yes, sir.'

'Good. Also, you mentioned a box?' Petion nodded, and Etienne smiled. 'Excellent. I will send someone to collect it, it sounds intriguing.' Petion nodded again, and Etienne dismissed the three travellers with a glare, allowing them to leave in Petion's company.

Nobody dared say a word.

Henri floated amongst the stars. Some distant part of his consciousness was aware that he was really still at home, but mostly he allowed himself to drift with the ebb and flow of stellar tides. After a short time, or perhaps a very long one, vague forms appeared in the blackness. Though they were invisible and incorporeal, Henri could sense them nevertheless: huge pillars and blocks, which gradually became more real as his mind became attuned to them. Something began to approach him, something as unreal and imperceptible as the formless pillars, but nonetheless alive with vibrant intelligence. It began to speak, directly into his mind . . .

Henri awoke with a start, not recalling the vision beyond the point at which his terrible benefactor had appeared. He did recall, however, as if it were a searing brand burnt into his brain, what he had been told.

Standing up as the unnatural flames died among the ashes, he stepped back to a wall cabinet and lifted another bottle to drink from; a rum bottle in this case. He knew he had to tell the cards, to find out what he needed to know. Wasting no time, he sat at the desk and unwrapped his precious tarot pack, laying them out in an inverted cross pattern. When there were seven cards face down on the table, he began turning them over, muttering to himself, 'A man is here . . . He has friends . . . He meddles in others' business . . . Ah, he has compassion . . . He has many guises . . .' Henri frowned at this one, not fully understanding, before turning over the next two cards, the Hanged Man and the Tower struck by lightning. 'He will cause trouble . . . Death and destruction to follow – but there is nothing about who it is!' Henri snarled in frustration. Momentarily frozen, he was struck by the compulsion to turn one more card, to divine the identity of this troublesome meddler. Feeling a peculiar reluctance to do so, he reached out and slid one card from the pack. It was as if he could feel its identity before he even turned it face up; he gasped.

The image of the skeletal figure, carrying a scythe and an hourglass, was unmistakable.

Chapter Four

Under the harsh red lights of the night illumination, Major Paul Richmann strode through a warren of disturbingly angular tunnels. The purloined briefcase was held firmly in one hand, a grim black crust surrounding the rim of a steel cuff which hung limply down the side.

Steel toecaps echoing sharply on the rock floor, he turned the corner and ascended a short spiral staircase, which opened at the top on to a cave with a row of wooden doors set into one wall. Moving unhesitatingly to one marked simply '6', he slipped inside.

The room within was quite small, and yet was packed with mechanical devices resembling bastardized typewriters. Several men and women worked at the machines, and one of the women rose from a plain desk as he entered. 'Your business?' she asked.

'I'd like to have the contents of this case examined, recorded and decrypted.'

'It will have to wait until morning. We are rather busy at the moment.'

'I'll do it myself if you have a spare seat.' He looked pointedly at several empty spaces.

'You know that is forbidden.' She clutched the case more tightly. 'Only decrypt staff are permitted to operate the cipher machines.'

Richmann shrugged; working the machines was boring anyway. 'Suit yourself.' Without so much as a backward glance, he left the room. At a loose end, but not ready to rest, Richmann prowled the tunnels until he found his way, perhaps because of a subconscious decision, to a pair of large steel doors that closed off the firing range from the rest of the complex. From within, a few half-hearted cracks could be heard. On impulse, Richmann slid one door aside and stepped through.

Inside was a long, low cave, the walls piled high with sandbags in an attempt to dampen echoes. Only one other man was using the range, a brown-haired naval officer whom Richmann didn't recognize, and who was firing a Luger with cold precision at a plain circular target mounted on the far wall. As Richmann approached, the man lowered his gun and eyed him in a rather aloof, Prussian sort of way.

'I thought I was the only one who enjoyed using the range at odd hours,' Richmann said.

'I find that practice makes perfect – a lot of practice.'

'Really? You must be new here.' Richmann smiled to himself at the thought of the reactions of most of the men to being assigned a session shooting at balsa circles.

'I am Leutnant Dietz. I'm being transferred from second officer's position on U-29 to first officer on another boat.'

'For which you have to wait in this rancid hole.'

'I'll make the most of my time.'

'Glad to hear it. Mind if I shoot?'

'I'm always interested in seeing people do what they do best.'

'Someone's been talking about me.'

'You are Major Richmann, I take it?'

'That's right.'

'Fascinating.' Dietz nodded to himself. 'So you're the one who fights for money instead of his beliefs,' Dietz said, watching Richmann's reaction.

'That's where you're wrong,' Richmann answered, keeping his face unreadable. 'I do fight for my beliefs – I believe I should have great wealth, and I've only got one talent that I can exploit to get me that.' Hanging his leather jacket over a chair, Richmann checked the weapons he carried. In a shoulder holster was a Steyr 1912 automatic, an Austrian pistol which was well-regarded by the military, but needed ammunition that was too rare and specialized for it to be widely used. Strapped in a specially made holster against his right thigh was a Winchester 08 rifle he had modified himself, removing most of the stock and cutting the barrel down to about eight inches in length. 'Now, if you don't mind . . .'

Silently, with a strangely calculating expression on his face, Dietz stepped aside to allow Richmann to use the same target. Tugging the Steyr from its holster, he checked the magazine and charger, and slipped the safety off. Taking an informal stance, he squinted at the target and squeezed off all eight shots in rapid succession.

The series of heavy impacts ripped along the width of the target, and, with almost agonizing slowness, the top half toppled over and fell to the floor. Richmann pulled back the slide on top of the gun, and ejected the magazine, before slotting a new charger into the bolt-way and slapping another magazine into the butt. This done, he replaced the gun in its holster, and gave Dietz a brief glance. Taking up position again, he drew the Winchester from its holster and fired in one smooth movement.

The left-hand third of the remaining half circle disintegrated in a blast of splinters. Richmann swiftly recocked the gun with a peculiar hand movement that threw it against his fingers just enough to work the lever before slapping it back into his palm so he could fire again. This time the right-hand third was ripped apart. With a final shot, the one remaining piece of the target was blasted to splinters.

Richmann slid the gun back into the holster on his thigh. 'That's what constant practice does, but personally I don't think static targets are worth the trouble.'

Dietz looked at the shattered remnants of the target scattered across the floor. 'Something tells me you don't use standard issue ammunition.'

'Damn right. I have my own recipe that gives a bit more of a kick.'

'You enjoy killing, don't you?' Dietz asked softly.

Richmann paused in the middle of pulling his jacket back on, and then completed the motion before answering. 'Some people once had a hold on me,' he began quietly. 'It was a long time ago. They thought they were so superior, and that they could control my life, always telling me what to do and what not to do.' His lip curled at the memory, the words coming out contemptuously. 'Eventually I grew sick of it, until one day they tried to prevent me from getting something I was owed. So I killed them.' He grinned, his eyes lighting up and a thrill running down his spine at the mere thought. 'It was glorious! I realized that now *I* could control *their* lives. The ultimate control; the power to end their very existence.' Richmann's grin faded, leaving an expression of simple contentment. 'Since then, I've practised my chosen craft until I'm the best, and when someone owes me, I can just take what I'm owed whether they like it or not. I suppose now there's not really much else I am good at, after all these years of specialization.' He shrugged again. 'Anyway, I'll leave you to your practice.' Richmann headed for the door.

'We'll meet again, Major,' Dietz called out. 'I can see a usefulness in you.'

'Submarines would make me claustrophobic.' Richmann left, closing the door behind him.

'No need to worry about that,' Dietz murmured, half to himself. With a little chuckle, he scratched his chin.

Heat, warmth, life. It felt a need for all those things, but was trapped in its own slumber. Instinct caused twitches of life, but without a conscious self there could be no waking, and it had no conscious self.

Not any more. But . . .

Instinct told it that it should be itself again.

Instinct took basic actions of its own, operating purely on the psychic wavelength that was its realm and its prison.

Deep in the heart of the Earth, far below the firing range and the docks, stone moved in an unlit womb of rock.

Chapter Five

Captain Petion held open the door of the Royale, apparently the only hotel in Port-au-Prince, while Ace and Benny entered the shadowy lobby. Despite the earliness of the hour, it was surprisingly humid inside. Perhaps it always was: the flowery wallpaper was spotted with irregular patches of damp, and the varnish was peeling from the long reception desk on the right-hand side of the lobby. A wide door at the far end led to a dining room which was presently closed, while a staircase with a threadbare carpet led upwards on the left. A few comfortable-looking but battered chairs were arranged randomly throughout the central space of the lobby. The clock behind the desk had stopped, at midnight, sometime in the unknown past – perhaps last night, perhaps a hundred years ago.

Nobody was around, so Petion stepped over to the desk and rang the service bell, as the others looked around in dismay. 'Why don't we just use the TARDIS as our rest stop, Doctor,' Benny asked in a low voice.

'In the first place, the good Captain here took the key. Secondly, staying here will allow us to sample the local culture to the fullest possible extent.'

'Sample bacteria culture, maybe,' Benny muttered to Ace.

'Yeah, I'd recommend staying out of the showers here.' Ace moved over to the Doctor.

'I'm beginning to think Norman Bates must have served his apprenticeship here,' he greeted her.

Ace laughed softly, then broke off as an interior door opened, to admit a rather irate mulatto, in hurriedly donned finery.

Petion stepped up to him. 'These three *bla* – foreign guests will be requiring rooms, if it isn't too much trouble. The treasury will pay, of course.'

The mulatto glared back. 'Our normal opening hour is nine in the morning, not,' he said, glancing at a pocket-watch whose gold plate had mostly gone, leaving it a dull grey, 'six-oh-five.'

'Oh, I am terribly sorry, but your door was open, so we thought we'd come in rather than wander the streets for a few hours,' Petion said.

'Probably wise, for *blancs*,' the mulatto answered stonily, either missing or ignoring the undertone in Petion's voice.

'Yes, well, I would also have found it irritating. The course of justice isn't furthered by guiding foreigners around town because hotel-keepers are objectionable, if you catch my meaning.'

'Well, I wouldn't want to get in the way of – '

'I'm very glad to hear it. Now, three rooms.'

Ace leaned forward. 'Preferably ones that aren't flea-ridden; unless you enjoy eating through a straw.'

The mulatto stood silently for long moments, finally saying, 'I have two. For how long?'

'Oh, a week say?'

'Very well.' He leaned over to pick up a large book, which he opened and turned to face the Doctor. 'You'll have to sign the book – all three of you.' While they signed, the mulatto turned to take two keys from the almost full board behind him, handing one to the Doctor and one to Benny. Then he glanced at the book. 'Real full names, please,' he said wearily.

The Doctor merely raised an eyebrow while Ace fixed him with a dangerously flat look. 'That is my real full name,' she said.

At first it seemed that the mulatto might argue the point, but after a moment, he simply said, 'I'll have some-one show you to your rooms.' He turned to the internal phone, an old stalk model where the mouthpiece was in the stand, and the earpiece was separated by a length of cable and hung on a hook. Muttering too quietly for any of them to hear what he was saying – '*blanc*' was about the only word any of them could make out, since he seemed to be saying it louder for their benefit – he rattled the side hook until he got an answer, and spoke into the phone. '*Blanc*' featured several times again.

When he put the phone down, he turned back to the Doctor. 'Fifteen dollars a week, each – in advance.' He held out a hand.

Petion hunted about in his pockets and soon pulled out some paper and a pen, with which he wrote an IOU from the military budget, adding, 'Keep the change.' The mulatto's already sour expression became silently angry.

After a short wait, a black employee in faded hotel livery appeared, and, following the snarled orders of the mulatto, led the quartet up the stairs in the direction of the rooms. As they climbed, Ace drew level with the Doctor. 'I've never heard a language like that before. It seemed to be part French, part I don't know what.'

'You wouldn't have done. It's Creole.'

'Creole? At least I've heard of it, then, even if I've never heard it.'

'Yes. It's an argot, you see.'

'Isn't that something to do with silver?' Ace said.

'You're thinking of argent. An argot is a language which has evolved or been developed so that outsiders can't understand it. Creole in particular is a mixture of French and several African tribal languages which the seventeenth and eighteenth-century slaves evolved to keep their plans for revolution safe from their masters.' He uttered the last word with visible distaste.

'Yes,' Benny agreed. 'Definitely a case to make one wonder whether the "gift of tongues" was a curse or a blessing.'

The Royale was not at all busy. The Doctor was led to one room, Ace and Benny to the other, though the rooms had connecting doors. The rooms would have been considered mediocre but passable elsewhere, though the manager had assured them that these were in fact the best rooms available. Somehow, they believed him. Papered in floral patterns, with flea-ridden rugs scattered over a fairly smooth wooden floor, each room contained a large bed, completely enclosed by fuzzy white netting, a sink, and a large and creaky ceiling fan. French windows opened on to a balcony, and the rooms shared a bathroom which had only a few spiderwebs in the corners.

'It's quite nice,' Benny managed to tell Petion with a reasonably straight face.

'For someone like me, perhaps. I know you will be used to better things. General Etienne – ' his mouth crooked wryly, wrinkling the strange little triple scar that marked his left cheek ' – has asked me to . . .'

'Keep an eye on us and report back?' The Doctor grinned.

'I'm afraid so. I see no reason why I shouldn't offer you a guided tour of the city, if you like.'

'I'll tell you what, Captain. You come back about, oh, seven-thirty, by which time we'll have cleaned up a bit, and that'll give us a few hours before the main heat of the day. All right?'

'Good enough,' Petion replied, after a thoughtful pause. 'I will return in an hour and a half.' With a faint bow to Ace and Benny, Petion stepped back outside and closed the door.

When his footsteps had died away into the morning stillness, Ace opened the door a crack. 'He hasn't locked it. I'll just go after – '

'No.' The Doctor sat heavily on the end of the bed. 'Do either of you,' he paused as if searching for a word, 'hear anything?'

Benny shook her head. 'Just the usual sounds of an island harbour.'

Ace shrugged. 'I don't hear anything either, but this place gives me the creeps a bit.'

'I don't really mean hear; I mean hear with your mind.' His expression twisted in puzzlement. 'Actually, I'm not really sure what I mean.'

'But you hear whatever it is?' Benny looked just as mystified.

'It's as if I can sense voices or sounds, just on the edge of hearing.'

'You mean like hearing the neighbours arguing through the wall of the house?' Ace put in.

'Yes . . . Whatever it is, though, I doubt it's anything of this Earth. The closest thing I've experienced is being on the fringes of a group of telepaths, and there aren't many of them to the pound on this planet. Or not in this time zone, at any rate.'

Benny sighed resignedly. 'I take it the words, "We can't leave until we find out what's going on," are about to leap out at us?'

'No, actually I was thinking more along the lines of "We can't leave because I haven't got the TARDIS key." Since you mention it, though, this telepathic noise-pollution has piqued my curiosity somewhat. Hopefully, when Captain Petion shows us around town, I should be able to get a better idea of where it's coming from. Also, of course, I'll be able to keep an eye on the TARDIS key.'

'Unless he dutifully hands it in to his superiors,' suggested Benny with disdain.

'He won't. I think if he were going to, he'd have done it back there. It seems to have equally piqued his curiosity.'

'I suppose he didn't seem too enamoured of the General,' Benny admitted slowly.

'I'm not surprised. General Etienne's going to murder a couple of hundred people any day now.'

'What?' Ace and Bernice chorused.

'Political prisoners he'll have executed.'

'Is this another of your mystical observations?' Ace demanded.

'A simple matter of history, but one which occurred in such an out of the way corner of your planet that people took no notice.'

Ace looked up with hooded eyes. 'I'm taking notice.'

'No!' The Doctor's head snapped up and fixed her with

a steely glare. 'This is a matter of recorded history: it has happened; it will happen; it must happen. None of us can stop it, and we must not even try.' His eyes bored into hers. 'Do you understand me?'

'Just like the Putsch?' She nodded, her expression a mixture of disgust and weary sadness. 'All right, I won't try to stop it.'

The Doctor remained glaring for a moment, trying to determine whether or not she meant it. Then he nodded. 'Good. I'd stop it myself if I could, you should know that by now.'

'What happened to Etienne afterwards?' Benny asked idly.

'He disappeared in the ensuing rebellion. Who knows?' He cut himself off, silently cursing himself for failing to spot the obvious. Behind him, Ace smiled.

A faint sea-mist rose with the sun, though it did not provide much respite from its heat. The sound of the all-pervading drums faded, though not entirely, and the rhythm changed to suit the new day. Somewhere out to sea, beyond the horizon, a small group of ships lay at all-stop.

Mostly transports, with a couple of small frigates, they all flew the US flag, which hung limply in the lifeless air. Colonel Mortimer stood glaring helplessly at the horizon. It seemed that he was to be disappointed; rather than being sent off to Europe, he and his men were left to swelter just out of sight of Haiti.

Mortimer felt almost insulted. All that training and equipment lavished on his Marines, and it looked like their only opponents would be what most of his men described as 'No-good niggers.' He cursed whatever fates had led him to this, and turned, heading for his bunk to dream of more glorious campaigns and worthy opponents. A sudden sound made him pause, and look nervously around.

Just for an instant, he could have sworn he heard someone laugh softly, but all around him there was only the shimmering emptiness of the Caribbean.

Scratching at his greying moustache, Mait sat by a small wicker table which held his telephone, idly doodling on a pad. As he had expected, the phone rang after a very short time. 'Mait,' he answered. It was Henri. 'Ah, I have been expecting your call,' Mait added pleasantly.

'I have received word from Richmann,' began Henri. 'He and his superiors are satisfied with the night's work. The Englishman's papers have now been dealt with, he says.'

'Excellent. The next time you speak to him, you may mention that there will be, shall we say, a power-vacuum, in two or three days at most.'

'Sam took the bait you held out?'

'Naturally.'

'Mait . . .' Henri's voice took on a new edge, which Mait, if he hadn't known better, would have sworn was a sign of nervousness. 'Mait, there is something else I must tell you. I cast the *obeah* today, after being in contact with *them* . . .'

As Mait's expression grew grimmer by degrees, Henri told him what had happened earlier. When he was finished, Mait thought for a moment before speaking in a low voice: 'I have not worked for two hu – for all this time to be stopped by some *blanc*. Leave the matter in my hands, and I will discover whether there have been any new arrivals.' He paused. 'If so, Carrefour will take care of them.'

Chapter Six

Dream images flickered ephemerally through a mist of subconscious sensation. Landscapes faded transparently, fourth-dimensional senses perceiving them as they were and will be. Newborns were bent with age. Somewhere, sometime, the images were constant in a way that was as alien to the dreamer as the other images would be to a man. A blue box . . .

Resigning themselves to a stay in Port-au-Prince, the Doctor, Ace and Bernice had all cleaned up before gathering again in the Doctor's room to await Captain Petion's return. When the youngish mulatto Captain did return, at precisely seven-thirty, he too had evidently washed and shaved. He was also wearing a rather flashier and slightly less practical version of his colonial-style uniform.

'Ah there you are, Captain.' The Doctor gave him a grin. 'Right on time.'

'Of course,' Petion smiled back. 'Now, where should I take you? Have any of you been in Haiti before?'

'Yes,' the Doctor admitted.

'Ah, in that case – '

'But not yet.'

At this, Petion looked at him in bewilderment.

'Er, I think,' Benny began hastily, 'the Doctor means you should just lead us wherever you think would be most interesting. For myself, I'd love to see the harbour.'

'The harbour is certainly interesting in its own way.' He trailed off and thought for a moment. 'But, it is as good a place as any to start. If you will accompany me?

President Sam was jerked into wakefulness by a knock

on the double doors of his office, which rapidly opened to admit the bull-like form of Etienne. 'Hmm? Oh, it's you.' Sam straightened himself up and rang the bell for a servant, before turning back to Etienne. 'What news?'

'My men have finished carrying the bullion down to the yacht, just in case.'

'Excellent.' Sam paused to order the servant who had entered to bring breakfast. 'General Etienne, how is it that this morning I receive a message informing me that men of my army are deserting to join Bobo, when you have mentioned nothing of this?'

'Who – ' Etienne flushed. 'No, I can guess who.' He silently wished he had killed that little *blanc* who had hinted that he would inform the President. He also silently hoped that he would survive this discussion long enough to take action later. For now, Etienne's animal cunning rushed to the fore as he tried to think of an excuse for why he had failed to prevent the desertions.

'Well?' Imperceptibly, Sam's hand shifted towards the desk drawer that held an old Lebel revolver.

'I did not wish to worry you with such bad news. I have men hunting them down at this very moment.'

'Very well.' Sam decided there wasn't really much point in punishing this fool. 'At least it is only the Cacos who have been deserting. Their machetes will be of no use against firearms.' He leaned back in his chair, and drummed his fingers on the desk. 'Where are the men who went to the harbour?'

'Still there, guarding the yacht.'

'Get rid of them and replace them with men who don't know what's in there. By the time you get back, I will have thought about what to do next.'

'Yes, sir.' Etienne stood with a feral grin and a dimly flickering flame in his eyes. 'I will take care of them personally.' He lumbered out surprisingly swiftly.

'It's like throwing a bone at a dog,' Sam muttered confidentially to the servant who was now bringing in a breakfast tray. The servant looked blank. Sam sniffed the eggs happily, then paused. 'Just taste those, will you?'

* * *

Ace half-successfully stifled a yawn as she watched the morning fish-market get under way, the rising sun dimmed to manageable proportions by mirrored sunglasses. She had been surprised that, although these people looked at the travellers with the wariness of the long-term exploited, none of them had been in any way uncivil. True, they hadn't exactly welcomed them into their families, but there had been none of the brutal hostility that she had seen in the eyes of General Etienne. This had been true of their entire journey down the Rue Grand, past several Catholic churches – not to mention one huge white cathedral in the exact centre of town, which Petion had said was less than a year old – and the Moorish-style wrought-iron towers that dominated the Iron Market. Finally, they had reached the southern end of the harbour, where each morning a wide expanse of waste ground was turned into the fish market.

Only a few vessels were at anchor in the harbour, mostly battered fishing boats, though a halfway decent-looking cruising yacht was also present, and apparently under guard. Rising above them, clinging precariously to the curving slope of the bay, were a mixture of buildings from stone houses to falling-down shacks. Strangely, they had all been whitewashed to resemble gleaming marble, regardless of the type of building they were. Ace felt it had the air of a colonial town gone completely to seed – the bougainvilleas most noticeably. Northwards along the harbour, in the direction they were slowly walking, Ace could make out the large silos and warehouses of foreign companies, while in the centre of the wide open harbour-front itself, the two-storey US customs receivership squatted silently, its business slow. Her attention was drawn from this scene, however, when she noticed the Doctor's somewhat distant expression. Benny noticed it an instant later, and all three of them stopped. Petion halted too, but continued pointing out the busiest areas, since he stood in front of the Doctor and couldn't see his face.

'Prof – Doctor?' Ace said.

'Shush.' His head jerked around in fits and starts, as if

trying to ascertain a direction. 'It's coming from up ahead; or rather, it's coming from someone or something that's been up ahead. The trail's a bit faded, but it's definitely there.' The Doctor glanced around. He hadn't felt anything like this since the Dark Tower. 'Captain?'

'Yes?' Petion faced him.

'What's in those buildings over there?' He indicated the warehouses.

'Those are simply storage warehouses for the foreign companies who trade our goods. Those nearest us are the French.' He squinted at the area. 'Those are two of my men . . . What are they doing there?'

'Let's ask them, shall we?' The Doctor set off eagerly across the road, glad of the excuse to investigate those buildings.

The two scruffy soldiers, who had been glancing warily about the compound, drew themselves to attention, more or less, as Petion approached. The captain led the two off to one side for a moment, then returned to his charges. The two soldiers set off for the office door set into the side of the large warehouse. Petion began to speak in a low voice as he led the others over. 'My men have been sent here by the police office. They received complaints of intruders and missing persons from the French last week.'

'I'm glad to see they were quick off the mark,' Benny commented.

'It seems there were . . . political considerations.' Petion shifted uncomfortably, and continued, 'A while ago, General Etienne tried to persuade the French to allow us to use their compound. They refused and fired shots when the great oaf tried to force them. Since then, he has persuaded loyal officers to be unhelpful towards them.'

'Does he think they're rebel sympathizers?' Ace put in.

'No, they shot at them also.'

The Doctor cocked an eyebrow. 'Your tone doesn't seem to show much respect for your superior.'

Petion froze for an instant, feeling those unreadable eyes on him. 'Perhaps,' he tried finally, 'I no longer feel entirely comfortable with his style of command.'

'Perhaps I begin to feel more comfortable with yours, then,' the Doctor said.

'I – ' Petion seemed to freeze again, before settling into a more businesslike manner. 'My men say there is no answer at the office, and after searching the compound they can find no sign of life. I intend, therefore, to break in – I am within my rights to do so. I suggest, however, that your friends may prefer to remain here.'

The Doctor glanced over at Ace and Benny. 'I doubt they would do that.'

'Very well then.' Petion stepped over the door, whose tiny panes of glass were dusted over to such an extent as to make them totally opaque. He tried the handle first, but was unsurprised to find the door locked. Drawing his revolver, he waved the others back beyond the range of any splinters that might fly off, and shot the lock out. The door rocked on its hinges, yielding easily to the kick which Petion delivered.

The door opened on to a stuffy room thick with the buzzing of flies and the tang of copper. As the Doctor, Ace and Benny followed Petion cautiously in, Benny fought down an impulse to turn and dash back out. She looked across at Ace, who was glancing about coldly, and determined that she wouldn't show any such timidity in front of her.

The room was built of crudely fashioned planking, and was dotted with rough-and-ready furniture. The floor was scattered with dented pots and smashed crockery; small pieces of glass were strewn across the tabletop, though Benny couldn't see what they had been a part of, since the windows seemed intact. It took her an instant to realize with a hollow feeling that the dry black crusts stuck to the wood here and there were dried bloodstains. Finally, despite her best efforts, her eyes were involuntarily drawn to the ragged mound off to the side. It lay between the door and a shattered cabinet whose gaps revealed a pair of rusty rifles. Something skittered away from it as the Doctor, Petion and Ace approached it. Petion seemed disgusted, Ace looked coldly angry, while the Doctor's features, as usual, were unreadable. Following them, Benny forced down a sensation of nauseated surprise that a human cadaver could be spread over quite such a wide area of flooring.

The Doctor knelt beside the torn corpse. What remained of the face seemed to show an expression of utmost horror, though it was difficult to tell. The torso had been ripped open in a most revolting manner, which meant there was little bloating of the tissue, but made the stench worse, and there were innumerable tiny glittering carapaces visible among the discoloured wounds.

Petion stood, looking down on the body. 'What could have happened?' he ventured weakly. 'I have never seen anything like . . .'

'Maybe,' tried Ace, smothering her disgust with anger at the needlessness of it all, 'some kind of animal. The wounds look a bit like claw marks.'

'No,' the Doctor said slowly, 'I don't think that's quite the case.' He drew out a magnifying glass and squinted through it at the edge of a wound, grimacing as he tried to ignore the scuttling parasites. 'Not claws exactly. Look at this area here.' He offered the glass, but even Ace shook her head with a gulp. 'The flesh has been put under more pressure to break the skin than a sharp clawtip would need. You can tell by the bruising.'

'Then what?' Ace asked. With a sudden certainty, Benny knew what the Doctor's answer would be.

'Fingers,' he said simply.

Petion's eyebrows shot up in disbelief, and he stammered for a reply. 'Fingers? Do you mean to suggest that a man tore him apart like this? That's impossible.'

'Not a man, several men.'

'But the strength needed – '

'It only takes eight and a half pounds of pressure to break even the largest bone. Given sufficient time and a subject probably either knocked out, paralysed with terror or simply held down, then it's certainly possible for someone with sufficiently insane fury to inflict this kind of damage. The question is why? If they were rebels, or soldiers for that matter, they'd have weapons.'

'You talk about it with a creditable lack of emotion,' Benny said in disgust.

'I have to,' he answered, turning so she could see the look in his icy eyes. The Doctor stood up, and looked towards the table. Moving over to it, he carefully brushed the glass splinters with his fingertips, and glanced up to the shadowed rafters. A shaft of sunlight entered up there, becoming lost amidst the more solid wooden beams. 'That's how they got in,' he pointed out. 'The skylight.' He switched his attention to an open book on the table. It was stained with blood, but otherwise pretty much undamaged. 'That's interesting. It seems he was interrupted while writing his journal. I wonder . . . It may mention something that would explain this.'

'Yeah,' Ace interrupted, 'maybe he kept up a running commentary.'

'I believe I should take that, Doctor. It is evidence, after all.' Petion held out his hand for the book.

'All right, here you go. You can hand in a nice report to the General, and I'm sure he'll take it from there.' The Doctor proffered the journal.

'The General. Ah, perhaps not.'

'Perhaps not indeed,' the Doctor agreed, dropping the journal into a pocket. 'We'll get back to the hotel, and peruse this account in private, eh?'

'Very well.' Petion nodded with a degree of uncertainty. He called to the two soldiers, and ordered them to stand guard and admit no one while he reported this discovery. The two soldiers glanced at each other hesitantly, but then accepted the order.

As the others exited, Ace paused in the doorway, her attention drawn to the wrecked gun cabinet. Thoughtfully, she removed a Browning automatic from it, hefting its weight in her hand. Reaching a decision, she slipped the gun into her empty holster, adjusting the fittings to

55

do so, and put several ammunition clips into her pockets. Thus armed, she followed her friends out.

The journey back to the Royale was uneventful, despite the threatening sound of gunfire from distant streets, and the hubbub of frightened crowds. It occurred to Benny to ask why the crowds were made up almost entirely of women in rough denim dresses, and children. Petion replied that most of the men had been press-ganged into one army or the other. Ignoring the disapproving glare of the mulatto behind the reception desk, the foursome ascended directly to the Doctor's room, where they all found seats – Benny and Petion on chairs, Ace perched on the dresser, and the Doctor at the end of the bed.

Carefully, the Doctor pried apart some pages, which had been stuck together with the blood. Then, flicking through it, he determined which were the relevant pages, and, after a glance at the expectant faces of the others, he spoke: 'Are you comfortable? Then we'll begin.'

'Very funny, Doctor,' Ace said.

The Doctor grinned, and began to read from the crinkled pages.

The Journal Of Francois Lacombe: I have never been a man of letters, despite having always done well at school as a youngster. It had been my intention, when I first came to this isle – which I then considered to be a blessed paradise, though I now know it to be an earthly extension of Hell – to catalogue my experiences in a regular diary. Looking back through the earlier pages, I see with a touch of sad dismay that I grew tired and gave up on my diary after a mere dozen days.

It is perhaps this very lack of determination which prevented me from acting earlier to forestall the events which I must now recount. I have recovered this journal from my travelling chest, and set pen to paper, because not only do I wish to leave a record of what has happened here – I fear I shall not be able to explain in person – but also because I feel it is my duty to warn whomsoever

56

should find this account, of what I believe to be a matter of the gravest import, on which action must be taken.

What action, I cannot recommend, for even now, I do not truly understand what evil fate has befallen myself and my companions. However, I shall detail my experiences in the hope that some future reader, if any, will understand and determine what should be done.

I have lived and worked happily here in the compound for nearly two years, having left my home in Alsace in the August of 1913. The work was hard, supervising the construction and maintenance of both the ore chutes and the cranes and railcars which run from the silos and warehouse to the waterfront, where our ores are shipped back to France. There were many of us then, but in recent months our workforce has been depleted as the company has withdrawn most of the men due to fears over the island's political stability. For some time now, there have been lethal fights outside our very gates, and the endless, insidious drumming from the voodoo temples behind Port-au-Prince has filled our ears with ever-increasing vigour and ominous roaring.

By the beginning of last month, June, there were only six of us left, everyone else having been returned home or moved to other places of work. The six of us volunteered to remain behind as a sort of combined guard force and caretaker. Ah, what a foolish decision I made! When M DeSalle, the manager, left with the last of the workers, he left us with sufficient provisions for several weeks, and with orders both to ensure that all company equipment remained in working order, and to protect it from any damage which might be caused by either the government or rebel forces in the conflict which we were all certain, and unfortunately rightly so, would burst upon us. To protect ourselves, he left two rifles, two shotguns, and a revolver for each of us.

From the very first, we decided that there should always be two men on guard, armed with the shotguns, while the rifles were locked in a cupboard for instances of dire emergency. I must confess to having felt some measure of unease at the prospect that we may have been forced to use these weapons against men, even blacks. Latterly, however, this emotion was replaced with relief that I had some means to defend myself. This attitude lasted until yesterday.

The first few weeks went by hectically, though with hindsight they were a haven of calmness and sanity compared to what was to follow! On several occasions we had to fire shots to drive off intruders who were so unwholesomely ragged that they could only have been members of the rabble who follow General Bobo. I do not mean this to say that we felt particularly friendlier towards the government forces, since they were as corrupt and brutal as the rebels. When they too attempted to take over the almost vacated compound, we managed to drive off the soldiers simply by firing shots in the air. They promised to return, but have yet to reappear. It is perhaps because of this event that they were less than cooperative towards us when, a few days ago, we reported the terrifying situation in which we had found ourselves.

Our first intimation that something was amiss, or more so than usual, came on Bastille Day. Claude, our Breton cook, had delighted us with a particularly fine meal that night, to celebrate the anniversary. Claude is – was – a fine cook, though a little fond of the cooking wines and sherry which more properly should have been restricted to use in the dishes themselves. I will not impinge upon your doubtless finite patience with a description of that meal, but will say that the particular method used to cook the fish and the other dishes accompanying it required longer hours at the stove than Claude would normally consider. It did not help that our stove is a truly antediluvian contraption, which runs on a perverse mixture of coal and oil. As a result, if things are not watched carefully, a great deal of smoke can be produced by the inferior user. Claude was too good to allow this to happen, however, but even so, there was a certain amount of unavoidable heat and steam which bathed the cook at his post. It was no surprise to any of us, then, when

Claude announced his intention, after we had toasted his health many times, to take a walk on the beach side of the compound to get some much-needed (and much-deserved) fresh air.

He had been gone from our communal hall only a few minutes when we all clearly heard a cry, the tone of which could only have come from a frightened man; as Claude was the only man we knew of out there, we all immediately rushed out to see what had so affected him. To our shock, and I find it difficult to believe even now, there was no sign of Claude. His footprints were clearly visible in the sand, and yet they ended a few hundred yards away, as if something had snatched him from the very air. We all spread out to search for him nonetheless, but, as we all feared, there was no sign, until Jean held up a hand for quiet. As the hard-working Parisian was our supervisor, we complied with no qualms. 'Do you hear it?' he asked. At first we were puzzled, until gradually, with an air of stupefaction, we all realized we could hear a faint noise which sounded like screaming. Every one of us stood in absolute silence, the silence of the grave, trying to determine from which direction the sound came. Eventually, Jean dropped to his knees and put an ear to the ground. The screaming stopped then, but Jean swore that it was Claude's voice, coming from under the ground! We searched all the more frantically after that, but to no avail. With the hour of eleven approaching, from which time the *cochon gris* are at their boldest and most deadly, we returned to our office-cum-living-quarters, and barred the door against the night.

For the next day or two, we were sick with worry over what had happened to Claude, but I will not bore you with the details of our prayers for his safe return, or our vigils at the windows overlooking the beach. It was some two days later that Joseph, our burly carpenter, who had been into town for supplies, burst breathlessly in with the news that he had seen Claude in an almost death-like sleep beside a fish stall at the harbour. None of us dared truly believe it, but we all volunteered to go and fetch him back. Jean stepped in with a firm hand, however, and assigned mechanic Antoine to accompany Joseph to bring Claude back. As they left, Jean brooded fiercely about the fate that would await the apparently somnambulent Claude if he proved to have been drunk that night. Our elation proved to have little foundation, however, since as the sun gradually sank into the fiery sea, there was still no sign of the trio who should have returned to salutations many hours ago. It was with heavy hearts that we retired that night to await the next day's developments.

His face grimly set, Jean decided that we would notify the local authorities of our predicament that very morning, in the hope that they would in some way be able to render some assistance. The three of us went to the police headquarters in the shadow of the palace, and there related the very same story I have set down here, albeit with the more preternaturally mysterious aspects left out for fear of ridicule. Alas, we were to be foiled here also, as the Lieutenant who heard us out did so with undisguised contempt for his foreign visitors. We, who had made this island what it is today! I could not help but feel that his eyes bore the look of one who is afraid of something, but all our wiles could not persuade him to do more than say he would pass on our concern. Disheartened, we returned to our compound to carry out our regular work. Simon, a bluff labourer, was now standing in as an impromptu cook, but the depression which he shared with the rest of us, ensured that the food was never more than edible. I still remember that evening with a small degree of fondness, however, for it was the last truly sane day we were to face.

After that meal, as the sun's rays faded and allowed the darkness to creep back into the sky, we became aware of a faint scratching around the edges of the door and windows. At first we thought little of it, assuming simply that some half-starved dog had come to forage for scraps at our dustbins. This impression was soon to be dispelled, however, when we heard the distinctive sound of footsteps, yet with a curious slur to the sound. I could only feel that whatever was outside was dragging its feet in a most unhealthy manner. Suddenly, we all started as the scratching resumed. This time, however, it was a fierce, insistent rasp, and the boards outside creaked with pressure. Silently, Jean signalled to Simon and myself to pick up our guns. This we did, I choosing a revolver, Jean and Simon taking up shotguns. Cautiously, when the scratching paused, we approached the door, and Jean quietly unlocked it. On a count of three, he threw open the door, so we could all rush out and –

We all froze in the grip of heart-wrenching horror. Jean stood on the boards outside, while Simon and I were rooted to the spot in the doorway. Rising from the positions where they had been working their nails ragged in an attempt to gain entry, were three forms who could only be our missing men. The horror, however, was in their eyes, which were entirely devoid of the spark of life with which we recognize our fellow man. Their bodies were tensed in animalistic postures, ready to spring, and their teeth and nails were caked with a dark substance whose nature I dare not speculate on.

Jean's paralysis ended, and he stepped forward, with a relieved cry of 'Antoine!' The cry died in his throat as the burly figure, who I admit must once have been our Antoine, surged forward with the speed of a panther, and wrenched the gun from Jean's hands, before plunging those grimy fingers into his eye sockets. Whatever happened next that caused the repulsive oily ripping noise was obscured from my view as Simon raised his gun to ward off the ghouls who had once been Claude and Joseph. They showed no fear of the gun, simply advancing with that terrifyingly silent pounce; Simon fired both barrels, the roar of the shotgun drowning out his fevered prayer. I confess I could not persuade my body to obey the directions my brain gave it, as I saw the shotgun rip a hole clear through Claude's chest. The hole was several inches across, and I could make out fading daylight through the gaps between shattered ribs and missing vertebrae. The repulsive dead flesh and slippery organs formed a baroque frame for the sunset – *and he still came on!*

Screaming wordlessly, I began blasting shot after shot into the oncoming figures, as Simon struggled to close the door, which trapped a ferociously flailing arm. Dropping my smoking revolver, I snatched up one of Claude's cleavers, and hacked at the arm with the maniacal fury of one who is so terrified that all moral sense has been subverted by the pure instinct to survive. In moments that seemed like hours, the arm parted from the body and flailed blindly as I tossed it out in the last instant before Simon slammed the door and slid the bolts along.

Though some unnatural strength kept our former comrades from death, we seemed to have inflicted some amount of pain on them, for they fled into the night in eerie silence. For our part, Simon and I slumped wordlessly against the table leg, shivering despite the heat. We both know that they will be back.

If the authorities do not respond before those once-human creatures return, this will be the only –

'It ends there, on the most bloody page. They must have come back while he was writing.'

'And the other man?' Petion asked.

'Presumably dragged off by the assailants. Makes one wonder, doesn't it, Captain?'

'I don't know what you mean.' Petion's voice, however, was edgy, and he looked away.

'Yes you do. "Once human"?'

'Such things are the stuff of myths which *blancs* use as a reason to look down on us. There is no truth in – '

'Isn't there? We both know better.'

Petion was distinctly uncomfortable. Nobody ever wanted to admit to someone else that they believed in tales told to frighten children, particularly not the extent to which the very mention of such things brought on an attack of nerves. Petion did secretly believe, though, as did everyone else on the island. Petion couldn't deny what they had all seen, however, and the account in the journal had the ring of truth. Reluctantly, and with great distaste, he nodded. 'There is a man who also asks these same questions – an American working at the university.'

'Who is this man?'

'His name is Howard Phillips. He is here as a teacher of pathology at the university medical school.'

'Well, in that case, don't you think we might give him a look at the late M Lacombe?'

'Very well, Doctor.' Petion raised his eyes to the cracked ceiling and sighed resignedly. 'I will arrange it.'

Chapter Seven

Accompanied by a squad of his most trusted men – ones he knew he could beat in a fight – General Charles Oscar Etienne moved heavily through the swirling crowds of the fish market, in much the same way as an icebreaker passes through pack ice. He'd had little contact with military establishments outside his own, and felt there was nothing unusual in someone of his rank walking with only a few men through the streets filled with both loyalists and rebel supporters, all of whom hated and feared him.

Shouldering aside with glee any raggedly dressed fisherman or denim-dressed woman who got in his way, he entered the harbourmarket area. The fact that the sun had risen to a point where it was giving out the full force of tropical summer, combined with the thronging mass of sweaty peasants, made the air stifling, which did nothing to soothe Etienne's already unstable temper.

Batting aside the last of the fishermen like flies, Etienne and his men emerged into a clearer area of rough wooden promenades and jetties. At the end of one of the longer jetties, a somewhat battered late-Victorian steam yacht rose and fell slightly with the motion of the waves. Etienne's dark brows furrowed as he clumped along the stained wood towards the yacht. Where, he wondered, were the men he had left behind on guard? Could they have thought to run off with some of the gold? Admittedly, he could hardly blame them for allowing the obvious thought to cross their minds, but on the other hand, everything they might have taken meant less for him, and that was inexcusable. Muttering a vicious Creole curse, he snapped at the sergeant who nervously waited behind him. 'Spread out! I want to know where these pigs have gone!'

The soldiers spread out across the planks, glancing expectantly at the crowds, who mostly ignored them. Etienne stepped to the edge of the jetty, where the yacht bumped gently against the sandbags and the tightly coiled hawsers which prevented it being damaged by the wood of the jetty. He stood in thought, hesitating before stepping across the gangplank, as if something in his subconscious were trying to warn him of some danger.

He looked back at the soldiers, who were alternately either searching through stalls and assorted clutter, or hitting protesting fishermen and traders with their rifle butts. Below him, there was the sound of water lapping at the rotting posts which were sunk into the bay, and a faint soft thudding, as if one of the sandbags had come off. Suddenly, Etienne realized what was troubling him, and drew his revolver just in case. Leaning carefully over, he confirmed what he had noticed earlier; all the sandbags and hawsers were hanging from the jetty as intended.

Cocking the hammer, he waved to recall his men, who scuttled back hurriedly. Pointing the gun down before him, he craned his neck out beyond the edge of the jetty and looked down. There, being washed against the support posts with each wave, was the torn form of one of the guards, floating serenely minus chunks of flesh the barracuda had already taken. He had no doubt that the other man had suffered a similar fate, whatever it might have been.

Etienne had some suspicions, but he decided it would be wiser to keep them to himself. Still, there was no harm in checking. 'You!' He pointed to a soldier at random. 'Get aboard, and see if the other man's below.'

'Yes, sir.' Swallowing nervously, the scruffy soldier edged across the gangplank as if afraid it would snap under him. Stepping on to the quarterdeck, he glanced about.

'Go on,' Etienne shouted. The soldier nodded, and approached the slatted door that led below. Without further delay, he turned the handle and went in.

Several minutes passed before he reappeared, looking

slightly woozy. 'There's no . . . no sign of . . . any – '
With an unfocused glance at his hands, he stepped
unsteadily towards the gangplank, but never reached it.
Without so much as a sigh, he slumped to the warm deck
and lay still, sightless eyes gazing accusingly at Etienne.

For his part, the General knew the look of death when
he saw it. '*Merde*,' he muttered. 'Sergeant, stay here.
Make sure no one goes aboard. The rest of you, come
with me.'

Etienne felt anger boil in his veins. Not at the loss of
the men, but at the loss of the gold. Not only that, he
realized, with a certain amount of trepidation, but now
he had to tell the President. Hoping that someone would
get in his way and give him an excuse to kill in order to
vent some of his anger, Etienne snarled wordlessly and
lumbered off back towards the palace.

The bright light of the late morning sun glittered icily
from the tiny scales which sheathed the almost purely
muscular form of the black snake as it coiled with decep-
tive calm around a small stone.

It tensed as it felt the shifting of pebbles all around,
which signified the approach of some larger creature. The
tiny tongue flicked out, tasting the air, and scenting the
tang – albeit far more faintly than usual – by which the
snake knew, in some wordless reptilian manner, that a
human had halted near it. Unconcerned, its pinpoint eyes
remained focused on the dry tufts of scrub grass that
clustered around the nearby dead tree, either unaware or
uncaring of the fact that Carrefour's expressionless eyes
were also trained on that area.

Carrefour, now dressed in home-woven shorts and
shirt, had settled into a comfortable cross-legged position
atop a broken wall with the same silent fluid grace that
characterized the snake's own movement. Without looking, he stretched out one long arm, and retrieved a fallen
branch from the undergrowth, methodically breaking off
superfluous twigs with his fingers, all the time keeping his
eyes fixed on the grass.

Carrefour admired the snake's tireless patience, a trait he himself continually strove to develop. He knew that in the same situation, after a short time, Henri would be pacing restlessly, while after a little more time, even the patient Mait would almost certainly have either become irritable or simply fallen asleep. He, on the other hand, knew how to deal with the boredom of concentrating on one still subject for lengthy hours. He had, after all, had plenty of time to practise.

He knew that the snakes were used to him by now, since he was a regular visitor to this forgotten site, and had been since . . . Well, since as far back as he could remember. Sometimes, in formless dreams on those nights when with assistance he managed to sleep, he felt there was something he should remember, but he always put it out of his mind when consciousness returned. He often visited the site, anyway, and no longer had to look around him to discern the layout of the house foundations, or the positions of the walls and fences which once marked the boundaries of the plantation which had become no more than a nest for the snakes. Faint cries echoed in his mind, as insubstantial as the smoke he knew he would have smelled, had he not realized that his concentration was slipping, and blanked his mind of all but the patient observing.

Carrefour allowed himself a small smile as the snake altered its position slightly, without the slightest sign of tension, after tasting the air. He had seen that tiny movement so often now, that he could almost feel the snake's own icy anticipation of the appearance of its prey. The smile was a sign of his calmness, he thought. He despised the way in which most men taunted each other, or shouted, screamed, laughed, or cried in the heat of the moment, letting their emotions get the better of them. The appearance of a tiny bewhiskered nose at the edge of the grass was something he saw as confirmation of the worth of calm and patience. The snake struck like a bolt of black lightning, delivering its fatal sting to the rodent, which didn't even have time to make a sound of fright.

In an instant, it was as rigid as if it were carved from stone, and as lifeless.

The snake began to feed, as devoid of hate or animosity as Carrefour aimed to be – as Mait had taught him how to be. Carrefour uncoiled himself from his boulder, now that the branch he had been toying with was reduced to a single straight length with a tiny fork at one end. Smoothly, he moved over and stabbed the stick down, trapping the snake in the fork, just behind the head. In a flash, he snatched up the reptile and held it firm, staring it down and stroking its head. Gradually, the snake stilled, and stiffened. Still smiling, Carrefour set off away from the ruined plantation, and away from the figures that seemed to mock him from the shadows.

President Jean-Vilbrun Guillaume Sam gripped the rail of the balcony tightly in order to still his shaking hands. From the hills above the city, the telltale smoke was rising in thicker, and closer, clouds with each passing day. Below, some of his soldiers were brawling with a mass of people in the streets outside the palace. This too got worse every day, and he dreaded to think what might happen if he weren't able to get out of the palace before General Bobo arrived.

Cries rose from below, as his men began to use rifle butts and bayonets on the thronging mass. Even the ferocity of his supporters' bloodletting didn't assuage his fears, however, for he knew that no matter what the circumstances, if he were still there when Bobo's supporters decided to make their move, he was a dead man. Almost all the previous revolutions on the island had proved that to be the way things were done.

He was drawn from his waking nightmare by the sound of gunshots and briefly ducked, but then noticed that it was the returning General Etienne shooting indiscriminately into the crowd in order to get through them. Sam rushed back inside and, followed by his bodyguards, descended towards the entrance hall.

Etienne was also afraid of what the rebels might have to say about him, and of what Sam's reaction would be to his news. Inside, he also seethed at those who made him feel so uncomfortable. Approaching the palace, he and his men began firing into the crowd, occasionally hitting one of the guards as well, which drew a laugh, from him at least.

He didn't really feel any better, however, despite finding an excuse to indulge in the bloodshed he craved like a drug. As the crowd began to realize what was happening, some people within it began to scream and shout, and a few hardy souls hurled bricks and pieces of wood at the guards, at Etienne and, since they were people with mixed political viewpoints, at each other. Impassive, bloodthirsty or afraid, the guards didn't hesitate to join in the shooting, causing the crowd to panic.

Etienne and his men took the opportunity to push brutally through the panicking crowd, who were fleeing in all directions. It was only a few more moments before they ducked into the palace, and slammed the doors shut on the chaos outside. Ordering his men through to the barracks, Etienne tried to arrange his message into a suitable form, as he walked to meet President Sam who was standing at the base of the stairs, their fine red carpet now threadbare.

'Well?' Sam's voice was tight.

'Bad news, sir.' He paused to think of a way of softening the blow. 'There has been a . . . problem with the yacht.'

'Problem?' Sam's jaw tightened.

'When we arrived, the guards were already dead.' He spoke tersely, betraying the annoyance he felt at having been deprived of the opportunity to kill them himself. 'The man I sent aboard died of a *coup l'aire*.'

'Are you certain?' Sam could barely control his voice; if the rebels had even one *bocor* working for them . . .

'The man was struck by no weapon. No one else was even there.' Etienne's eyes broke into wildness, and he visibly fought an urge to shake. 'It can only mean that *they* have placed a curse on the boat!'

Sam wanted to shout at the General to forget such superstitious peasant nonsense, but found that he couldn't; not when he knew it to be true. He paced under the chandelier that had once gleamed, but whose gilt had faded long ago. Unlike his own. 'If I cannot get out, then my only chance is to try and take them with me. If we can make an example of some traitors . . .'

'We could arm the militia.'

'No! Not with so many of them deserting. If this goes on I won't even have enough men to guard the jail! I don't – of course! How many of the criminal scum do we have?'

'A couple of hundred, I think.'

'Interesting,' Sam said, with a smile that even Etienne stepped back from. 'We will show those peasants what will happen to anyone who proves to have disloyal tendencies. Kill them.'

'How many?'

'You disappoint me. I'd have thought you'd reach the conclusion as quickly as I did. All of them,' he snapped with a dismissive wave. 'Anyone in the jail who has even mentioned the name of that diseased ape Bobo.' He stopped, a strange look on his face, thinking to himself. 'In fact,' he began again, 'even the ones who haven't so much as heard of Bobo. Shoot them all, and leave their entrails for the birds.' Face icily calm, he turned away sharply, and stalked off darkly, back up the stairway.

Etienne thought about it for a moment, his lips moving silently. Slowly, an evil grin spread across his features.

The shabbily uniformed guards wasted no time in kicking the prisoners awake, and hustling them out of their cells in groups. The prison, an old fortress with thick stone walls, was home to more rats than prisoners and guards combined. The guards, who stalked through the corridors which were lined with barred doors, had all grown used to the rank stench that pervaded the very stones of the walls themselves. Snarling curses at the filthy wretches who were their unfortunate charges, they moved through the prison, rattling truncheons along the bars before unlocking the doors and going in to prod the scrawny, underfed prisoners into sluggish activity. 'This is your lucky day,' the lieutenant in charge cried, 'you won't be spending another night in this rathole!' A few of the more optimistic or naive prisoners smiled at this, but most of them, probably guessing what he meant, simply cowered away even further.

General Etienne stood atop the wall, watching with a hungry look as the prisoners emerged, dressed in whatever stained rags they had been wearing at the time of their arrest, which for some had been years ago. Most of them blinked and tried to cover their eyes, as the full force of daylight struck them for the first time in months or years. To Etienne's annoyance, the muddy courtyard was too small to contain more than a third of the prisoners, so he reluctantly ordered the lieutenant to start taking groups of prisoners outside, to stand them against the outer wall of the jail.

When there were as many prisoners lined up as the guards could safely keep an eye on, Etienne called a halt. The prisoners cowered against the wall as the guards looked on expectantly, having been surprised to find themselves issued with ammunition for their rifles. Etienne laughed. 'Fire!'

Both inside the courtyard and outside, the guards opened fire on the terror-struck prisoners, the bullets tearing through the ill-treated bodies and blasting tiny chunks of bloody plaster and brick into the air. Drawing bayonets and machetes, they then moved in on their helpless victims. Most of the prisoners were only wounded, since the guards were ill-trained, and they cried for pity as Etienne's troops ripped open their quivering torsos, kicking the warm offal aside, leaving clouds of buzzing insects to descend on them.

When the first groups were finally still, and cooling

despite the sun, the next batch was brought, pleading now that they knew what was to happen.

Charles Oscar Etienne simply laughed, caught in the throes of fear-spawned madness, as he watched his men systematically shoot and disembowel well over two hundred starved and unkempt prisoners, most of whom had been guilty of no more crime than wondering aloud what a change of government would mean for them.

It was as if the entire population of the island had briefly stopped to listen, allowing the sharp crack of rifle fire to carry across to almost every corner of Port-au-Prince. In the Doctor's room, four people's heads jerked at the sound. 'The rebels making their move?' Ace asked.

'No.' Petion shook his head. 'It's coming from the barracks – or the prison.'

'It's Etienne,' the Doctor said quietly, 'emptying the prison.'

'You mean he's killing the inmates.' Benny shot Petion a revolted look.

'He's a brutal pig of a man,' Petion ventured, 'but I never dared to fear he would go that far.' He glanced down at his uniform as if seeing it for the first time. The thought occurred to him that after such a massacre, anyone in government uniform was likely to get lynched and hung from the nearest convenient tree. Fear and nausea washed over him. 'I only wanted to serve my country as my father did,' he began slowly. 'Perhaps it doesn't deserve such service.'

'Captain!' the Doctor snapped in a tone he had heard the Brigadier use frequently; it certainly seemed to get Petion's attention. The Doctor had been going over the details in the journal again, trying to gain some inkling of what it was that had happened there that seemed to have left a telepathic trace for him to pick up. The last thing he needed, therefore, was for Petion to sink into a fugue. 'We don't have much time before – ' He stopped himself, and then realized that Petion wouldn't have time to spread the prediction about. Besides, he thought, Eti-

72

enne and Petion already thought him to be working for British Intelligence, and such information was the intelligence world's stock in trade. Thanking his lucky stars that none of them had noticed that the date on the documents he had shown them was about sixty years in the future, he caught Petion's gaze with icy blue eyes. 'We haven't much time before Admiral Caperton lands his force of US Marines.'

Petion started, but his attention was held firm by the Doctor's steely gaze. 'You mentioned an American pathologist,' the Doctor continued in a low but firm tone. 'You must take us to him immediately.' Petion nodded in bemused agreement as the Doctor paused, before resuming in the same tone: 'First, you will give me back the key you took when we first met.'

'I – ' Petion's hand had taken the TARDIS key from his pocket and proffered it to the Doctor before he knew what he was doing. Petion stared at his hand in amazement as the Doctor retrieved the key and caused it to vanish like a magician's favourite card. He shook his head to clear the cobwebs. 'To get to the university we'll pass that blue box where I met you,' Petion informed them.

'Excellent,' announced the Doctor, jumping to his feet and reaching for his umbrella. 'Let's go, then. More haste more speed, or we'll be lucky if we're worth two birds in a bush.' The two women rose to join him at the door, and Petion moved to open it for them. As he held it open for them, Petion received the Doctor's wink with a smile which suddenly froze. Grey eyes, he thought. I could have sworn they were blue . . .

Business in the city's marketplace still continued, but at a rather more hurried pace, since everyone wanted to stock up on essentials and return home to check on their families. The wary glances the Haitians gave to the pale foreigners who worked for the ore companies and the sisal and sugar companies were more open now, but there seemed to be some kind of realization that the foreigners were as scared of the developing situation as they were themselves.

Major Richmann, hands in the pockets of a safari jacket, leaned comfortably against the shadowy trunk of an ancient and solid tree, which had a good view of the street containing the foreign consulates. The street was packed, both with locals running to and fro and fighting among themselves, and with foreign workers seeking refuge or reassurance.

Somewhere, a hoarse voice cried out a lament for the helpless prisoners murdered by Etienne, while just down the street, a snarling figure exhorted the crowds to take revenge, and beat the soldiers of the government to death. As the cries struck chords with the populace, an increasing number of bricks and bottles began to be thrown at the few government troops who had been trying in vain to keep peace on the street.

Richmann chuckled to himself as the snarling figure drew closer, and resolved into Henri, dressed in the simple clothes of the local people. Henri made a card appear with a flick of the wrist, and glanced at it with a thoughtful expression. 'The *blancs* would seem to be in for a disappointment of some kind.'

'Figures.' Richmann smiled wryly. 'They'll all be begging for passage off the island, and there are only two ships.' He looked around at the black man, allowing some curiosity to show. 'So, do you see this newcomer you want rid of?'

'I haven't seen him in person, but I hope to sense his presence.' Henri ignored Richmann's condescending expression. 'There has been no sign so far.'

'You know, you don't have to do this personally. If Mait says he'll take care of it . . .'

'One can never be too careful,' Henri said.

'Exactly why I don't like to have you here, Henri. You've got a big ceremony to perform tomorrow night, and I'd hate to see anything happen to you – beforehand.' He fought to keep his tone level as he added the last word.

'You seem to be amused about something.'

'Just thinking of good times to come, Henri, since I've got some interesting news reports to give to the wire services; not to mention a fascinating story for each of the foreign embassies. Actually, I'm sort of surprised you're not rolling around with laughter, considering how you should be able to see everything in greater detail than us mere mortals.'

'Compared to most of my countrymen, I am presently in paroxysms of laughter,' Henri replied sourly. He gave Richmann a calculating sideways glance. 'Perhaps,' he said slyly, producing a fan of cards, 'your future would provide some cheer.'

'At least it's nice to know *I* have one,' he said, refusing to pick one of the cards nevertheless. Turning his back on Henri, Richmann searched the crowd for . . . whatever. Presumably, newcomers would be even more confused than anyone else. He found that he was now having to concentrate more forcibly on focusing on the faces, and realized that he was tired, having stood here watching for hours on end. He shook his head, deciding it didn't matter, since it wouldn't affect his ability to kill this stranger if by some chance the person saw and recognized him. After all these years, he reflected, he could probably do it in his sleep.

Pausing only for the Doctor to doff his hat to two elderly men playing cards outside a tiny tin house, the foursome rounded the clump of bougainvillea, and all but Captain Petion stopped short. When he realized that the Doctor, Benny and Ace were no longer following, he too stopped.

Petion looked puzzled and not a little edgy; Ace muttered something that was unintelligible and probably obscene; Benny shot Petion a dark look and cursed herself for not keeping a closer eye on this example of the career military type; and the Doctor simply raised his eyes to the heavens with the resigned look of one who knew that something bad was bound to happen to them sooner or later.

The TARDIS was gone. 'Etienne,' Petion muttered, in the tone usually reserved for the vilest of insults.

'Not quite what I'd expected,' commented Benny, who'd been on guard against any potential ambush since leaving the hotel.

'Happens all the time,' the Doctor shrugged. 'He'll have it at the palace, and that's not going anywhere. Come on.' He strode off.

Benny glared at his back. 'This isn't precisely the sort of living history I'd hoped for,' she grumbled.

Carrefour, now dressed in more formal finery, stood back from Mait, who reclined comfortably in a wicker chair. 'A snake?' Mait questioned in a soft voice.

'I can get in with it, Mait. No one can hide things from me; their very look tells me everything.'

'Such as that the *blancs* are staying at the Royale rather than one of the embassies?'

'Precisely.'

'All right, Carrefour, but don't take too long. I'll have Bobo move out today.'

'It will take but a moment.' Carrefour silently left Mait's study.

Mait leaned back, and tried to shut out the faint tang of the sea that reached him even here, about as far inland as it was possible to get in Haiti. *Even the smell of the brine is disturbing these days,* he thought to himself derisively. From a nearby table, he lifted a thick book bound in something like pigskin, and flipped through it to the page he required. Nodding to himself, he rose, and twitched aside one of the Arawak wall hangings to reveal an alcove. Inside was a small gold and silver mechanism, perhaps two-feet high and one-foot on a side, that resembled a complex clock. Tiny gold and silver rods and cogwheels twitched and ticked softly to themselves. In place of a normal clock-face, however, was a circular convex mirror a few inches across, and other mirrors orbited on stalks and occasionally formed conjunctions of concentric mirrors.

Mait passed his hand across the face of the central mirror and closed his eyes in concentration. 'Bobo,' he called softly. 'Bobo, there is panic and confusion throughout the city. You must make your move now.' His voice gradually hardened. 'You will march now, Bobo. You will march now.'

Satisfied, Mait passed his hand across the mirror again, and replaced the wall hanging with a smile. The Arawaks were fine artisans, given the proper encouragement, he thought. If only some of them had survived. He hadn't had a decent intelligent conversation since the last Arawak died, he opined silently to himself. How long ago was that? He couldn't recall, except that it was sometime before his dislike of open water forced him to move to this sprawling house. It didn't matter, he felt; they, and his people, would be avenged before long.

He lifted the telephone receiver from a cane table, and dialled a number. It was time to inform others that Bobo was moving.

Chapter Eight

The world was strange when viewed through binocular eyes, relying solely on reflected light for vision. Each time, the experience seemed new. Each time, it was new. There was always a sense of discomfort and shying away, but not something that could be truly noticed. It was like the changing of direction by a tick crawling across the skin. It wasn't important.

Dreams provoke autonomic reactions. A dream of a chase causes the muscles to twitch and spasm. A dream of a feast causes a hunger reaction. And a dream of life? Of ruling?

Deep down, in the heart of the world, and the heart itself, something stirred unconsciously in the mindless throes of fading sleep.

The first heavy drops of the afternoon rain had begun to plaster down the dust and make the heat slightly more tolerable by the time Petion ushered the Doctor, Ace and Benny into the shelter of a stuccoed cloister in the small university grounds. 'At least it doesn't seem to be hurricane season,' Ace groaned thankfully.

'It is,' Petion answered sardonically, 'but we're still waiting for the first one.' Without further ado, he led them along the walkway, and down a few worn steps under a creaky-looking archway. Beyond was a long low building of Spanish-looking design, whose white walls had become dulled and pitted. Petion led them directly towards it, and the others noted a sign above the screen door which announced in both English and French that this was the hospital-cum-medical-school. The Doctor paused to shake out his umbrella before going in, while Petion held the door.

Inside, a strong smell of disinfectant greeted them in the open-plan reception area. Three double doors led off to other areas, and a huge fan gently swirled the air. A black nurse looked up from the desk as they entered, and Petion told her in passing that they were going through to see Dr Phillips. From the way the nurse nodded and returned to her business, it seemed obvious to the three travellers that Petion must have been to see Phillips before, and more than once.

The captain beckoned for them to follow him as he went through the left-hand door, and down a long corridor with closed doors on either side. Eventually, after a few more twists and turns past storerooms and the like, they emerged into a wider chamber. The walls had been white-washed rather than plastered or stuccoed, but they retained occasional unidentifiable stains. Despite the cloying smell of disinfectant, there was a faint hint of something sickly sweet in the air. Benny noted that this was attributable to the presence in the centre of the room of the body they had discovered earlier. A trolley containing instruments and other medical paraphernalia stood to one side, while a tall white man in a stained coat and apron was feeling about somewhere in the gaping chest cavity with rubber-sheathed hands. As he worked, he spoke slowly and clearly into the horn of an odd-looking device which Benny recognized, after a moment's thought, as an ancient wire-recorder.

The man stopped in mid-sentence at the sound of their footfalls, and glanced up. 'Oh, it's you, Captain,' he said in a more normal voice with what the Doctor's experienced ear identified as a New England accent. 'I thought you'd be along. I gather you found this poor devil.'

'Indeed I did, Doctor Phillips. I have come, however, for a different purpose. Three,' Petion hesitated for the briefest moment, 'guests wish to speak with you. This is Doctor . . .' Petion trailed off in puzzlement. 'Actually, I don't think I caught your name.'

'I didn't throw it. Doctor John Smith, but I prefer just to be called Doctor.'

'A doctor of medicine?'

'Well, a doctor of many things . . .' The Doctor hesitated. He had taken a medical degree under Lister, but tended to discount this qualification when visiting more sophisticated times, since it was in a relatively basic type of medicine. However, he had taken the degree some forty years ago, as the chronometer flies, so he wondered whether medicine had advanced enough for him to deny it now. Finally, he decided that there could certainly be elderly physicians practising in this time zone who had taken degrees under Lister or his contemporaries, and so he was probably knowledgeable enough by this time's standards. 'A doctor of many things,' he repeated more certainly, 'and medicine is certainly one of them.'

'You got your degree in Edinburgh, I take it?'

'Glasgow actually. Why did you ask if it was Edinburgh?'

'Your accent, of course. Where else would a Scotsman get the best medical teaching?'

'Ah, of course. Actually I'm not Scots, I'm from Gallifrey originally.'

'Gallifrey?' Phillips' brows furrowed in puzzlement, then smoothed again. 'Oh, Ireland then.'

'No! If I had a grotzit for every time an Earthman thought that . . .' the Doctor muttered under his breath.

Phillips had by now moved on to Benny, who couldn't help thinking a little guiltily that such a tall, thin man with lank hair and a gaunt, weathered face looked a little cadaverous himself. 'Bernice Summerfield,' she told him, 'but most people call me Benny.'

'Delighted to meet you, Benny.' He smiled, and his eyes twinkled somewhat. 'Are you also a doctor?' he asked with a slight hesitation, which Benny knew from her studies must have been because of the scarcity of female doctors in those decades – they were allowed, but not really encouraged.

'No, I'm a history professor.'

He was a little taken aback, but, assuming she just meant she was a schoolmistress of some kind, he quickly recovered. Finally, he glanced at the other woman. There, he stopped: she was an unusual woman, dressed in a strange, western-style duster coat with a waistcoat underneath and a low-slung holster just visible on one thigh. She carried herself like an old soldier.

Ace smiled wryly at his confusion, and mischievously wondered what his reaction would have been had she worn her usual combat suit. 'I'm Ace.'

'Pleased to meet you, Miss, er, Ace.' He smiled genuinely. 'What do you do?'

'I look after them.' She jerked her head at the others.

Phillips would once have been a little put out by these strangers, but had seen too many strange things in too many countries, to allow himself to be bothered by such trivia as a woman who seemed like a soldier. He smiled warmly at the trio, hoping they would forgive any lapse he had made. 'I'm Doctor Howard Phillips. I'm sure the good Captain here has told you that I'm the practising pathologist here, and I also teach the subject.' The trio nodded, and Howard continued, as he returned to the table with the cadaver, 'I hope you'll forgive me for not shaking hands, but they're a bit sticky at the moment, as you can see.' He paused in momentary concern. 'Perhaps, if the ladies would care to wait outside, there are things they may rather not see . . .'

'We already have. We were with Captain Petion when the body was found,' Ace said.

'Oh, well in that case, if you're sure. Oh, and call me Howard, by the way, all of you. Petion, are you going to stay?'

'I think perhaps I'd better. I don't think anyone in this uniform will be popular anymore, and in any case, General Etienne will wonder why I haven't reported back.'

'Don't tell me you're disobeying orders?'

'I think maybe it's time I was free enough to admit what scum I think Etienne is.'

'Dare I say "I told you so"?'

The Doctor interrupted by clearing his throat meaningfully, and the three time-travellers clustered around the shattered corpse. Benny tried to keep her face as composed as possible. It wasn't that she was unused to violent death, but she had already seen this mangled form, and wasn't keen to repeat the experience. However, she told herself, it wouldn't do to show anything that the others might take as a sign of weakness. She forced herself to concentrate on the conversation that had already begun.

'I had thought this might've been the work of an animal,' Ace was saying, 'because I've seen such wounds before, done by . . . big cats.' She shifted uncomfortably.

'Really? Haven't seen many cat-wounds myself. I wouldn't mind hearing a bit more on that subject, if you've the time.' Phillips shook his head, as if trying to clear his mind. 'As to this poor chap, it wasn't any kind of claws. If you look here,' he said, pointing to the same ragged edge as the Doctor had, 'the subdermal tissues are far more flattened than they would be if anything as sharp as a claw had made the incision.'

'I thought perhaps fingers,' the Doctor put in firmly.

'Fingers?' Phillips fixed the Doctor with a dark and thoughtful look. 'I suppose it's possible,' he admitted cautiously.

'This man has obviously been torn apart, and I'd guess fingers were the cause of death,' the Doctor repeated.

'Oh, he was torn apart, but neither fingers, nor claws were the cause of death.'

'No?' The Doctor was blatantly surprised. 'Heart failure brought on by stress?'

'Scared to death, you mean? No, total systematic failure. All this,' he waved a hand over the ripped flesh, 'happened afterwards. These, on the other hand,' he pointed to some lesser wounds on the cheek and arms, 'were made beforehand. You can tell by the way the blood has flowed in a more lively fashion than on the main wounds.'

'Poison?'

'More than likely.' Howard watched the Doctor as he

pulled out a magnifying glass, and studied the lesser scars with a practised eye. He wondered just how much the Doctor already knew.

'Fingernails,' the Doctor pronounced, looking up questioningly.

'My thoughts too,' Howard stated guardedly.

'Then someone, or rather several someones, tore him apart with their bare hands.'

'Why wouldn't men use weapons?' Howard said.

'They wouldn't if they were operating on base instinct and had no real intelligence – or had lost it.'

'You've been reading the wrong books before your visit, I think. Or perhaps listening to the sensational stories of the wrong sort of local raconteur.'

'Tetrodotoxin, Howard.' The others all looked at the Doctor in surprise.

Howard felt a sense of relief. 'Ah, so that's why you're here. I feared you might be newspaper reporters – or worse,' he apologized. 'The local rumour-market throws up the most dreadful nonsense, but as you seem to be above that . . . If you'll allow me to wash up, we'll be able to talk more frankly. Oh, Petion, would you mind summoning someone to take the body back to storage?'

Petion nodded and left. Howard stripped off his gloves, apron and white coat to reveal a cotton shirt and linen trousers, which matched the jacket hanging by the sink. Howard then began washing his hands, while the others waited patiently.

Benny, however, found herself drawn to the instruments on the trolley. Despite the climate, which was unkind to metals, the instruments were gleaming. Cautiously she picked up a bone saw, which seemed to her to be a coldly terrifying implement. She smiled to herself, fascinated by the sight of these museum-pieces in their native environment, so to speak. Despite this, she still felt rather chilled by the touch of the saw; even the most basic first aid kit in the TARDIS had an anabolic proto-plaser tucked away in place of these primitive-looking things. 'I'm glad I'm not sick,' she murmured.

She put the saw down as Howard returned, tugging on his linen jacket. 'We can talk in my office, it's this way.' With that, he escorted them from the room.

It had been a childishly simple matter for Carrefour to discover where the new arrivals were staying, particularly since they were the only white people to have arrived when everybody else wanted to leave. Dressed in top hat and tails, he entered the Royale, and glanced around in studied distaste.

When the bell rang, the mulatto who was in charge emerged, both puzzled and pleased by the notion that he was actually getting another customer, despite the present troubles. His smile froze when he saw the tall figure waiting at the desk, leaning casually on a cane. 'How may I help you, sir?' the mulatto asked with some degree of nervousness.

'Where are the new *blancs* staying? The ones who arrived this morning.' The voice was rich but soft and musical.

'Rooms thirteen and fourteen.'

'Ah.' The figure seemed to consider this. 'Their leader, then. Which room did he take?'

The mulatto paused, deciding that despite his strangeness, the odd little man had somehow seemed to be in charge. Besides, the others were only women, he thought to himself. 'Room thirteen, sir.' He tried to keep his voice as steady as possible. 'Will you require a key?'

'Not at all, I can enter the rooms.' The man grinned, and the mulatto felt an icy trickle run down his back.

With a flick of the thumb, Carrefour flipped a silver coin at the mulatto, who caught it fumblingly. Silently, Carrefour ascended the stairs. He was up there only a couple of minutes, and when he returned, he stopped at the desk once more. 'One more thing. Do you know where they have gone just now?'

'I believe Captain Petion said they were going to the university.'

'Thank you,' Carrefour purred as he left. Outside, he

stopped for a moment, pondering the significance of an army captain accompanying his quarry; and a captain who was noted for differences with his superiors, at that. Finally, putting his concerns aside for later consideration, he set off for the university.

Strangely, he no longer had his cane with him.

Howard's office was merely a small cubbyhole, which was barely large enough for all five of them to squeeze into. As they entered, the Doctor pulled a small memo pad from his pocket and hastily scribbled some notes. When he had finished, he handed the pad to Ace. 'Ace, you and Captain Petion go and find the TARDIS.' He handed over the key. 'When you get in, programme in these instructions, then come and meet us here when you get back, right?'

'Right.' Ace nodded, satisfied in a grim sort of way that the Doctor would trust her ability to look after herself. 'Come on then, Captain,' she said cheerily, and the two of them left the way they had come.

'Please make yourselves comfortable,' Howard invited in his rich voice, and the Doctor and Benny sat, glancing around the office. Various framed prints hung on the walls, and an overloaded bookcase sagged under the weight of many volumes, while every available inch of space was cluttered with papers and knick-knacks. Benny couldn't help noticing that many of the curios dotted around seemed more like archaeological souvenirs than anything related to medicine. Howard caught her gaze, and smiled briefly. 'My hobby,' he explained, 'though I have a very basic degree in anthropology, which I suppose meets archaeology halfway. My father always insisted I learn a second trade to fall back on.'

'They're fascinating pieces,' Benny commented.

'Yes. They may have some bearing on what we're about to discuss as well, believe it or not.'

The Doctor raised a questioning eyebrow. 'I thought perhaps we'd talk about *zombis*, Howard.'

'*Zombi*? Ah, from the Congolese *Nzambi*, you

know . . .' Howard leaned back to study the Doctor. 'You are correct to a certain extent, Doctor. Over the couple of years in which I've been here, I have seen several cases of tetrodotoxin poisoning. In those cases, the victim was apparently kept deliberately docile, and often used as a slave. For some reason, the relatives never want to see the victim again, even after he's recovered. I suspect that they are afraid he might bring some curse upon them if he returns home.'

'But they have never truly been dead, and the effect wears off?' the Doctor said.

'The major organs go into a sort of catatonic suspension, as far as I can gather, and the effect does wear off if the victim is not given regular supplementary doses of . . .'

'Of what?'

'I'm not really sure. The stuff's plant-based, but pretty much defies analysis. Someday, though . . .' He trailed off.

'Either way, a victim of this poisoning surely wouldn't display either the ability or the inclination to rip people apart?'

'No, in fact they are, if anything, weaker and more vulnerable than healthy people. However, I have recently encountered something quite different.'

'You mean victims of a different drug?'

'That's what I thought at first, but some of them – it's difficult to explain. Please follow me.' Resignedly, as if it were the only way, he led them through the hospital once more, to a lower level, where the rooms were more like cells, with barred windows in the doors. 'This,' Howard explained, 'used to be the mental ward, though there wasn't much use for it, in the normal sense.'

Benny wrinkled her nose at the stench that was perceptible through the doors, and even the Doctor looked unhappy about it. Howard led them to one door, and slid open the window. Inside was a malnourished woman in simple rags, who was finishing a plain meal. She ate slowly and dully, as if not truly aware of what she was doing. She was barely able to lift the spoon to her mouth.

'That,' Howard began, 'is a tetrodotoxin victim. We don't know her name or who her family are, but we're trying to bring her out of it. Usually it succeeds, and they become what's called a *zombi savane* – an ex-zombie as it were.'

'But surely there must be something more you can do than lock her up and feed her gruel,' Benny said, horrified. 'Wouldn't some sort of therapy – '

'We try. Her door isn't locked, as it happens, but she seems to prefer it in there for the moment. Anyway, this is what really puzzles me, and I suspect you'll be interested, Doctor.' He opened the window of another cell. Instantly, a contorted face lunged for the opening, pulled up short by a thick iron chain. The inmate was a white man, whose mouth twisted and snarled, though his eyes remained completely dead. He strained at his fetters with inhuman stoicism, his fingers stretched into talons. 'I am as uncomfortable with the idea of chains as you are, Miss Summerfield,' Howard began hastily, clearly noting the look on Benny's face as she opened her mouth to speak, 'but it is unfortunately necessary.'

'What makes it so necessary?' she asked with undisguised contempt.

'You see the scar on his chest?'

'Yes, is that what I think it is?' the Doctor asked slowly as they peered at the Y-shaped mark on the man's chest.

'It is. Those are autopsy scars.' Benny's eyes widened, as Howard continued, 'He was washed up on the beach a few miles outside town, and brought in here. It seemed an obvious case of drowning – a sailor washed overboard, perhaps – but I conducted an autopsy nevertheless, as part of one of the classes I teach. I discovered that he hadn't drowned at all – in fact, I couldn't find a cause of death. I believe it was finally recorded as misadventure, by the way. Anyhow, after the class I sewed him back up, hence the scars, and called two orderlies to take him to the morgue. They are now hospitalized with serious injuries. Apparently, they had got him into the drawer and were about to close the door, when he burst back out, and attacked them with no real motive at all. It took Captain Petion and seven of his men to get him down here.'

Benny frowned in horrified disbelief, while the Doctor leaned back against the wall, wrapped in his own dark thoughts. He looked at Howard from the corner of his eye. 'How many more cases have there been like this?'

'None here, but I hear that there have been some cases in the nearer towns and villages. It's impossible to get details, though, because the villagers are scared that Baron Samedi and the spirits of the Petro gods – that's the evil gods, in case you're wondering – are abroad in the countryside. It doesn't help that they have some sort of instinctive dislike of foreigners, and the *cochon gris* have got everybody afraid of their own shadows. The rebellion was just the icing on the cake, I suppose, though to be honest, revolution's an everyday thing here. I don't think anybody really pays much attention to who's the President at any given time.'

'Well, I can't blame them for their dislike of foreigners,' the Doctor announced, 'considering what the French in particular have done here since the slave-trade started. As for the *cochon gris*, it's high time I did something about – have there been no cases in Cap Haitien or Petionville?'

'Not that I've heard, though news doesn't travel particularly quickly here; except for that carried by the drums, of course.'

'It must be nearby then,' the Doctor said. Both Benny and Howard looked up, but were startled when the Doctor suddenly snapped his fingers decisively. 'Didn't you say your archaeological curios had a bearing on this business?'

'Yes, of course. Back to my office . . .'

While the Doctor merely glanced at the carved stone fragments with a nod and a look of recognition, Benny handled them with reverence, feeling the chill and gritty texture of the stone as she hefted its weight. She viewed the actual carvings with more trepidation, however, as they seemed to depict rather unnerving serpentine forms, some of which also had stylized wings, feelers, or other less recognizable limbs. Something stirred within her, trying to reach the surface thoughts in her mind, as if the carvings were somehow familiar.

'These fragments,' Howard lectured, 'came to light up on the mountain slopes on the same day as that poor fellow downstairs was brought in.'

'That's hardly a connection.'

'No, Doctor, but look.' He dug out a large, thick book from the bookcase, which creaked in relief, and laid it in front of the Doctor.

'Where did you get this?' the Doctor breathed in a palpable mixture of fascination and horror.

'From Crowley. I once had cause to give him emergency treatment for an ulcer, and he gave me this in lieu of payment.'

'The unexpurgated *Necronmicon*, eh?' The Doctor carefully opened the book, and flipped through the yellowed pages, whose spidery script seemed to defy the eye's powers of focusing. 'And with all Roerich's original illustrations,' the Doctor added tonelessly.

'It's something of a collector's item, or so I gather. Page one hundred and fifty-six is the one you're looking for.'

'Right.' The Doctor flicked through to the relevant page, and nodded silently as he saw the illustrations there.

Benny leaned over for a look, laying the carvings on the desk. She gasped in surprise, as she realized that the illustrations on the page were the same as the carvings, albeit less worn. They seemed to show unnameable creatures bricking themselves up in a representation of a citadel.

'The last paragraph on the next page, I'm told, reads – '

'It's all right, I can read it,' the Doctor said.

'You can? What language is it?'

'Eocene.'

'Well, what does it say then?' Benny demanded impatiently.

'It's a bit fragmented, but I'll give it a go. "Even as the . . . Great Ones," I think that is, "may return from their resting slumber, so the adept may, by use of the Ashes of Noah, and essential Saltes, call his fellow man back from the great beyond." It seems to be a rather roundabout set of instructions for bringing back the dead.'

'Doctor!'

'What is it, Benny?'

'These pictures,' she said, mentally kicking herself for being unprofessorially slow to remember, 'I know what they remind me of.'

'You've seen this before?'

'Not the book, though I've heard of it. The carvings, though, are identical to ones I've seen on both Veltroch and Exo Three.'

'Are you certain?'

'I've got holos in the TARDIS I could show you.'

'We might get round to that. Is there any chance – ' He stopped and looked at a bemused Howard. 'Might you excuse us for a moment?' Howard nodded and the pair stepped out into the corridor. 'Is there any chance the ones you saw on those planets were taken there by human colonists for some reason?'

'No way. The ones in the tunnels on Exo are carved into living rock and are millions of years old. As for Veltroch, there's a globe there covered in those carvings, and when we scanned it for its age, the readings went off the scale, which make it at least three *billion* years old.'

'How much do you know about them?'

'The archaeology journals are full of them, from many different planets. Some authorities reckon they're evidence of a star-spinning race at the dawn of the universe, while others feel they show that aesthetic standards develop along similar lines everywhere.'

'The first theory, it speaks of the Great Old Ones, doesn't it?'

'You know it does.'

'I'm just thinking, so imagine for a moment that I don't know. Tell me.'

'On most inhabited planets with these carvings, there are legends of ancient beings who ruled everywhere, before dying out. The legends also say that someday they may return, but that's a facet of legends about everything from Davros to King Arthur.'

'Did you know that Earth has such legends?'

'No!' She blinked in surprise; to think that Earth could also have such stories and she, a professor of archaeology – sort of, she mentally added guiltily – didn't even know it.

'The Terran version is more detailed, perhaps because it's more recent.'

'You know about these things?'

'More than most,' he said shortly. 'There is a certain significance in the frequency of discoveries of the legend's artifacts. I wonder . . .' He opened the door, and they both rejoined Howard.

'Howard,' the Doctor began, 'have there been any more findings of carvings like these?'

'So you think they're important too?'

'I know they are. Just answer the question.'

'Well,' Howard began, clearly slightly taken aback by the Doctor's sudden brusque attitude, if not a little offended, 'I believe the university museum has a few pieces.'

'There's a museum here?' Benny managed to sound interested, though she silently thought that it would probably be an uninteresting hovel.

'Yes, down past the front gate. It doesn't do much business even at the best of times, but it's there. It mostly has artifacts from the original Arawak inhabitants, and few bits and pieces from Columbus's ships and those that followed.'

'I think I'll go down for a look, then,' Bernice said.

'Benny – '

'Doctor, I can take care of myself.'

'All right, but be careful, and meet us back here at five.'

'Right.' With a friendly nod to Howard, she left, unaware that the Doctor was watching her with a concerned look.

'Well then, Howard, I'd like you to show me where these things were found, if you would.' The Doctor ended with his most winning smile.

Carrefour had been circumnavigating the university grounds, and came to the hospital just as Benny emerged. He paused in the shadow of a palm tree, observing her as she set off, stopping to ask directions of a nurse arriving for duty. From his concealed position, Carrefour gleaned from the snatches of conversation drifting across the grounds that Benny was headed for the museum. Had Carrefour waited a few moments, he would have found the Doctor as well, but instead he slipped away to a short cut he knew that led to the museum. As he moved, he took a jar of scented oil from one pocket and proceeded to rub it over his face and hands.

He moved wrapped in his own thoughts, deciding that the information the woman could give about the others would alone make what he was about to do worthwhile.

Chapter Nine

Transient flashes of thought coalesced briefly, but then were gone in fractions of an instant. There was a sense of wellbeing, of satisfaction, as if at the thought of the approach of some eagerly awaited occurrence.

They were not flashes of dreams, but of something perhaps approaching the nature of conscious thought.

Flashes of life.

The young man who had driven Richmann's car the previous night glanced about him uneasily. Something about the ancient caverns in which he and his fellows had made their base unnerved him to no small degree. Perhaps it was the unnatural smoothness of the walls, floors and ceilings, which gave the definite impression of having been deliberately constructed, although his superiors had assured everyone that these were natural caverns.

Nevertheless, that sense of artificiality was present, exacerbated by the sheer oddity of the shapes of the caverns. Perhaps, the man thought, that was why these were supposed to be natural caves: no human mind could have designed such forms, where the angles joining walls to ceiling were strangely canted, giving the impression of odd spaces at the edge of vision. It wasn't so bad in the main cavern, of course, since the corners there were hidden in shadow due to its sheer vastness; but, out here among the corridors and labs, the effect was very noticeable.

The young man carefully followed the signs hammered into the stone, since he knew, as did they all, that there were innumerable deeper caverns below, in which it was terrifyingly easy to get lost – or worse. Fortunately, the man thought with relief, his destination was not too far from the main cavern, and voices carried to him quite well, accompanied by the miscellaneous sounds of machinery and well-coordinated activity.

Before long, he emerged on to a flat landing – illuminated by a larger bulb than the ones in the corridors – which opened on to a pair of double doors with rubber trim round the edges. A skull-and-crossbones notice leered from the door at eye level, but the young man greeted it as an old friend, and stepped through the doors.

The scene that greeted his eyes could have been lifted from any of the gothic scientific romances of the previous couple of decades. White-coated forms busied themselves among long, specially built worktops which were cluttered with all manner of beakers, retorts, valves and endless lengths of glass tubing. The air was filled with the sounds of dripping liquids and the muffled chatter of masked scientists. Against the far wall were several booths with airlock-style doors, and glass cabinets, from whose ports thick rubber gloves hung like dead squids.

Picking up a filter mask from a pile lying under one of the many charts that adorned the walls, the man threaded his way carefully through the laboratory to the corner in which stood an almost skeletal figure with a grey widow's peak.

Professor von Stein turned at the man's approach and nodded, his dour expression visible through his mask. 'It's time for the test, I know, Leutnant,' he broke in before the young man had a chance to speak. 'I don't see why they couldn't call up on that damned contraption,' he finished, waving in the direction of a piece of electrical workmanship on the nearest wall.

'I wish they had,' the young Leutnant answered with feeling. 'However, I was to bring this to the lab.' He drew a thick, narrow envelope from inside his civilian jacket.

'The autopsy results for Doctor Karnstein?'

'Yes.'

'I'll leave them on her desk.' Von Stein stepped away from his position, and the Leutnant saw that he had been observing some rats in a cage filled with straw. As he watched, a faceless lab assistant opened a small door in the other side of the cage, and removed one of the creatures, clamping it into position on what was evidently a specially designed operating board. After checking the clock which was attached to the steel bars of the cage, he carefully took hold of one of the rat's back legs with a sinister-looking set of metal pincers, and twisted sharply. The Leutnant suppressed a grimace, then backed off hurriedly, for the crunch of breaking bone was not accompanied by the requisite sound of agony. The assistant made a note, and was putting the rat back into its cage when von Stein returned and beckoned to the Leutnant. 'Come on then, young man, we don't want to keep the General waiting.'

As they paused to remove their masks, von Stein lifted a small medical case from a cupboard, and left the laboratory. The young Leutnant followed, almost glad to be back in the caverns.

Captain Petion pulled Ace quickly into a doorway, as the people on the streets scattered at the sound of gunshots, leaving hens and the occasional goat to scramble for cover. The pair watched as unwashed men in scraps of mismatched uniforms bore a coffin hesitantly through the street. The coffin was followed by several wailing people of both sexes, who started at each shot from the gun of the bandolier-draped ruffian in front, who was announcing the coffin's arrival by firing in the air.

'What the hell is going on, Petion?' Ace said.

'A funeral, probably for one of Etienne's victims.'

'At least he let the relatives claim the body.'

'I doubt it. More likely they broke in and stole it back during the unrest.'

'Is he that bad?'

'I'm afraid so.' Petion glowered darkly, cursing himself for ever obeying any order from Etienne. 'I've brought shame on all of us by serving under him.'

'Cut that shit out,' Ace snapped, fixing him with a stare. 'Did you know he was like this before you joined up?'

'Well, no – '

'Shut up, then. At least you had the guts to quit when he went off his trolley. What about the others in the army, eh? The ones who're shooting everybody on his orders?'

'Well, they . . . I see what you mean.' He fell silent, somewhat mollified.

'Right. Now, where in the palace will they have taken the TARDIS?'

'The what?'

'The blue box.'

'Oh, that. I don't know, we – I mean they, have never confiscated anything quite like it.'

'Damn. We'll just have to ask someone where it is. Can we go now?'

'One moment,' Petion said, and glanced out at the street. 'All clear.' With no other sound, they both emerged from the doorway, and hurried along the edge of the street, skirting close to the walls of the buildings, until they finally came to a fortified gateway, where soldiers could just be made out behind piles of sandbags. Petion rapped on the gate, and a scruffy soldier appeared, his gun raised. When he saw Petion, however, he smiled and lowered the gun.

'Open the gate, Private,' Petion said in a commanding tone which was much firmer than he had expected it to be. Nodding wordlessly, the soldier unlocked the huge gate, and opened it just wide enough for them to enter, then slammed it shut again. Ace and Petion hurried towards the barracks' entrance to the palace.

Henri almost missed it, having fallen into a drowse through sheer boredom, but something caught his attention, and he snapped his head around to follow the movement. He saw a man in the uniform of an army captain entering the palace gate in the company of a young white woman. That in itself was strange enough, since most of the soldiers went to the brothels in the town proper, and wouldn't consort with the supercilious *blancs*, but there was something else . . . Abruptly, he realized what it was. It was the way she moved: not like a woman, but like a hunter, or a soldier – and Henri knew for certain that even the *blanc* nations didn't have women soldiers.

He snatched his cards from a pocket and flicked one into view at random. It showed a young queen with a sword.

Henri smiled, and hurried away.

Ace and Petion had barely entered the barracks, when two soldiers appeared. 'Hey, that's the Captain the General wants,' one of them exclaimed.

'What does the General want to see me for?' Petion demanded as the soldiers approached.

'Treason and desertion. You're under arrest.' They both lowered their rifles, aiming them at the stomachs of their quarry.

Ace and Petion slowly raised their hands. Ace could practically hear Petion seething, and knew instinctively that he'd never been in this position before. She raised her hands with a calm born of experience. 'You ready?' she asked in a conspiratorial whisper.

'What?' He relaxed as he realized what she meant. 'Yes.'

'Follow my lead then.' She remained silent as the two soldiers came up to them and prodded them with their rifle barrels. One of them opened his mouth to give them an order, and gestured down a drab hallway with his head. At that instant, Ace sidestepped, grabbing the rifle and pulling forward, with the result that the soldier practically dived face-first into her raised knee. He tumbled, spitting blood, while Petion rabbit-punched the other as he froze in surprise, then smashed him in the mouth with his own rifle butt. In a matter of seconds, they had locked the two soldiers into a linen cupboard and tossed the rifles into the bushes outside.

'This could complicate things,' Petion said dryly. 'Where did you learn to fight like that?'

'School playground.' She stifled a laugh as Petion's eyebrows lifted so high that they almost disappeared. 'Still,' she continued, 'you're right about this complicating things. We can't spend all our time dodging your ex-comrades.' She gave him a wolfish grin. 'I think that if Etienne's so desperate to see us, we'd better do as he wants – more or less.'

'No excuses, Lieutenant! I want Petion and that *blanc* bitch under lock and key within ten minutes, or you're sharkbait!' Charles Oscar Etienne slammed down the telephone receiver with an animalistic snarl, which froze in a twisted rictus as his office door slammed open, the glass pane cracking under the impact.

'I believe the phrase you're looking for is "Speak of the devil",' Ace commented, as she thumbed back the hammer on the revolver she'd picked up at the French compound. 'Shut the door, Petion.'

The Captain closed the door, and remained by it, keeping an eye on the corridor outside. 'Ace,' he said worriedly, 'perhaps it would be better if I asked the questions. I admit you did well against those guards, but – '

'I'm in a bad mood, Petion, so if you're about to say anything like "But you're only a woman," I'll shoot you too.'

'Sorry.'

Ace gave Etienne her best icy smile, and was rewarded with a glimmer of fear in his eyes, though he still looked more surprised and irritated than anything else.

He glared back, silently sneering at this woman who dared to threaten him. Even so, he could not help but take notice of the revolver which loomed, alarmingly large, in the foreground of his vision. He swallowed. 'Women shouldn't be allowed to play at soldiers,' he grunted finally.

'Listen, Etienne,' she said in a dreadful voice, 'I've seen more campaigns, more death, more horror, more bravery and more honour in the last three years than you'll ever see. What I've never seen in that time, though, is a supposed warrior and leader of men who's quite as moronic, bestial and dishonourable as yourself. In addition, I've had a very bad day, what with finding dead and mangled bodies, and being pissed off by your guards, so I'm in just the right mood to conduct a little interrogation.'

Etienne started back in his chair with a little noise at the back of his throat.

'What I want to know,' Ace continued, the gun pointed unwaveringly between Etienne's eyes, 'is what have you done with the big blue box you had brought in this morning?'

'Why should I tell you anything?' he snarled.

'I'd have thought because it's obvious that I'll shoot you right now if you don't.' Privately, without allowing any fluctuation of the muscles in her face, she willed him to talk rather than make her keep to her word. Etienne might get his kicks from killing unarmed men, but she wasn't going to let herself drop to that level. She had experienced a twinge of disappointment when she realized that he didn't have a gun in his hand.

'Kill me and you never find out where it is,' he sneered.

Ace smiled coldly. 'I said I'd shoot you, I never mentioned killing you. I've got six shots here, General. First I do your kneecaps, then your elbows, then maybe wrists or ankles.' She wondered how she could be saying this. Even this scum didn't deserve such treatment, though he might condone it. Behind her, Petion looked chilled by her threat, and her tone. 'After that, I reload and move on to more imaginative targets.' She shifted her aim, her meaning clear. 'So speak now, or forever hold your peace.' Come on you arsehole, she thought, don't make me do this.

Etienne's eyes bulged. 'It's in the armoury,' he shrilled. He clutched the arms of his chair tightly, his eyes fixed on the gun barrel. Ace noted the direction of his gaze, and felt wryly disappointed that she had put all that effort into the cold calculating killer-look, only for him not to see it.

'I know where the armoury is,' Petion put in.

'Good.' Ace stepped back to the door, not taking her eyes off Etienne for a moment. She and Petion stepped outside, and closed the door all but a crack. Keeping the gun on Etienne, Ace took a small spherical piece of plastic from one pocket, and balanced it precariously on top of the door. 'That,' she called in to the petrified General, 'is full of gelignite. Open that door, it falls, and boom!' She and Petion hurried off down the hallway.

Etienne sweated.

As they dashed through the stuccoed corridors, Ace glanced over at Petion. 'Wish I had some nitro with me.'

'Wasn't that an explosive you left on the door to Etienne's office?'

'Nah, it was one of them things you get for washing liquid. If we don't get to the TARDIS before he finds out, we're in the soft brown stuff.'

The two soldiers who were on guard outside the armoury looked half-asleep, and Ace and Petion were able to walk up and crack them sharply over the head without resistance. The doors to the armoury were unlocked, and as they carefully poked their heads round them, they saw that several men were inside being issued with ammunition. Unnoticed, they withdrew. At that point, a shot blew splinters from the thick door, and the unmistakeable voice of Etienne bellowed, 'Get them!'

Three guards were with him, crouched behind ancient suits of armour. Ace and Petion dived for cover behind the pillars to either side of the doors as several more shots howled up the corridor, blasting chunks of wood over the whole area. At least one hit one of the unconscious guards. Ace felt a stab of guilt at the thought that her action had left the guard defenceless.

'Inside!' she shouted, and stepped out from behind her pillar, loosing off shots steadily, knocking holes in the suits of armour with hollow booms, and causing the guards to duck back as she followed Petion into the armoury. The few troops inside glanced up, ramming rounds into chambers.

'Quick,' Petion shouted, 'they're just outside! Go and help the General.' Responding instantly to the commanding voice of a superior officer, the men dashed out. Ace thought she heard a couple of them fall in the ensuing volley of gunfire, as she slammed the heavy bolts home to lock the door.

The TARDIS stood in one corner of the armoury, a huge room filled with endless racks and cabinets of arms. Many of the storage spaces still held swords and pieces of armour, but there were plenty of rifles, revolvers, grenades, crates of dynamite and so on. In a dim corner, Ace could make out several small artillery pieces that looked positively Napoleonic, while some Maxims and Gatlings stood in a row against one wall. A couple of large cabinets were marked with warning symbols that Petion translated as meaning they held explosives.

The brief volley of gunfire outside had ceased, and there were inarticulate shouts and thuds as something heavy was slammed against the door. 'They'll take a long time to get through it,' Petion said. 'It's iron cored.'

'Great!' Her mouth crooked upwards. 'It'd be a crime not to take advantage of the time we'll have in here,' she began. 'Do you have a key to those explosives cupboards?'

'Yes.'

'Good. Open them, and I'll be back in a minute.' She fished the TARDIS key from her pocket, opened the door, and went in. Petion began opening lockers and cupboards filled with large boxes covered in stencilled danger signs. He had just finished when Ace returned, pushing a strange, basket-like wire contraption before her. Petion goggled at the thing, which rolled along on wheels which each seemed to want to go a different way. 'What is that thing?' he asked in amazement.

'It's a shopping trolley.' She couldn't keep the surprise out of her voice; hadn't these things been invented yet? 'Right, you saw that Frenchman; if we're likely to run into whatever he ran into, we'd better get some shopping done first.'

In a clearing between cane fields, where the earth was already drying out, Professor von Stein prepared an injection, watched by several men who stood around him in a semicircle. All the men wore tropical uniforms marked with the insignia of Kaiser Wilhelm's army. A group standing beside a skeletal scarecrow wore plain battle-dress and battered helmets, and were armed with long Kar 96 rifles, while the ones watching von Stein most closely were officers in full dress regalia.

Von Stein finished his preparations, and injected a fluid into the left arm of another soldier in unadorned fatigues. Having done this, he turned to a stout figure bedecked with medals, who proudly wore a close-cropped, red Van Dyke beard. 'Well, General, the subject is prepared. I have given a more diluted dose this time, with some minor adjustments to the formula.'

'Excellent, Herr Professor. Kapitan, you may begin the test.'

'*Jawohl*, Herr General.' This man, with the lean, scarred face of a professional fighter, waved the man in fatigues away. Nodding, he broke into a run, and vanished into the fields.

The General turned to the soldiers, who were hefting their rifles. 'You know the parameters of the test. You have been issued with live ammunition, and may fire at will when the target is sighted. Your task is to prevent Private Hauser from retrieving the flag at the old jetty and returning here. I know,' he lowered his tone to sound more companionable, 'that Hauser is your colleague and friend. If this test is successful, he still will be. If not, then be assured that he will not have given his life in vain, as these tests are vital to the war effort.' He glanced at an expensive gold Hunter he wore on a chain. 'It is time. Go now, and good luck.'

The Kapitan and his six men jogged into the fields after the first man. The General stepped over beside von Stein. 'You know, Herr Professor, you're not going to be very popular among the men if this goes wrong as well.'

'It was your idea to use my work this way. You were

102

supposed to be here to scout for locations for a submarine base.'

'I found one, but providence also delivered this little bonus, which is why I sent for you and Doctor Karnstein. Don't tell me you begrudge your country this service?'

'I'm not particularly bothered either way.' He shrugged. 'Apart from this damned climate, that is. As for Karnstein, who knows what goes on in her head?'

Ace dropped, carefully, a final box of small-arms ammunition into the shopping trolley, and wheeled it over to the TARDIS. Petion followed her, throwing nervous glances at the door, where the thuds had got louder and cracks had begun to appear.

'Come on,' she said, pushing the trolley inside.

'We won't both fit in there with that thing.'

'Are you ever in for a shock.' She disappeared inside.

Hesitantly, sure he'd have to squeeze, Petion went in after her. After the briefest instant of blackness, he emerged into a wide white room with some sort of machinery in the centre. Ace stood at the machinery, and the shopping trolley lay unattended to one side. With a gasp, Petion leaped backwards, into the armoury. Astonished, he walked cautiously around all four sides of the blue box, and went back in again. The white room was still there. With a weary look at him, Ace pressed a large red lever, and a pair of double doors slammed shut, sealing them in. 'What is this place?' Petion whispered.

'The inside of the TARDIS. The blue box,' she explained to his blank look.

'Impossible!'

'Yeah, but you get used to it.' She had taken out the piece of paper the Doctor had given her, and laid it on the console. Referring back to it frequently, she made a number of adjustments to the controls, before turning on the scanner. Petion looked at it in amazement, as the lock on the armoury door finally gave way, and a horde of soldiers tumbled in. General Etienne stalked in with them, his features contorted with rage. He made straight

103

for the TARDIS and rapped his fist on the door. 'I know you're in there,' he bellowed, 'it's the only hiding place. Come out, and I might let you live.'

Neither Ace nor Petion was going to fall for that one, however, and so neither of them was surprised when Etienne ordered his men to attack the TARDIS door with the sledgehammers they'd used on the armoury doors. The sound of the impacts echoed deafeningly through the console room, but Ace knew well that the soldiers would never get in that way.

Nevertheless, she decided this was the time to follow the Doctor's last written instruction. Turning the scanner off, she tapped a keyboard and watched one of the small monitors until the words, '*Hostile Action Displacement System – Emergency Manual Override,*' came up. The Doctor had informed her that using this system was the best way to guarantee that the controls would respond to her. 'Pity we won't be able to see their faces,' she told Petion, and pressed the '*Execute*' button. The faint hum that filled the air suddenly lowered in tone, and the glass column at the centre of the console slid smoothly into motion. Petion looked puzzled as Ace laughed.

Outside, the soldiers exchanged fearful looks as a deep grinding sound emanated from the blue box they were hammering at. Suddenly, as the grinding assumed a definite rhythm, the box faded away into thin air.

Etienne was so frozen in terror that he didn't even notice his men running off in panic.

In the console room, Ace jammed the interior door open, before returning to the trolley. 'Come on, I've got a lab set up inside, and I could do with your knowledge of local weapons.'

'I didn't think even the British secret service had this sort of thing.' He waved around vaguely.

'Oh, it's amazing what Q Branch comes up with,' she replied, wondering silently just what had been on the paper that the Doctor had shown Etienne when they arrived.

Though his breathing was quite shallow, Hauser's eyes darted around him like those of a hunted fox. He crouched at the edge of the cane field, looking down the overgrown slope that descended towards a rickety old jetty which hadn't been used for years. The jetty was perhaps half a mile away, but the plain red flag that had been rammed between two of its planks was big enough to be clearly visible over that distance. He nervously searched the intervening terrain: the nearest area was covered in scrub grass and low oily-leaved bushes; the last few hundred yards in rocks and boulders. At first he saw nothing, but then, at the last instant before moving, he noted a bush bending against the wind, and realized that at least one of his pursuers had circled around to block his path. Hardly had this realization penetrated his mind than he heard the faint sound of the crushing of leaves and grass behind him. Stiffening, he glanced back, and saw the heads of two of his pursuers approaching his position.

He didn't stop to think for long, since he wasn't armed, but decided that he might have a chance if he could get into the bushes and rocks below, where he might circle around them all. Taking a deep breath, he burst from hiding like a startled hare, dashing into the undergrowth while the first shots zipped past him. He hadn't gone far when he felt a heavy blow on his shoulder, which knocked him off his feet. There seemed to be no other damage, however, and he rolled up and bounded from bush to bush as more shots pounded into the vegetation around him. Another blow, which he saw was a shot from the man in front, caused him to stumble, and he rolled downslope, crashing headfirst into a boulder. Rising to his feet, he saw the others converging on his position, and he slipped aside as the firing started again.

Hauser dashed through spaces between the boulders, changing direction according to the sounds of pursuit. Finally, he reached an open space between the rocks and the jetty, which protruded out into the sea. There was no sound from elsewhere, and Hauser knew that his pursuers were waiting for him to go for the flag. He had no choice. Mouthing a last prayer, he sprinted for the flag, and was instantly pummelled by a flurry of what felt like heavy punches. None caused any pain, though, and he managed to grab the flag and run back to the rocks.

Now all he had to do was get back to the starting position.

In the clearing in the cane fields, General Froebe and Professor von Stein had been listening to the crack and boom of rifle fire for some time, until the soldiers eventually started to arrive back, out of ammunition. Froebe looked on eagerly, and von Stein crossed his fingers. A few moments later, Hauser walked slowly back out of the fields, carrying the flag.

The soldiers eyed him apprehensively, and not without cause. Hauser's body was ragged, his flesh torn by their bullets. His back and chest were just patches of ripped muscle and bone, but he still stood, and there was surprisingly little blood. Tiredly, he handed the flag to General Froebe, who looked at von Stein with glee. 'Excellent, Herr Professor. Simply marvellous. He doesn't even feel any pai – ' A gut-wrenching scream cut him off, and he whirled to see Hauser fall, coughing large gobbets of blood into the dust. He was choking, his face drained of colour; in seconds, he lay silent and still. 'Perhaps a formula that doesn't wear off so quickly is in order, eh, Professor?'

'I'll get on to it immediately, sir,' von Stein agreed wearily.

'As a matter of fact, you won't, not quite yet. Henri and Major Richmann have found us a suitable test site for the main project, so this secondary one will have to wait a bit longer.'

'When is the main test?'

'Henri has a ceremony tomorrow night, so we'll administer Phase One tonight, and Phase Two after twelve hours.'

'Yes, that should allow sufficient time for a certain

result, either way, and Henri can judge the effectiveness of the suggestibility enhancement.'

'Good; then I suggest you make sure your people are ready. And by the way, don't forget to deliver Hauser to Karnstein. I want to know what went wrong this time as, I'm sure, do you.'

Chapter Ten

The university museum turned out to be a low, maze-like building set at the edge of the grounds. Despite its small size, Benny looked forward to her visit to it as a source of double historical interest. After all, not only would she see objects of interest, but the chance to see how museums were run six hundred years in her past would itself be worth taking.

Ducking into the building, she found herself in a shadowy vestibule whose air was scented with the must of antiquity. An elderly curator seemed to be the only person in the museum; Benny reminded herself that people had other concerns at the moment besides visiting such places. Still, she would have expected at least one or two students to be about. She decided that someone ought to tell the local history professor how to get things done. She made a mental note to do so on general principle, and tucked it away at the back of her mind.

As Benny approached, the curator looked up curiously, perhaps surprised to see a customer at all. Benny went over to the booth in which he sat, and indicated the open interior door. 'Is there a charge to go in?' she asked. It went against her nature to even think about the possibility of entrance fees to such places, but she was aware that others had more commercial viewpoints.

'Entry is free, Miss,' he piped up. 'Would you like me to show you around?'

'That'd be fine. I'm honoured.' Somehow she sensed that the old man liked to show off his museum to whatever visitors actually appeared.

The curator nodded with a gap-toothed grin, and came

out of the booth's side door. He beamed at her eagerly. 'What would you like to see first?'

'I've heard the word "Arawak" mentioned a few times. What – '

'Ah, not many people today show interest in them. There's a selection of Arawak artifacts over here.' He led Benny through an arched area in which stood several suits of Spanish armour, posed to look like they were setting up a camp. Beyond the armour was an open area, where the displays consisted of wall hangings, pots, pieces of jewellery and other small knick-knacks. 'These are some of the bits and pieces that the *blancs* didn't steal or destroy when they first landed.'

'So the Arawaks were the original inhabitants of the island?'

'That's right. They were hunter-gatherers until the *blancs* started to arrive. Shortly after that, they had all been wiped out, or driven to other islands, then wiped out there. All gone in less than a hundred and fifty years.'

'That's disgusting!'

'That's the *blancs* for you.'

'No doubt.' By this time, Benny had more or less got used to the use of the word '*blanc*'. It often seemed to be used to mean simply 'foreigner' rather than as a deliberate insult. 'Do you – ' She broke off, having the sudden uncomfortable feeling of being watched. 'Is there nobody else here today?'

'No, n – no one. They are not interested in the past here.'

'A pity.' She looked around inconspicuously, wondering if she had truly heard the slight fearful hesitation in the old man's voice, or had only imagined it. 'Do you have any new exhibits?'

The old man tensed briefly, before visibly forcing himself to relax. 'There are a few pieces in the rear gallery. I doubt they will be of interest to you, though,' he added almost pleadingly.

'Show me.'

'They are through there,' he said, indicating another arch. He shuffled uncertainly.

'Aren't you coming, to give the guidebook tour?'

'I have some other work to do.' Clamping his jaws shut, he sidled off back in the direction they had come. Benny watched him depart consideringly. He definitely seemed frightened by something, as if he had somehow been warned off. Again she felt that sensation of being observed, though there was no one around, and it occurred to her that perhaps this hadn't been such a wise decision after all.

She shook her head, putting such thoughts out of her mind. If someone was in here watching and waiting, she could wait till he made his move, then one swift boot in the groin and he'd be as harmless as any of those empty suits of armour. Setting her jaw, she stepped into the area the curator had indicated.

Nothing happened. She glanced around and saw that there was no one there. Harrumphing to dispel her tension, she went over to a low table, upon and around which a number of stone pieces had been set out. They ranged in size from a few inches across to one huge block that could have filled an average doorway. Her attention drawn to the markings on the large stone's surface, she examined it first, drawing out a Holmesian magnifying glass and peering through it. As she had expected, the stone displayed a welter of strange serpentine carvings which were arranged in rows like a bas-relief cartoon strip. From another pocket, she pulled out a thick diary, and opened it somewhere near the front. Flipping pages for a second, she stopped and gazed at the sketch she had made six-hundred years hence on the planet Veltroch, which orbited the star Fomalhaut some seven parsecs from Sol.

The precise details of the 'plot' of the stone comic were obviously different, but there was no mistaking the fact that both the aesthetic style and the form of the creatures depicted, were identical to those on a rock on an alien world untold billions of miles away.

110

Benny suppressed a cold shiver that assailed her spine as she thought of the implications of her discovery, and instead concentrated on noting the details concisely under the Veltroch sketches. 'If I can just get back to the twenty-sixth century, my Nobel's guaranteed,' she said to herself. 'Maybe even a Magnees . . .'

She turned her attention to the table with the smaller fragments. A placard was propped against them, and she picked it up to enable her to read it under the dim lighting. It read: 'Soapstone carvings – possible Arawak tribal legends, engraved into stone for posterity. These specimens were discovered on the north side of Gonave Gulf near Port-au-Prince. No other information is known about these antiquities.'

'That's never recent enough to be Arawak,' she muttered, wishing she'd thought to bring a tricorder. Benny replaced the card, and brushed her fingers against her trouser leg. The curator couldn't have been particularly house-proud to have let the dust build up like that. She filed a second mental note to remind the curator about the responsibilities of the upkeep of exhibits. She noted that the stones were also a bit dusty. Picking one up, she wondered why she couldn't feel its surface when she wasn't even wearing gloves. Her breath stuck in her throat, and she had to force herself to draw each breath. She shook her head to clear the cobwebs, and started at a faint noise behind her.

The sound of soft footfalls behind her caused her to turn sharply. An unnervingly tall and calm form stepped out of the shadows, dressed in top hat and tails, with kidskin gloves. She tried to take up a defensive posture, but her legs had apparently gone to sleep; pins-and-needles assailed her, and she sprawled at the stranger's feet. Fuzzily, she wondered what was wrong with her, and what the stranger was up to. He looked down at her with a grin that was downright worrying, and leaned across to pick up the placard. He held it before him, and blew softly, spreading a cloud of dust through the air towards her and chuckling softly.

He crouched down beside her as her vision faded, and nodded to her. 'Sleep now, Miss. You've got a big day tomorrow. A beautiful day.' He laughed again, and the last things Benny saw at the end of the white, TV static tunnel of her vision were his gleaming teeth, which slowly vanished like those of a demonic Cheshire Cat.

The Doctor silently clutched his umbrella and watched Haitians from all walks of life jump equally quickly out of the way of Howard's bone-shaking car. Even with such primitive transport, it did not take long for them to get out of the city, though they had to duck a few times due to trigger-happy locals, and the car sustained a few holes, mainly to the rear bodywork. Fortunately, its performance wasn't affected, and they were soon out in the countryside, over the dusty ridge that backed the city, and into a narrow track that ran through the cane fields. To the south rose the Cibao mountains, and the Cordillera Central mountains, the beginning of which marked the border with the Dominican Republic. When out of Port-au-Prince, Howard turned left, and they covered about twenty miles before stopping at the point where the coastline veered to the left.

Howard got out of the car, gesturing at the rolling countryside all around. 'This area is the source of all the recent finds of those carvings.'

The Doctor got out, and scrutinized the lay of the land, which consisted mainly of cane fields inland, surrounded by areas of thick tropical growth, and of dusty scrublands towards the coast. 'Do you hear anything?' he said.

'Just the damn bugs.'

'No, I meant – ' He stopped, remembering the telepathic sensation he'd felt earlier. The new sound was like that, but more physical somehow; definitely a real sound. The Doctor wasn't surprised that Howard couldn't hear, since his ears were more sensitive than most humans', which proved advantageous now and again. It had its downside, of course, he thought acidly, since it made busy restaurants an absolute nightmare of revolting sound. 'It's more of a vibration, I suppose . . .' Handing his umbrella to Howard for safekeeping, the Doctor searched around for a moment, finally finding what he wanted. It was a smallish boulder a few feet off the road. Going over, he brushed off a few basking insects, and set his ear to it.

'Look, Doc, what are you doing?'

'Listening, so be quiet.'

'Oh.'

'And don't call me Doc.'

'Sorry.'

'Hmmph.' The Doctor concentrated, trying to blank his mind, to keep it open and receptive. At first there was nothing, but gradually, as the Doctor's conscious mind settled into a receptive mode, he began to discern a faint thrumming which sounded, or felt, constant, and yet seemed somehow to oscillate. Rising with a nod, the Doctor suddenly bolted about a hundred yards along the road, and ducked into the scrub on the other side.

Howard followed in consternation. He had visited the British Isles once and remembered them as damp and dreary. Had the hotter climate addled the Doctor's senses?

He found the Doctor crouched with his ear to another boulder, sighting along one outstretched arm. 'Er, Doctor? Are you all right? I mean, the heat – '

'I'm perfectly fine,' the Doctor protested crossly. Frowning, he picked up a few small pieces of stone that were scattered around. 'This type of rock should be quite a distance underground,' he said. 'Exactly as I thought.' He stepped back out on to the road, and pointed at a small headland that curved into the bay a short distance away. 'What's over there?'

'Nothing that I know of, except a ruined plantation that's overgrown. It was terraced on that hill,' he said, pointing.

'Are there any mines on the island?'

'Certainly not over there. There are some inland, in the foothills. Why do you ask?'

'The earth carries vibrations, signs of activity. Judging from triangulated readings, I'd say it centres on that area.'

'You could tell that?' Howard scoffed in disbelief.

'Yes,' the Doctor snapped irritably. 'I'd better go and take a look – ' He was interrupted by a distant thunderous rumble.

'Even in the tropics, you don't get thunder in clear skies,' Howard pointed out worriedly.

'No, that was a dynamite blast, and it came from Port-au-Prince.'

'Bobo! He must be making his move now!' They both dashed back to the car.

'We've got to get back to Benny,' the Doctor urged.

'Right.' The car started up, and they set off.

Chapter Eleven

Haitians of all political persuasions scattered in panic when the first shells, and even cannonballs, began to hit. Although Port-au-Prince was under fire from the oldest and most primitive of artillery pieces, which were so ill-preserved as to be as dangerous to their operators as to their targets, the effect was still terrifying to the populace, who were unused to the banshee wail that echoed overhead and preceded bone-crushing explosive impacts.

Henri paused briefly under an archway, a glimmer of sadness pulsing within him. He was delighted, of course, that the objective he and his colleagues had worked towards for so long was finally approaching, but it was disheartening to see such damage and disruption being inflicted on what was, after all, his home.

He rushed towards the corner building that housed the news and wire-service office, hoping fervently that Richmann would still be there. He was in luck; just as he reached the corner, casting nervous eyes upwards at another screech, Henri saw a glowering Richmann come out of the building. Kicking aside a couple of fleeing peasants, Richmann came over to Henri, a cold scowl on his face. 'What the hell is going on? This isn't supposed to start until dawn.'

'There has been a change. One of the *blanc* women I told you about has entered the palace; the other has been taken by Carrefour.'

'Hoo-rah,' Richmann drawled sarcastically. 'What about the man?'

'I'm told he has left the city with the American from the university hospital. He will probably return, however, now that one of the women is ours.'

'Are you trying to tell me,' Richmann began dangerously, 'that these changes in plan have been made just on the basis of your superstitious intuition that the newest arrivals on the island are somehow dangerous?'

'Mait knows the value of my power of *obeah*.'

Richmann, clearly less impressed with Henri's powers of fortune-telling, snorted. 'General Froebe knows the value of following a logical strategy,' he replied pointedly.

'The General approved the order.'

'Oh? And was he given the choice before the order went out, or simply informed that it had been given?' Richmann couldn't keep the scoffing tone out of his voice.

'It is a moot question,' Henri snarled, eyes burning. Richmann smiled understandingly, and Henri's blood pressure soared. 'Your orders, Colonel, are to prepare an ambush for the man and the American. I recommend taking up position at – '

'You recommend nothing, Henri! You don't tell me how to carry out a military operation, and I won't tell you what you can do with your cards.' Before Henri could reply, Richmann turned and stalked off, batting civilians aside. Richmann seethed at Henri's arrogance, and consoled himself that with any luck he wouldn't have to stand for the superstitious fool's whims for much longer Drawing a gun from a shoulder holster, he prepared to fight his way through the streets if necessary; it would be nothing compared to what was to come, he thought.

Henri watched him go, trying to calm himself down, distressed at how easily he had succumbed to Richmann's taunts. Still, he thought, as long as Richmann considered him a superstitious peasant, he wouldn't consider him a threat. Or at least, not until it was too late . . . Calmed a little, he too walked off, in the opposite direction, safe in the knowledge that no one in their right mind, regardless of politics, would dare to stand in his way.

Jean Vilbrun Guillaume Sam sat at his desk, head in hands, apparently oblivious to the events outside. He knew he was a dead man, no matter what happened – it

116

was just a matter of time. He had called for Etienne some time ago, and was still waiting; it gratified him to think that he would at least have an excuse to send the stupid pig on ahead of him.

When the door opened, he looked up expectantly, his hand straying towards the drawer that held his revolver. Instead of Etienne, however, he saw a young lieutenant, barely out of his teens. Sam's hand stopped, but didn't withdraw. 'Where is General Etienne?' he asked softly.

'I do not know, sir. He seems to have vanished.'

'Vanished?' Sam laughed hollowly. 'I might've known he'd be the first rat to desert this sinking ship.' He waved around grandiosely. 'All right, you'll do. Order an immediate and indefinite curfew. Allow one hour for the announcement to circulate, then shoot anyone who violates the curfew.'

'The announcement wouldn't even reach half the city in that time,' the young officer protested hesitantly. 'You'd be ordering us to shoot anyone on the stree – ' His speech ended with the full stop of a heavy bullet in the face. Without a further sound, he toppled to the carpet.

'It's going to be hell getting that stain out.' Sam looked at the revolver as if seeing it for the first time. He breathed heavily as images of the fates of previous presidents replayed themselves in his mind. He considered whether the gun offered him an alternative; whether it would be better to shoot himself now and be done with it, or fight on and try to take some of his enemies with him.

Decisions, decisions, he thought.

General Etienne not only had to duck, but also had to hunch his shoulders in, just to fit in the narrow tunnel that led from the palace cellars. Though brutish and simple, he was by no means stupid enough to fail to recognize what fate would await him when the rebels broke in. There was no doubt in his mind that they would break in, since there hadn't been any failed revolutions on the island

117

during his time. There had been quite a few successful ones, however.

He had briefly considered going out fighting anyway, but had been held back by the thought that he should deal with those immediately responsible for his predicament. To Etienne, this could only be one person – the *blanc* who had threatened to betray him to the President in the conversation which Etienne now interpreted with the benefit of hindsight.

Of course, there had been the event with the woman and that blue box, but if Etienne concentrated hard enough, he found that he was able to think that he'd imagined it. At least, he reflected, his men would be thankful for an enemy whom they could see, and who wouldn't disappear into thin air. He himself would see what tricks the *blanc* had to save himself.

It took only a couple of hours for the news to reach Washington DC. The stocky man who was President of the United States was informed of the news from Haiti in the Lincoln Suite of the White House, which comprised the living quarters for the President and First Lady.

Within ten minutes, Woodrow Wilson had consulted with his chiefs of staff in the war room, and decided to go ahead with the contingency plan. Though there had been some concern as to what the world's reaction would be, Wilson had smoothed it over with assurances that the world community couldn't deny that America had the right to protect the few hundred of its citizens in Haiti, and to defend the various mining and import/export concessions that had been granted to them.

'Besides,' he added confidentially, 'Haiti's only six hundred miles from Florida, and right in the middle of the Indies. Now, I don't want their niggers giving our niggers any funny ideas.'

The morse message reached the waiting ships a couple of hours after that. Marine Captain Glen, who was Colonel L V Mortimer's number two, found his superior in his cabin, reading a letter poker-faced. 'Still no change, sir?' he began understandingly.

'Not really, but the painkillers are having less effect now.' With a grunt, he sat up and tucked the letter away. 'So, what is it, Captain?'

'Orders from Washington, sir.' He proffered a slip of paper.

'Well well. We're to go in immediately, eh?'

'The Admiral's ship has already signalled ours. He intends to make a dawn landing.'

'Willing to trade the risk of a night of hell in the hope that the niggers'll be too tired to fight us off afterwards? All right, Captain, dismissed.' When Glen had gone, Mortimer rose, and took his Browning automatic from its holster. Rooting out the cleaning kit for it, he went to work thoughtfully, the letter all but forgotten.

Benny had been in something of a fog since her visit to the museum. Although she could have sworn she had blacked out, she still somehow recalled the journey on which she had been taken by the tall man and a few others. She had seen them through a strange fuzzy blankness, as if they were constructs of her subconscious which were being projected against her closed eyelids. She felt a sensation of floating, since the poison which had claimed her had blocked all physical feeling, and she could not move her head to see the men who were carrying her.

After a seemingly interminable journey through what sounded like continual thunder, low walls of tangy wood rose up around her, and she realized in horror that she was being lowered into a coffin. Chill dread settled in at the base of her skull and directed the activities of her roiling stomach, as she tried in vain to move her mouth, or even blink. Surely she couldn't really be dead; couldn't they see that? She still had so much to do, so many worlds to explore, discoveries to make, fathers to find . . .

Something briefly blurred her vision of the tall man, who silently wiped away the tear she could not even feel, before he lowered the lid over her face, cutting off all light.

She could no longer see what was happening, and certainly couldn't feel anything. The coffin muffled all sounds from outside, and she wondered if they were going to leave her here, or whether she was being taken elsewhere. The thought crossed her mind that perhaps they were burying her, and she silently shouted at herself not to think that, even though it was the most natural supposition she could make.

Ace had hung her coat over a chair in her lab, and was busy rearranging the workings of several weapons with the aid of a set of jeweller's screwdrivers. Occasionally, she glanced across to check on the progress of the chemicals bubbling away on the other side of the room.

'What is this made of?' Petion asked with a note of admiration.

'What?' She turned, and saw that he was examining her combat suit. 'Oh that. It's woven kevlar fibres mainly. Protects against shrapnel from frag grenades and shit like that.'

'Fascinating.' He was obviously comparing the slightly elastic design with Ace's figure. 'I suspect it's very fetching.'

'You want to see?' she asked with a certain degree of mischief.

'Doesn't matter,' he shrugged. 'I was mainly thinking of its military application.'

'Really?' She didn't believe a word of it.

'Really,' he replied firmly.

She looked back at him curiously. 'Don't tell me you're – '

'What?'

'You know.'

'Oh! No, worse than that, I'm afraid. I'm married.'

'That usually doesn't matter to guys,' she commented blithely.

'It does to me.' Petion's voice dropped to a softer tone.

'Do you worry about her? With all this shit going on, I mean.'

Petion smiled, his scar crinkling, as he thought of the woman with the sunny smile . . . 'Often. But for now she lives over the border in the Dominican Republic. Her aunt lives there and gave her a room, so as to avoid the strife here. I took her there myself while off duty after being injured by a faulty grenade.'

'Probably just as well she got out. I sometimes wonder what it would be like,' Ace said softly. 'Get married, have kids, stay in one place and one time . . .' Be a mother, she thought, but what kind? 'It's not for me, though. Not yet.' A thought struck her. 'I've been meaning to ask,' she began hesitantly, 'if it's not an indiscreet question, that is. That scar – surely it's not from the grenade?'

His hand twitched towards the scar, almost reflexively. It was just below his left eye and consisted of three sloping cuts, and a fourth bisecting all three. 'No, it isn't. It's something that's difficult to explain to *blancs*. My parents were something of traditionalists, and in Haiti it is a tradition that if a baby is born more fit and healthy than average, the mother will add a blemish, such as a scar, in case the *lou-garou*, the werewolf, should take a liking to such a perfect child.'

'That's obscene,' Ace growled, the hairs on the back of her neck prickling at the thought that a mother could do that.

'Not to us,' Petion answered dismissively. 'It's better than being eaten alive.'

Abruptly, the all-pervading background noise in the TARDIS altered, and when Ace and Petion dashed back to the console room, they found the time rotor grinding to a halt.

As Ace tipped the door lever, Petion nodded towards the doors. 'I'll go first, in case some of them are still out there.' He couldn't bring himself to believe what Ace had told him about the TARDIS's ability to move. He was surprised therefore, after drawing his gun and edging out carefully, to find himself standing in the deserted mortu-

121

ary room where he had introduced the three travellers to Howard. Behind him was the solid bulk of the blue box, and he walked around it again, still disbelieving.

'Any sign of the Doctor or Benny?' Ace emerged behind him.

'No, but they may be elsewhere in the building,' he answered distractedly, tapping suspiciously on the nearest corner of the TARDIS.

'I hope so – listen.' Outside, the evening was shattered by the sharp sounds of gunfire, and the occasional explosion. Needless to say, these events didn't silence the persistent drumming, though they did sometimes drown it out.

'I'll go and check Howard's office,' he said.

'No, I'll go. You round up as many others – nurses, patients, whatever – as possible and get them together in as few rooms as you can. Then we'll see how defensible we can make this place.'

'Right.' Without hesitation this time, he set off.

Ace looked back at the TARDIS door and weighed the key thoughtfully. 'I get the feeling we're in for a long night', she said.

Mait received Henri's report dispassionately, before letting a slow smile spread across his face. 'So, control of the *zombis* through the mind mirror is completely effective. I'm sure Froebe is also pleased.'

'So I gather.'

'Were there any problems?'

'Two of the *zombis* collapsed upon their return and could not be revived. The French had wounded them and they were too dead.'

'That is to be expected. Still, the test was a success, and I am not displeased that a French area was chosen as the site. Very well, convey my congratulations to General Froebe – I'm sure he'll be anxious to convey his to me for the sake of protocol.'

When Petion returned, Ace had brought out from the

TARDIS the four Vickers guns that she had liberated from the palace armoury, and was checking their actions for signs of wear or damage. He hurried over, followed more perplexedly by several nurses and patients, and handed her a note. 'I found it in Howard's office,' he explained.

Ace took the note and read it, finding that it told her where the Doctor and Howard had gone. 'They're not back yet?' she asked.

'It seems not.' He indicated the people with him. 'These are almost all the people who are here, except for a few who couldn't walk, but I'm having them moved to the ward nearest here.'

'No sign of Benny either?'

'None.'

'Strange.' Ace furrowed her brow and thought about it. Going by past experience, there was a high probability that something had happened to the others, and her first instinct was to go and search for them. She knew, however, that getting herself into trouble as well wouldn't help them; going by the sounds of fighting outside, she knew that it would probably be almost suicidal to risk going out tonight. Clenching her fists until the knuckles went white, she reluctantly decided that it would be better to stay here and hope that the Doctor, Howard and Benny made it back. When she looked back at Petion, she saw that he was watching her with a sympathetic expression. She realized that he must know exactly what was running through her mind. Straightening, she pointed to the Vickers. 'Get as many able bodies as you can and set up these guns in the most advantageous positions – you know the layout better than I do.'

'As the highest-ranking military officer, isn't that my decision?' he asked softly, with a faint smile.

'Doesn't experience count for anything? I've fought in more battles than you'd be likely to believe.'

'Really?' Petion glanced back at the TARDIS. 'I think I might believe any number.'

Chapter Twelve

Something was disturbing all efforts to continue resting. Primitive sensations skittered here and there, triggering twinges of irritation that carelessly boiled away.

The Doctor ordered Howard to stop the car at the top of the road leading down into the city, weighing up the risks of being attacked by one side or the other.

'We weren't attacked by any villagers,' Howard pointed out reasonably.

'The villages only really pay lip service to the capital, since the *Bizango* rules them,' the Doctor answered. Howard cocked an eyebrow, intrigued that a newcomer could know such a thing, but the Doctor didn't notice as he continued: 'In the city, it'll be complete chaos. Do you have any weapons?' the Doctor asked resignedly.

'Just this.' Howard reached back and pulled out a double-barrelled shotgun.

'It'll have to do. Get out,' he ordered. As Howard got out and went around to the other side of the car, the Doctor slid over, and examined the rudimentary dashboard. 'I'll drive, so you keep an eye out and use that thing if you have to. Try just to frighten with it,' he added as an afterthought.

Richmann had found a couple of his men in one of the city's bars, and dragged them out to take up position around a junction in the northern poor quarter. The two men, who were completely sober despite their time in the bar, moved away to stand against the cracked plaster walls of the buildings to either side of the main road, glancing quickly around the corners to check for traffic.

Calm and untroubled, Richmann sat in the shade of a palm tree, and relaxed. He felt no fear that either the militia or the rebels would molest him or his men, since all the troubles were occurring in what he thought of as the richer areas. Here, he could see only the occasional flutter of movement, as the fearful denizens of the area tried to keep out of the way and out of trouble.

He strongly suspected that the course of action he was taking was the one that Henri had been about to suggest earlier, before Richmann had walked off. This hadn't stopped him following the actual strategy, but Richmann wasn't about to let anyone tell him how to do his job – that was a matter of principle. He spent the next few minutes wondering how much more of Henri's ungiven advice he would be following.

He was drawn from his reverie by the faint chugging of an engine. He stood, cocking his head to estimate the speed at which the vehicle was approaching. It seemed to be moving quite rapidly. He gestured to his men, who drew back from their corners and pulled out Lugers from concealment.

Whistling softly to himself, Richmann drew his Steyr automatic from its holster beneath his leather jacket, checking that it held a full magazine. Returning the Steyr to the holster, he reached into the holster on his right thigh and slipped the cut-down Winchester free. Slipping ammunition into the Winchester, he strolled out into the centre of the road, and stood casually, facing north, the shortened rifle held loosely but firmly in his hands.

Due to the modifications that the Doctor had made to his own vintage car, Bessie, he found that he had forgotten just how slow the genuine article's top speed was without intervention from superior technology. The journey in Howard's car forcibly reminded him of that limitation, however, as he struggled to get the thing going over thirty miles per hour. Muttering very unscientific speculations in a number of alien languages about the car's origins and usefulness, the Doctor kept his foot down and did his best to avoid the holes in the road.

Howard alternated between scanning their surroundings for signs of hostile action, and glancing worriedly at the Doctor, all the time fearing for his car's safety at these maniacal velocities. There didn't seem to be any sign of anyone at all, and Howard wasn't particularly surprised, since neither the government nor the rebels were particularly interested in the hovels hereabouts. Abruptly, the car breasted a small rise in front of a junction, and Howard's eyes widened as he saw a man standing in the middle of the road, who, it seemed, they were about to run down. Before he could give a warning, the Doctor slammed on the brakes.

Richmann tensed as the approaching engine noise reached a peak. Suddenly, a car appeared at the end of the short stretch of road beyond his men. Richmann stood his ground, certain he would be able to jump out of the way if things went wrong. With a screech, the car began to slow as the brakes were applied, and Richmann could clearly see the startled faces of the occupants as it slewed to a halt only a few feet ahead. Smoothly, he worked the action of the Winchester, and swung it up towards the centre of the windscreen.

Time slowed to a crawl for Howard, as he saw the gun swing up, its wielder moving a half step forward and a half turn round. Recognizing that he had no time to position his own gun, Howard ducked down, the enemy gun already beginning to flare at one end.

The Doctor too ducked, almost cracking his head on Howard's skull, as a hot blast of air drove a shower of glass splinters over their backs.

Without raising his head, the Doctor threw the car into reverse, inadvertently hitting one of the Luger-toting men who had stepped out behind them. The other one began loosing shots into the car, sending bullets slamming into the backs of the seats. Then the first man stalked forward, blasting several more shots into the car; the radiator disappeared in a cloud of steam, the bonnet was blown off, and the car suddenly lurched downwards and circled as half the wheel nearest Howard was blown away. Howard finally got his gun into position and fired one barrel at their original assailant, causing him to dive headlong back behind the palm tree. He began to aim at the other man, who was reloading his Luger, but was stopped by the Doctor's hand on his shoulder. 'The wheel,' the Doctor hissed. Nodding his understanding, Howard grimly fired the other barrel at the half-wheel in front of him. The half-wheel disappeared in a blast of sparks and blue smoke, causing the car to lurch again. The Doctor immediately threw his weight into the steering wheel and floored the accelerator, sending the battered car down the street at a lopsided angle, the exposed wheel hub throwing up a constant stream of sparks.

Richmann and his remaining man ran a few yards after the departing car, blazing away with a frustrated volley which only succeeded in blowing a few holes out of the bodywork and setting fire to the rear-mounted spare wheel. Richmann halted, white-knuckled and tight-lipped. 'Shit!' he snarled, whirling back to face his men. The one who had accompanied him chasing the car simply glowered in the direction it had gone, while the other one, who hadn't fired a shot, writhed by the roadside, trying to clutch a leg which trailed at an unnatural angle.

Richmann strode over to the injured man, and glared down furiously. He gave the bad leg a gentle kick, to be rewarded with an agonized moan and the information that it was certainly broken, probably in two or three places. Richmann glared back down the road at the settling dust, and seethed that two men with only a double-barrelled shotgun could get away from *him*. He looked down angrily at the man who had been so uselessly injured. Unable to restrain the anger that welled up within him, Richmann swung his cut-down Winchester round and, with an animal roar, blew the man's head open like

a dropped melon. For a few seconds, as the body crum-
pled into the dirt, Richmann stood quaking with fury,
veins throbbing with hatred. Gritting his teeth, he fought
it down. 'Damned idiot!' he spat at the sticky patch in
the dusty road.

Evening turned into night with considerable speed in the
tropics, and by the time Howard's smouldering car crawled back into the university grounds, it was almost fully
dark. They had run into a few mobs of scuffling Haitians,
but fortunately, they were mostly without firearms and so
the Doctor and Howard had been able to drive through
them, sending the mobs scurrying out of their way. The
car, however, had picked up a few more dents, and none
of the windows existed any longer.

A number of dark figures ducked into the surrounding
bushes as the car screeched to a halt outside the hospital's
front door. Almost immediately, there was a brief burst
of machine-gun fire, which destroyed the three remaining
wheels. 'One group or the other must have taken over
already, Doctor,' Howard said.

'I very much doubt it.' Cautiously, the Doctor poked
his head out of the door. 'Ace!' he called.

'Doctor? Is that you? Hang on a mo.'

'I thought as much,' the Doctor muttered darkly. 'I
think it's about time I had a talk with her.' He and
Howard climbed out of the car, which reacted with a
series of creaking sounds and the hiss of escaping steam,
and hurried over to the door. Ace opened the door just
wide enough for the pair to enter, and slammed it shut
just as a brick arced over from the darkened bushes. 'All
right Ace, what's going on here?' the Doctor said.

'Well,' Ace flinched a bit at his severe tone, 'we got
into the palace, persuaded Etienne to tell us where the
TARDIS was, and flew it back here. Just like you said.'
She smiled innocently.

'And where did the machine gun come from?

'That arsehole Etienne had stored the TARDIS in his
armoury, and I thought it would be best not to waste the

time we had in there. It's just as well I did, 'cos by the time we got back, this place was virtually surrounded.'

'Who by?'

'Rebels out front, militia out back. I think that they each think this dump's occupied by the other.'

'And now we're stuck in the middle. I presume you took more than one gun?'

'I've got four old Vickers guns set up in strategic positions, so neither group should be able to get in. Petion and a few of the hospital staff have rifles and handguns as well, and all the patients have been brought into the middle rooms for safety.'

The Doctor had to grudgingly admit to himself that she'd done well, but another thought was nagging at him. 'When you said "persuaded" Etienne, what did you mean by that?'

'I just threatened to blow his ba – ' She stopped at the look that crossed the Doctor's face. 'I threatened to shoot him,' she finished.

'And did you?' he asked dangerously.

'No.'

'Good,' the Doctor said, relieved. 'I disapprove of killing at the best of times, Ace, but, and this is vitally important, you must *never* kill anyone with a role in recorded history if you can possibly avoid it. That is more important for your planet than any other considerations.'

'What?!' Howard recoiled in surprise at the direction the conversation was taking.

'What historically important person ever came from Haiti?' Ace asked, ignoring him.

'Er, look, what do you mean by "your" – ' Howard continued, rather flustered.

'Well, it was a Haitian who first deciphered the Rihanssu language that allowed a peace treaty to be drawn up, and ended an interstellar war with Earth in the twenty-seventh century. Have you killed anyone?' he asked urgently.

'Not that I know of; we're firing at knee height.'

'Oh, that's all ri – What! Fire above their heads!'

'Look, Doctor, Ace.' Howard finally managed to get their attention by laying a hand on each of their shoulders. 'What do you mean by "your planet" and all that talk about the twenty-seventh century?'

'Ah, that.' The Doctor grimaced; he had completely forgotten Howard and now regretted speaking so openly. There was only one thing to do – brazen it out, and hope that Howard found the facts too ridiculous to believe. 'Well, actually, Ace is from nineteen eighty-six, Benny is from the twenty-fifth century, and I'm not from this planet at all. As a matter of fact, we travel in time and space.'

'Oh.' Howard's eyes blanked over. 'I think I'll have to think about that . . .' Is this man insane, he wondered, or am I? Aliens? Time-travellers? Utter nonsense, surely? And yet, the Doctor seemed so matter-of-fact about it, so sincere. But then, he reminded himself, so do those who believe themselves to be Napoleon, or Alexander, or God. Howard sighed.

'Why don't you come with me,' the Doctor suggested, seeing his expression, 'and I'll show you the TARDIS. Ace, you and Benny continue with what you're doing until the Marines arrive in the morning, and please stop making that face.'

'What face?'

'That one when I mentioned Benny. Can it be that you two aren't getting along?'

No, it's not that.'

'Good.'

'It's that she's not here.'

'You mean she never came back?' The Doctor sounded horrified. 'Howard, how far is it between here and that museum?'

'A few hundred yards. She shouldn't have had any problems.'

'Unless she ran into one of those groups . . .'

'I wanted to go after her,' Ace added, 'but Petion wouldn't let me.'

'Quite correct of him, too! I should never have let her go off in the first place.' He paused for a moment, before

130

letting his breath out in an uncharacteristic snarl. 'We'll just have to leave that problem until morning as well. Reset those guns to fire warning shots, and try to keep us safe till dawn. If my memory doesn't deceive me, Admiral Caperton's Marines should land around then. Come on, Howard, and I'll show you the TARDIS.' Together, they set off.

When Benny's fuzzy vision flared, she imagined that it was one of those near-death experiences that people talked about. Or perhaps not just near in her case. She still felt that she was floating – or, more accurately, she thought that she was floating precisely because she couldn't feel. She was not expecting the vaguely defined figure that coalesced as her vision cleared.

Father, she first thought as the figure of a grey-haired man resolved itself. So she was dead after all . . . Then her vision cleared further, and she saw that the man looking down on her was much thinner than her father had been, with a more skull-like face and thinner hair. She realized then that the coffin lid had simply been lifted off, letting in light from a long strip-light that hung from a plain rock ceiling. The thin man, who was dressed in a white lab coat, examined her eyes with the aid of a magnifying glass and a small torch. She found that she could not even blink under the harsh glare. Next, the man lifted a six-inch needle from somewhere beyond her field of vision, and jabbed it down sharply, while watching her eyes. She strained, but still couldn't see what happened, and couldn't feel where the needle had gone in.

The man glanced down at the needle. 'Little bleeding,' he commented in a noticeably Teutonic accent. 'What did you use?'

'A *coup poudre*,' came the lilting answer.

'Diodon and sphoeroides?'

'You would use such terms, yes. Absorbed through the fingertips, before you ask.'

'How long ago?'

'About three o'clock.'

'Hmm. You say she is working with the British?'

'With a man who claims to be a British agent.'

'All right. She'll recover by midday, I should think. Put her in the infirmary until then – strapped down, of course.'

'Of course, Professor.'

Recover by midday? Benny relaxed in relief, though it didn't show in the slightest.

The village didn't even have a name, and wasn't placed on any maps of the country. Its two-dozen or so crumbling one or two room houses squatted in the scrubby hillside clearing like old termite mounds. They were far enough from the city for the sounds of insurrection to be too faint to disturb anyone but the few scrawny goats which wandered listlessly around their enclosures. No lights shone in the village, since darkness was for sleeping as far as the villagers were concerned.

The night air was still and mercifully cool, a gentle breeze blowing in from the coast below. A few clouds drifted above, forming only briefly before dissolving again. And then there was something else.

It slipped smoothly through the blackness, a faint throbbing heartbeat announcing its coming to a couple of village dogs, who strained in vain to make out what it was with their inadequate monochrome vision. They began to howl and bark, rousing the villagers from their beds, and starting babies crying. Underfed farmers emerged from their homes, rubbing their eyes and searching for suitable throwing stones. They stopped their search, however, when the faint throbbing finally penetrated their consciousnesses. Questioning each other, they milled around, looking upwards with tired eyes.

The first wisps of vapour came unnoticed, but not for long. It was only a matter of moments before one man twitched his nose at some unfamiliar scent, and turned to see what it was. Rather than completing the movement, however, he simply spun limply into the dust without a sound. Shocked cries were choked off as his fellow villagers followed him into oblivion, softly caressed by the spreading gossamer folds of vapour which billowed ever more thickly through streets in which even the babies' cries faded into silence.

In the darkness above, something dark also faded away.

Chapter Thirteen

The rest of the night had passed quite quietly at the university, and the Doctor, Ace and Petion had taken turns on watch. Howard had, after a quick tour of the TARDIS, retired to his office with a brandy bottle he had been saving for a special occasion.

Off in the distance, sharp cracks of gunfire and the occasional dull blast of dynamite interrupted the rural drumming. Around three am there was a huge blast from the direction of the palace, which woke even Howard from the slumber into which he had fallen.

The great double doors of the palace had been smashed inwards by a hammerblow from an American Civil War vintage sixty-five pounder naval gun, which the rebels had somehow recovered from the sunken *Atlanta*, transporting it on an ox-drawn cart since the wheels were missing from its carriage axles. As the plaster dust settled, dazed guards emerged from the interior of the palace, only to be cut down by the machete-wielding *cacos* who had brought their knowledge of the palace to the rebels. A few shots rang out, killing one or two rebels, and those rebels who had guns returned fire, albeit hitting some of the *cacos* as well as the guards.

The guards were ill-trained and fearful, with little combat experience, while what the rebels lacked in training and tactics was more than made up for in sheer ferocity and homicidal bloodlust. It was a matter of only a few minutes before the rebels reached the President's quarters, and stopped to await General Bobo, who had made clear his intention to take over personally.

Bobo was surprisingly young for a general, being only

in his early thirties, and had unremarkable features atop his muscular frame. He was dressed in yet another variant of an old French colonial uniform, this one blue, with occasional spaces between the somewhat tarnished medals. He wore a grim expression, not showing the elation with which he looked forward to killing President Sam, and taking over as ruler of his country. He paused outside the doors, taking stock of his men, careful not to give any sign of his thoughts. He only wanted the best for his people, of course; to save them from the unjust regime of Sam. Of course, he would probably have to raise taxes to rebuild his ideal country, and shoot a few of his highest officers before jealousy got the better of them, but that was only natural. The people would understand, he thought; if they didn't, they were obviously supporters of the maniac Sam, and would be properly shot. Those who spoke ill of him would find it difficult to continue such activity without a jaw to move, he considered, and made a mental note to put one of the Secte Rouge in charge of security. They'd enjoy that, he knew.

Bobo was in for a shock, however, for when he kicked open the door to Sam's office, he discovered that the President had already taken the matter out of his hands, having blown his own brains out. He now sat slumped in his chair, fate having painted a faintly mocking smile on to his clammy skin that spoke of joy at having outwitted his executioner. Cursing, Bobo emptied the contents of his revolver's cylinder into the lifeless form, which shuddered in a parody of its former fearful existence. Only then did Bobo step fully into the room, and allow his followers after him. 'Tell the people I have executed this most unworthy of Presidents,' he ordered in a surly manner. 'In fact, take the body out into the streets and shoot it again.'

The dull orange glow of fires added scant colour to the moonlit visage of Port-au-Prince's whitewashed buildings as seen from Gonave Gulf. Colonel L V Mortimer, USMC, scanned the city as part of his preparation for landing. The ship he was on was, he and his men hoped, hidden from view in the shadow of the large island in the centre of the gulf. Mortimer had attended a staff meeting with Admiral Caperton which had lasted through the night. The meeting had determined that Mortimer's ship and one other would simply sail into the harbour, dock, and begin debarking troops to secure the city and protect any foreign citizens they found – particularly Americans from the university and the dockside customs receiver-ship, but also any others if there was an opportunity. The Admiral's flagship would set men ashore at Cap-Haitien on the east coast, where the Admiral would establish a garrison in Henri Christophe's hilltop fortress known simply as The Citadel. The other ships would remain offshore, and dispatch launches to set men ashore around the coastline of the gulf, to make their presence felt in the countryside, as well as to circle around and prevent the escape of any rebels or corrupt officials.

The main concourse of the docks was deserted, most of the combatants having gathered around the more important buildings and streets in the city. As a result, the Marines experienced no resistance as they jogged down the hurriedly lashed gangplanks, and spread out across the docks. Mortimer, armed with a Browning rather than a rifle, called out orders to his squad, and directed them to positions around the two-storey customs building.

Observing his target through cold eyes, Mortimer strode ahead, pistol ready, marking the positions of the dark figures who could be made out scrambling about the building. He almost outpaced his men as they approached the customs building, from whence there came sounds of hand-to-hand combat. Waving his men into a pincer formation, Mortimer surprised the small group of mach-ete-wielding rebels who were trying to wear down the staff of the building. They turned on the newly arrived Marines in surprise, and yet with considerable ferocity, hurling themselves at the armed men, who coolly gunned them down, their machetes being no match for rifles.

Mortimer himself killed two or three, moving with a sort of mechanical fluidity, ignoring everything but each man whom he targeted.

In a matter of minutes, the attackers had been routed, only a few surviving to run back into the streets where the morning had yet to dispel the darkness. Mortimer reholstered his gun, satisfied at a job well done, and striving to contain the excitement he felt at the combat. He spotted a familiar face, and beckoned him over. 'Glen, pass the word for the main party to head directly here. We can use the receivership warehouse as a staging post.'

'Right, sir.' Captain Glen headed back towards the ship.

The large goods doors opened then, and several white men rushed out, cheering. The customs staff greeted the Marines warmly. 'About time someone put down them niggers like the mad dogs they are,' someone cried, raising a laugh from his rescuers.

'We know what to do with mad dogs, right enough,' Mortimer drawled, nodding towards the nearest of the fallen blacks, who had already attracted a brace of flies to the sticky wounds in his face. 'Who's in charge here?'

'I am,' answered a burly man with greying hair. 'Fred Johnson, manager.'

'Colonel L V Mortimer,' the hawk-like Marine responded with a faint smile. 'With your permission, I'd like to use your warehouse as a staging area and base of operations, while we secure the area and send in protection for other American interests in the city.'

'Okay, I suppose, Colonel. We're a bit understocked anyway – business hasn't been so good since the trouble started.'

'I guess not. Thank you, Mr Johnson.' Mortimer found a junior lieutenant and began issuing orders to have his maps of the island, tactical notes, and sundry other items brought in. It was just a pity, he thought, that he'd now have to sit tight here, while his men were facing the enemy.

It took the Marines a remarkably short time to set up

defensible emplacements on the wide dockside, before Mortimer sent his men into the city, ordering small groups to leapfrog each other in order to secure the university and consulates. A larger group was dispatched to the palace, to enforce a curfew and arrest both the leaders of the rebellion and the officials of the corrupt government.

The sun had barely begun its climb into the sky when there was a renewed flurry of activity outside the university hospital. A sudden volley of shots broke out, the sound no longer muffled by windows, all of which had been shattered during the night. Ace woke at once, drawing her gun and spinning about on the carpeting of plaster chips and glass fragments, searching for the source and target. To her surprise, the gunfire didn't seem to be directed at them, and she wondered if the rebels and soldiers had finally got around to fighting each other directly. Looking around, she saw that the others were all awake as well. The Doctor was using a pocket mirror to see what was going on outside without sticking his head out of the window, Howard was over by a small stove cooking several breakfasts, the hospital staff were milling about seeing to their patients, and Petion was being shaved by an orderly using a piece of broken glass. Ace was uncertain whether or not to say anything that might disturb his concentration more than the noise outside did.

'We don't have much longer to wait.' Ace jumped; she hadn't heard the Doctor come over. 'Things are moving on apace,' he finished.

'Meaning?' she said.

'The fighting outside. They're not fighting each other, you know.'

'That American invasion you mentioned?'

'Exactly.'

'They haven't changed much, then?'

'Not really. They come in, widen a few roads, build a couple of schools, and keep a firm hold over what they see as a bunch of "upstart blacks".'

'Nothing unusual there, then.'

'No, just the usual bigotry and oppression.'

The gunfire outside died down as the Haitians scattered. Seconds later, there was a loud bang outside.

'Grenade,' Ace commented. After a few moments of silence there was a series of sharp raps on the door, and a voice called out, asking if anyone was inside.

Howard looked up sharply. 'An American voice,' he said in wonder, as if he were surprised to find that he was still alive and about to be rescued, after the previous night's events.

'You'd better open the door, I think,' the Doctor said dryly, and Howard left with a nod.

'I wonder which side they'll be on,' Petion murmured, with a hint of worry in his voice.

'Strictly speaking, neither. They'll arrest pretty much anyone involved with either the rebellion or the government. I think, though,' the Doctor said, eyes twinkling, 'we'll be able to persuade them that you're on the same side as the rest of us.'

At that moment, Howard returned, grinning, accompanied by a Marine sergeant and a man he introduced as Marine Captain Glen. They tensed somewhat upon sighting Petion, but Howard hastily interposed himself between them. 'This is Captain Petion,' he began, 'formerly with the militia, but didn't like what he saw. He's with us now.'

'Captain.' Glen nodded perfunctorily, still with a hint of suspicion.

Howard went on to introduce his staff and patients, before ending up at the Doctor and Ace. 'This is the Doctor, he's a Brit investigating some occurrences here.'

'Such as the disappearance of your envoy?' Glen suggested.

'Perhaps,' the Doctor replied evasively. 'At the moment, I'm investigating many things.'

'And this is, er, Ace,' Howard finished. 'One of the Doctor's assistants.'

'A secretary, perhaps?' the sergeant surmised with a suggestive look.

139

'His bodyguard,' Ace said coldly, not liking his jumping to conclusions one little bit.

'Dressing like some Dodge City card-sharp might be your idea of fun, but bodyguard?' The sergeant laughed aloud. His laugh was sharply curtailed when Ace lunged forward, snatched his rifle from hands that were too surprised to grip it tightly enough, and smashed him in the groin with the butt. As he doubled over, she kneed him in the face, and had her own pistol levelled at Glen's stomach before he could react. There was an uncomfortable silence, during which the Doctor watched Ace with a look of worry.

'Any of you arseholes want to add to Rambo's comments here?' she asked icily.

'As one captain to another,' Petion said, with a conspiratorial smile, 'I recommend you take her word at face value.'

'Yeah, sure,' Glen muttered uncertainly. He watched Ace warily as she stepped back and put her gun away. He had always thought that the British were even more conservative than the Americans about what women were allowed to do. Still, it took all sorts. 'Quite a looker,' he whispered back to Petion.

'Hadn't noticed.'

'Oh.' Glen glanced down at the sergeant struggling to get up while clutching his aching groin. 'Neither had I.'

'Excuse me,' the Doctor broke in, 'but have your men taken all the university?'

'Pretty much. Why?'

'I want to pay a visit to the museum. Part of the, er, case I'm working on,' he added hurriedly.

'Oh, right. I'll send a man along with you, just in case.'

'Don't bother.' Ace smiled sweetly, and slipped her mirrored sunglasses on as she headed for the reception area.

'Come on, Howard, you can show us the way.' The Doctor led Howard to the door, but was stopped by Petion.

'If you don't mind,' Petion said, 'I'd like to come too.'

The Doctor shrugged, and they left together.

Mait awoke gasping for breath in a black wave of pain, belatedly realizing, as it faded, that it was pain in a dream. He got up stiffly, finding a steaming coffee pot beside his four-poster.

In the most shadowed corner of the curtained room, the darkness stirred, and slid forward. 'Good morning, Mait. Welcome to another beautiful day.'

'What are you doing here, Carrefour?' Mait wasn't particularly concerned, since the tall man had proved his loyalty many times. He was, however, presently supposed to be with General Froebe's men.

'The situation has changed, Mait. The Americans have invaded, and are rounding up both the rebels and governmental forces.'

'What?' Mait was momentarily nonplussed, but soon recovered, as he mentally ran through the possible effects of this on his plan. 'That has been possible for some time. So long as they are kept busy in Port-au-Prince until the morning, we can continue with only minor alterations.'

'As you say, Mait.'

'Use your . . . influence to arrange to have the Americans kept busy tonight, so that the ceremony may occur in peace. I will visit Henri, even though he lives uncomfortably close to open water.' Mait shuddered involuntarily. 'And I will make sure he keeps Richmann out of sight so that the Americans do not realize their worst fears have already come true.'

'As you wish, Mait. And after the ceremony?'

'Afterwards . . .' Mait sighed in expectation. 'We will be as those we follow. The Americans will have no power over us then.' He smiled unpleasantly. 'And neither will Froebe and his men, once they have shown us the way.'

The Doctor led the way into the museum, followed by Ace, Howard and Petion. The place was unlit, with pools of darkness shrouding the exhibits. The Doctor produced a small but powerful pocket torch and swung it around, briefly illuminating each exhibit in turn.

'What are we looking for?' Ace asked.

'Carvings, statuettes, that sort of thing. But they'll be carvings of a most odd nature.' He paused for a moment. 'Or a most unnatural oddness, depending on how you look at it. Either way,' he added more earnestly, 'they'll undoubtedly be tucked away in some suitably black and hidden corner.'

They slipped through the museum like ghosts dodging the approach of dawn, all but ignoring the Arawak and Spanish exhibits. Finally, on turning a corner, they entered a small area in which a large slab of stone stood beside a table covered in smaller fragments. The Doctor walked over and played the torch over the large stone. As the light flickered across its surface, the already uncomfortably organic-looking reliefs seemed to writhe and slither in an even more lifelike fashion. Ace repressed a shudder, while Howard looked on unaffected, having seen the stones when they first arrived at the university. Petion looked astounded in a repulsed sort of way. Privately, he wondered who had carved these things, and hoped it had not been some ancestor of his.

'It certainly predates the Arawaks,' the Doctor said. 'I'd say these carvings were at least fifteen million years old.' His voice was uncharacteristically hushed.

'Bullshit,' Ace scoffed. 'Even I know man hasn't been around that long.'

'No, and remind me to wash your mouth out,' he continued absently. 'These were never carved by the frail hand of man, so to speak.'

'How do you mean?' Howard asked in indignation. 'Not carved by man?'

'No. I'm not the first visitor to this little planet of yours, you know.' He stopped, peering at the stone, and altered the angle of the torch. A faint glistening showed up on the surface of the carvings. 'Aha. I thought as much.'

'Coated with poison?' Petion asked hesitantly.

'Yes. Topically active, no doubt. Look at these smaller

pieces. They're all coated and some of them are disturbed. Benny will certainly have picked up some of these things to examine them, and she'll have absorbed the stuff through her fingertips.'

'You mean she's dead?' Ace snapped.

'I doubt it. Why take away the body if she were? Do you have any empty nitro canisters?'

'Yeah, here.' She handed over a small metal cylinder.

'Doctor,' Howard began slowly. 'If your friend isn't dead – '

'I know,' he said sharply. Ace noticed that Howard and Petion were both looking at him strangely. 'I'll want to analyse this to confirm it,' he continued, carefully using a pen to roll one of the small carvings off the edge of the table and into the canister. He dropped the pen in after it, and screwed the lid down tight.

'What's going on with you lot?' Ace demanded. 'Benny may be a bit of a dipstick, but if something's happened to her – '

'Ace.' The Doctor looked at her with pained eyes. 'If this stuff is what I think it is, someone may be trying to turn Benny into what the people here would call a *zombi*.'

Ace felt as if she'd been struck. Killing someone was one thing, but this was worse; there was no honour or morality in it at all. Not trusting herself to speak, she settled for gripping the butt of her gun with white knuckles.

'I should have realized at once – that Frenchman who was killed, the same poison must still have been on the skin of his attackers, and it would almost certainly still have been strong enough to affect him as well! Howard, Petion,' the Doctor asked desperately, 'can either of you put me in touch with a *houngan* of the *Rada Loa*?'

The other two men looked at each other. 'There are a few places where we might meet one such . . .' Howard replied.

'But,' Petion interrupted, 'travelling the streets today would be almost suicidal, what with all the fighting. And even if you did find a *houngan*, he most probably wouldn't agree to talk to you, since no one here has any sympathies for the *blancs* who have always exploited us.'

'Well, that's all right then,' the Doctor stated grimly, 'because neither have I. Ace, you can come with me. Howard, get back to the hospital. They'll need you back there to take charge and you can make sure the Marines don't compromise the defences you've set up. Petion, take me to a *houngan* of the *Rada Loa*.'

Chapter Fourteen

Benny was shoved down into a leather-covered chair in an office carved from the living rock. Before she could move or speak, the two guards who had brought her retreated back into the corridor, leaving her alone in the office. It never occurred to her to worry about what was to be done with her, though she wryly thought that the hospitality of the military establishment seemed to be a constant throughout human history. Instead, she found herself drawn to a large open window cut into one wall. It was all in one piece and couldn't be opened, and she judged it as being thick enough to resist breaking, even under the impact of one of the chairs.

Outside, she could see a small three-port dock, with a nest of sinisterly squatting tanks on the far side. Men crawled over the area like ants over an anthill, and several small handcarts rolled along here and there. The scene was illuminated by large floodlamps bolted on to the striated walls of the huge cavern which enclosed the whole place. Up above, the roof was wreathed in shadow, but Benny sensed the presence of something huge, lurking in the darkness. Pulling herself away, she looked over at the filing cabinets against one wall. She went over and tried one of the handles, but the cabinet was locked. Idly, she wondered if there was anything around that she could open it with. She checked, but saw only a few photographs of a passing-out parade, a map, some pens and a blotter. There was nothing that could be adapted for lock-picking, not even a paperclip.

'There is nothing in there that would matter to you anyway,' came a faintly amused voice. She spun around.

'You never know, I have a wide range of interests. You're General Froebe, I take it?' she said.

'Indeed.' He circled the large mahogany desk and seated himself. 'You seem to have the advantage of me, Fraulein . . .'

'Summerfield. Professor Bernice Summerfield.' She shrugged, knowing the name would do him no good, since she wouldn't be born for another half a millennium.

'Professor of what?'

'Archaeology.'

'Which university?'

'Heidelberg.'

'Ah, the famous British sense of humour.'

'Who says I'm British?'

'Your accent is unfamiliar, but we know you are working in concert with a man carrying British Intelligence identification.' He smiled patronizingly. 'If you would like to tell me what you have discovered so far about your missing envoy, I would be interested to hear it.'

'Our missing envoy?' Benny thought, trying to recall her knowledge of this period of history. 'You had him killed, of course.'

'Of course. A deduction worthy of Holmes himself,' he replied straight-faced.

'Thank you. Are you about to hand over a signed confession, then?'

'What were you doing in the museum?' he asked, ignoring her taunt.

'A bit of housework: dusting, that sort of thing. All those old things get rather dusty and so on if they're not looked after.'

'I am disappointed,' he sighed. 'I had hoped I wouldn't have to give a woman the full benefit of our facilities.' He pressed a button on the desk, and two guards came in.

'Aha. Now it's time for the electrodes and rubber hoses, eh?' She tried to sound flippant, though she suddenly wondered if she hadn't gone a bit far.

'Nothing so crude. We'll give you a course of injections of a solution of scopalamine and quinine. That will give us results with no mess.'

'Those will have side effects,' Benny said slowly, forgetting to even try a witticism.

'Well, you will become something of a vegetable, unfortunately, but I'm sure our guards, so lonely this far from home, will find a use for you even in that state.' He nodded to the guards. 'Take her back to the medical centre and have Dr Karnstein meet me there in one hour.'

The guards nodded and ushered Benny out.

Carrefour sat on a low wall that stretched out from the side of a building, leaning his back against the building's wall and tootling to himself on a child's flute. Along the street, he saw a small group of men drifting aimlessly towards him. Most were armed with large stones or pieces of wood which had had nails or shards of glass stuck into them. A few had stained machetes, while two even had old militia rifles. Their shadows stretched far ahead of them in the morning sun, and he leapt down on to the shadow of the leader. The group halted, eyeing Carrefour with a mixture of fear and confusion. Carrefour gave them a wide grin, and stepped down the shadow path to their leader. 'Good morning,' he said quietly, locking eyes with the leader. 'I would like you to do a little service for me, and you will do it. You'll enjoy it, in fact.' He chuckled softly.

'What service?' the man asked fearfully, as Carrefour had known he would.

'Take your men. Show the Americans that we do not appreciate their presence. I would be most grateful.' He stepped meaningfully off the shadow on to a patch of sunlight.

The man swallowed nervously. Brought up in the outskirts of the city, his grandparents had often told him stories of how a *bocor* could trap your soul through your shadow. And even this man had heard of Carrefour, who had committed the almost unheard of crime of zombifying another *bocor*, rather than just killing him. Too frightened to speak, the man nodded vigorously, as did his men, and they walked off stiffly, none wanting to be seen to be more afraid than the others.

Carrefour watched them go, and reseated himself, rolling the flute between his fingers. As if its touch ignited memories, he heard the crackle of burning wood, and felt its heat through his flesh. He ran a finger along the lowermost surface of the wood, his fingertips brushing the marks that spelled out his name, and it echoed in his mind with the voice of his father, who had carved the instrument many years ago. The miniature flute was the only object Carrefour retained from his childhood, and the only one which he even remembered with any clarity. It had been his only possession when he had fled his home as it burned.

His home had burned with the same anger that the men responsible had felt, the anger which Carrefour had striven to purge himself of. Putting the thoughts out of his head, he settled back to wait for the next people who could keep the Americans busy. Almost without realizing it, he began to play a soulful, haunting melody.

The rats had been cleared from the lab when the Leutnant returned with a message for Dr Karnstein. Instead, the naked corpse of Hauser lay on a central table, the chest cavity spread open, and several organs glistening purply on gleaming dishes to either side. Trying to avoid gazing at the grisly sight, the Leutnant sidled over to the statuesque Karnstein, and handed the envelope to her.

As he left, the image of scarlet, oval glove-prints on white paper went with him.

Stepping back from the autopsy she was performing, Dr Ingrid Karnstein unfolded the paper to read the message.

Professor von Stein raised an eyebrow questioningly. 'Bad news?'

'Just a nuisance interruption. Some girl Froebe wants interrogated after lunch,' she said.

'That's an important facet of our work, Doctor, lest

you forget. Anyway, you shouldn't be surprised – you said yourself that there was a risk that the two men affected by the drum explosion would be found and their condition understood.'

'That's all right for you to say, since you've always worked in passionless chemical engineering.'

'We've had this conversation before. You volunteered for this assignment – never forget that.'

'Oh, I never will,' she answered with a hard edge to her voice. After all, she thought, how can I forget the day I agreed to enslave most of Europe? 'At the time, we were supposed to be coming to use neurotropic qualities of tetrodotoxin and datura to save lives by slowing the bleeding of our wounded soldiers. I did *not* volunteer to have that perverted into a weapon that will kill or turn innocent people into mindless automata!'

'An additional bonus that will save our men's lives, since no one will be able to shoot at them,' von Stein shouted.

Karnstein was too repulsed to even try to answer. She returned to her gory work, which had become less disturbing than her conversations with von Stein.

When she had been strapped back on to the bed beside a tray of sinister-looking instruments in the medical centre, Benny had tensed her muscles as best she could, before the guards had fixed the buckles and left. As soon as she was alone again, she relaxed, the pressure of the straps easing slightly. 'Must make a note of this,' she muttered to herself. 'Dear diary, history isn't what it used to be.' She began to wriggle slightly, to see if she could get her hands free, but it was no good, the straps were still too tight. She tried her legs next, and they moved a bit within the straps, but her boots prevented her from pulling her legs through the loops. 'Bugger! Wait a minute . . .' Turning her feet towards each other, she pushed the toe of her right boot against the edge of the left, while scraping her left heel against the tabletop. After several long moments of ankle-straining effort, her left boot popped off and thudded to the floor. Her heart froze in her throat, and she stilled completely, trying to determine whether anyone had heard and was coming to investigate.

Nothing happened.

She wriggled her left leg a bit more, and her foot slipped free. Allowing herself a small triumphant smile, she started the same process on the right boot. It soon hit the floor as well, and both her legs were free to move. This time she didn't wait to see if anyone would come, but swiftly glanced to the small instrument tray. A set of surgical tools and syringes lay on the white-sheeted top, and she focused on a scalpel with a small but wickedly sharp blade. Shifting into an uncomfortable position in which her back was slightly turned to the tray, with her hands still strapped down, she turned her head at a painful angle to watch the tray. Carefully, she slid her left leg off the table, and over to the tray, the leg almost on its side and bent at the knee to reach the tray, which was almost level with her hip. Straining slightly, and with teeth clenched, Benny lifted her foot above the instruments and lowered it with extreme care towards the handle of the scalpel. On the first two touches, it shifted, and she couldn't get a grip on it, but on the third attempt, she clasped it between her toes. Keeping a tight grip, she slowly swung her leg back into a normal position, laying the scalpel down on the end of the bed. 'What do you know, those ballet lessons paid off . . .'

She then pulled the scalpel towards her hips, raising her buttocks off the bed so she could pull foot and scalpel up underneath her. When the scalpel was level with her hands, she nudged it to the left with her foot, and settled back down, finally grasping the handle with straining fingers.

The hard work done, it took a matter of moments to cut through the strap holding her left hand. She then unbuckled her right, and stood up, dropping the scalpel into a pocket, just in case. Pausing only to pull on her boots and recover her other belongings from a shelf near the door, she cautiously slipped out of the room.

Benny found herself in a rock-walled tunnel, with bare bulbs hanging from the ceiling at regular intervals. Odd sounds of voices and activity came indistinctly from the distance. The tunnel to the right turned left after a short distance, while the tunnel to the left led to a crossroads. Uncertain which way to go, Benny gradually became aware of a gentle breeze blowing from the right. She had spent her share of time in caves digging for archaeological pieces, and realized that she was probably too deep underground to feel a breeze from outside. The dock below, however, contained water, which meant there could be an opening to the sea. That being the case, the breeze she felt was probably being caused by air which had got in at low tide being forced out at high tide. If that was so, then going right, towards the breeze, would take her deeper into the caves. She set off towards the junction to the left.

Once there, she paused, debating which way to go. 'This is as bad as that castle on Khul,' she muttered. 'That was a real nightmare, that one.' Sighing, she turned left.

Petion had to duck as he preceded the Doctor into an adobe-style blockhouse, which was refreshingly cool inside. An open doorway on the opposite side gave a bright rectangular view of an area of beaten earth open to the sky. A stout woman, whom Petion had spoken to a moment ago, indicated that they should sit on the scraggy cushions situated around the walls. 'He will see you in a moment,' she said without explanation, and went out, leaving the trio in the dim room.

Ace glanced around, noting the clay bottles and pots sealed with wax that were stacked together in rickety cupboards. Plant material was everywhere, hanging to dry from the ceiling, piled in bowls, tied in bundles . . . She didn't recognize any of it. Bizarrely, above an altar spread with objects she couldn't identify, and didn't want to, there was a crucifix, and a cheap reproduction of a painting of St Patrick. She wondered darkly if all this wasn't just a waste of time, when they should be out hunting for clues to Benny's whereabouts. The Doctor sat with an unreadable expression, which presumably meant his patience wasn't being strained. Petion looked both nervous and comfortable at the same time.

For his part, Petion was feeling no actual fear as such, but these trappings of a bygone age, which could represent good or evil depending on the choice of the individual worshipper, instilled in him a definite sense of wariness. He was content, however, in the knowledge that this man had only ever been known to serve the *Rada Loa*, those good spirits who were often associated with Catholic saints when the people felt it necessary to show some respect for the official state religion without compromising their traditional beliefs.

After a few moments, a man entered, his face set in a grim expression that, while not malicious, certainly didn't show any sign of sympathy for their cause.

'This is Clairvius Dubois,' Petion announced quietly. 'Hopefully he may give us the help we are looking for.' He inclined his head respectfully, turning to Dubois. 'This is the Doctor and Ace,' he said simply. 'They are working with Dr Phillips, and we all need your help, if you will give it.'

'I have helped Phillips in the past, because he is unlike the other *blancs*. How do I know you are as worthy as he? Even now, I hear that *blanc* soldiers have again invaded our country.'

Petion opened his mouth to speak, but the Doctor got there first. 'We don't share the others' aims here. We need your help to cut short the troubles that will follow.'

'By subjugating us more quickly?'

'By ending the brutal acts that would turn the whites against you and encourage them to clamp down harder.'

Dubois raised an eyebrow. 'Such as?'

'How many *zombis* have been created recently?' he asked blithely.

Dubois's expression went hard. 'This conversation is over.' He stood and began to go out.

'More than the few the *Bizango* intended, I'll warrant,' the Doctor said.

'What?' Dubois froze.

'You may not know who, but you do know that some-one is creating – unauthorized, shall we say – *zombis*, don't you?'

'Who exactly are you?' Dubois's voice was hushed and cold.

'Me?' the Doctor asked innocently. He leaned forward, holding Dubois's gaze. 'I'm the one who's wondering why whites are turning up as *zombis* – and whites who have no official record, at that. I'm the one who's looking for a friend who may well be in the hands of the *cochon gris*. And most importantly to you, I'm the one who'll have to put an end to all this nonsense. Does that satisfy you?'

The aging *houngan*'s grim facade held for a moment, then dissolved into a spray of laughter lines as he smiled. 'To talk to me like that, you must be who you claim to be – no one else would dare do such a thing!' Stepping briefly outside, he called for a bottle of Clairin to be brought, and the woman who had shown them in brought it instantly. 'I will admit to some curiosity as to how you know so much about the *Bizango*, Doctor.'

'I have enemies in high places. I've also been here before.'

'Ah. Dr Phillips told you of the *zombis* he has been studying, I take it?'

The Doctor nodded. Petion handed Ace the bottle and advised her in a whisper not to smell the stuff first. Nat-urally she did, and it almost made her eyes water.

'It is true,' Dubois continued 'He asked me in as an advisor, and I realized at once that they were not the work of the Bizango.'

'Well, you should know,' the Doctor commented slyly.

'What?'

'Surely an outsider, even another *houngan*, wouldn't have made such a distinction "at once"?'

'Very good, Doctor. And you are right, I am an *Emper-eur*. I had enquiries made as to the origins of the *zombis*, but no one knew where they had come from. We did discover, however, that one called Mait – his officially registered name is Gilles Lemaitre – has built up a small but powerful network of his own, and that they have performed many *cochon gris* ceremonies.'

'*Cochon gris* . . .' The Doctor nodded in contemplation. 'So they're a splinter group working for their own evil purposes rather than for the island's status quo?'

'Yes. We have no proof that the *zombis* are their work, but they are the only suspects.'

'Haven't you done anything about it?' Ace put in.

'Mait is too well-protected for even us to get at.'

'Hmm, and that's saying something,' the Doctor said. 'Do you happen to know where he lives? I think I'd like to have a look into this.'

'He has a large villa in the Cordillera Central. I doubt if your missing friend will be there, however.'

'Where else could she be?'

'There is a small cemetery, where they have held ceremonies almost every night recently. Either Henri Duval or Carrefour is always in attendance – they are Mait's right-hand men. If they intend to make a *zombi* of her, they will do it there.'

'Tonight?'

Dubois shrugged. 'Probably. Usually it takes three days, but in a hurry . . .'

'One more thing,' the Doctor began slowly. 'Do you know anything of the Old Ones, or the carvings that are in the museum?'

'I have heard legends, told by old men who should know better, but I have no knowledge of such things personally. As for the carvings . . . They are much like the legends, but as to what that means – '

'I know what it means, and I think this Mait of yours thinks he knows what it means. We'd better get over there.' He pulled out a tatty map from an inside pocket. 'If you'd point out the villa on this?'

'If you really think you can get in, I will come with you. This is as much my business as yours, Doctor.'

Dubois's tone brooked no argument, even from the Doctor.

'Oh, I can get us in, all right.' He held up the TARDIS key, rubbing it thoughtfully. 'But I have a few things to do first. We'll also want to sit in on the *cochon gris*'s ceremony tonight, if there is one.' He clapped his hands to emphasize the decision. 'Right. You'd better make what preparations you need, Dubois. Can you meet us at the university hospital in one hour?'

'Certainly.'

'You've been most helpful, thank you. Come on Ace, Petion, we'd best be getting back.'

As they left, Ace looked back thoughtfully. 'Do you think we can trust him?'

'Yes, he's *Bizango*,' the Doctor said.

'So? What the hell does that mean?'

'The *Bizango* are a sort of neighbourhood watch in Haiti. They hold the odd kangaroo court to deal with those who have caused trouble but aren't what the state would consider criminals – people who con their own families out of earnings or land, that sort of thing. Defendants often end up being zombified and forced to work as slaves. Hard labour, I suppose. These *cochon gris*, on the other hand, are zombifying purely for their own ends, not to mention interfering in the, er, governmental process. So, the *Bizango* will come down on them like a ton of bricks if they get the chance, for both the unauthorized *zombis* and the rabble rousing.'

'And the Secte Rouge?'

'The *cochon gris*'s strong-arm division.'

'How come the *Bizango* aren't interested in the revolution?'

'Because to them, one government is as corrupt as any other. But at a local level, people's attitudes and the *Bizango*'s system remain pretty much unaffected by what happens in the city, so they simply aren't interested in who's President.'

'You seem to know a lot about it.' Ace's voice turned faintly suspicious.

'Only from the sort of dry texts that Benny hates so much. The present situation, apart from the fact of the American invasion, is as much a mystery to me as to you.'

'Really?' She stopped and halted him with a hand on his arm. 'Is it just coincidence that as soon as we arrive all sorts of weird shit starts happening? Or have you found a new game to amuse yourself?' She didn't even try to keep the bitterness out of her tone.

The Doctor looked at her with an air of hesitant concern. 'No games, Ace. Not this time.' For a moment he looked lost. 'Nobody knows anything about the Old Ones, not even the Time Lords. All I do know is that it seems someone here does believe that they still have an influence.' He smiled crookedly. 'I suppose when you look at it that way, it could be considered that they have an influence by proxy, as it were.'

'So that's why you want to have a look round this Mait's place?'

'Yes . . .' He took on a strange, thoughtful expression. 'Mait . . .' he muttered. 'I wonder . . .'

Mait shrank into his chair on Henri's verandah, staring out gloomily at the glittering expanse of lake below. Henri returned from inside with a bottle of Clairin and two mugs. 'You'd think I would be over this by now,' Mait said darkly, eyeing the lake.

'A near-drowning isn't the sort of thing that one forgets easily. It's bound to leave its mark on a man. Even you,' Henri added.

'But it was so long ago, when I was a boy . . .'

'It's hard to think of you as a boy.'

'Why? How old do you think I am, Henri?' Mait's face took on a whimsical look.

'I don't know, sixty, maybe sixty-five.'

For a long time Mait didn't answer, until a low chuckle gradually worked its way from his throat. 'As young as that, eh?'

'Well, I – '

'Don't worry,' Mait told him, amused by his baffled expression. 'Suffice it to say that I'm older even than that.' He took a swig of the spiced rum, and set the mug down carefully. 'I am here on more important business, however.'

'The ceremony tonight?'

'I would like you to have your Secte Rouge followers in attendance again. The emotions that are stirred by a human sacrifice will be useful to us, in order to be certain we have enough power for the *Wete Mo Nan Dlo*. Therefore, you can perform the ceremony as set, I will attend as *Empereur*, and Carrefour can handle the sacrifice at the appropriate moment.'

'One o'clock?'

'Yes. The Secte Rouge should have found us someone by then.' Mait smiled to himself. 'It's also possible, of course, that our victim may willingly come to us,' he added mysteriously.

'The *blancs*, you mean?'

'Yes. Make sure the guardians are alert tonight. When the fear and agony the *blancs* feel is transferred through the mirror . . .' He left the sentence hanging as he helped himself to more rum.

Chapter Fifteen

General Froebe was entertained by visions of a luxurious country estate as his imagined reward for services to the Kaiser, as he escorted Dr Ingrid Karnstein through the tunnels.

Karnstein had proved attractive but uninteresting company since her arrival. She simply got on with her job rather sourly, and coldly logged reports which were clinically critical of the conditions in the complex. Froebe had at first been surprised, thinking of how many people would kill to get a posting to the tropics. That was before he came to recognize that Karnstein was using this by-the-book method of criticism to show displeasure at the nature of their business.

Karnstein seemed to have been born to fit the caricatured image of a hospital matron, determined to do a patient good even if it killed him. When war was first declared, and she was co-opted into the military, he imagined that her first reaction had been that it was typical of these men to mess up her promising career like that.

In short, Karnstein appeared to feel that while she had to do her job – by the book, of course – she didn't have to like it. Her attitude irritated Froebe more than anyone else's had ever done in his military career. He longed for her to either finish her job and go back to Germany, or do something blatantly treacherous so he would have an excuse to get rid of her. Anything but this fragile, walking-on-eggs relationship.

The truth was, Froebe's almost entirely military life had left him unable to cope with anyone who wasn't either a bloodthirsty volunteer, or a conscript to be whipped into shape. Most importantly, to his way of thinking, he preferred his staff to be men.

He reached the medical centre with a sense of relief, and pushed the door open, holding it for Karnstein, since even though he disliked her, he couldn't neglect his duties as an officer and a gentleman. He nearly let the door shut on her face in surprise, when he saw that the woman was gone. '*Scheisse!*' He hit the alarm button by the door, and bells started ringing throughout the complex.

Karnstein examined the cut bonds with a look of amusement; she seemed almost glad that the woman had escaped. Froebe stormed off back down the tunnel towards the approaching sound of booted feet, shouting orders all the way.

At each junction, Benny took an upward-sloping tunnel with the strange breeze at her back. Nevertheless, she had to retrace her steps several times, though she still made sure to pick routes which moved ahead of the breeze.

She hadn't thought about how much of her hour remained, until bells started ringing, and she realized that they must have gone for her. She had passed numerous rooms cut into the rock during her journey, and had noted several tunnel opening with chains stretched across them, hung with danger signs. She had no intention of following any of those routes. She was suddenly aware of approaching hurried footsteps, and scurried back into the last room she had passed, which wasn't locked and turned out to be a storeroom for spare cables and bulbs for the lighting system. Peeking out, she saw three white-coated figures approach, two hurrying along in front, the last trailing a few yards further back.

Hefting a large, heavy pair of cable-cutters that had lain on a shelf, she let the first two go by. Worriedly judging her moment, and hoping fervently that the other two heard nothing, she slipped out behind the third man, and cracked him over the head with the cutters. He fell into her arms without a sound, and she dragged him back into the storeroom.

There, she checked for a pulse, fearing for a moment that she had killed him. Finding a faint pulse, she divested him of his white coat, and tied him up with a length of cable. 'See how you lot like it,' she muttered. Tossing her safari jacket aside with a regretful air, she shrugged on the purloined lab coat, picked up a dusty clipboard from the shelf, and stepped back out into the corridor. She paused a moment, uncertain whether to follow the other two or go back the way they had come. She settled for following them.

It took only a few seconds for Benny to rush on and spot her unknowing guides. Hanging back so they were just at the limit of vision, she followed them through the tunnels of the complex, occasionally passing other personnel or soldiers, who ignored her to concentrate on their search for the fugitive. And they're supposed to be the experts on camouflage, she thought ironically.

Eventually, they came to a large set of steel doors, watched over by a single guard. This confused Benny at first, until she realized that they must have been going deeper into the complex, while Froebe would have assumed she was making for the outside. They wouldn't be expecting her to go further into the lion's den.

She stopped at the corner as the two scientists approached the doors. The guard seemed to have been daydreaming when the two scientists approached. Unconcerned, he raised a hand to stop them.

'Team Delta,' one of the scientists said. 'Here to check the potency of the first shipment.'

'Right.' The guard drew a notebook from one pocket. 'Precisely on schedule. Wait a moment – '

'What's wrong this time?'

'It says here there should be three of you.'

'What do you mean?' The scientists exchanged weary looks and glanced back to check on their comrade.

Who wasn't there.

They looked at each other in surprise. Then the other

scientist, silent until now, pointed back up the corridor. 'There he is, last as usual.' They laughed, and the guard admitted them, smiling sheepishly.

As they entered, the guard beckoned to Benny. 'You're late,' he called.

Benny wasn't going to pass up an opportunity like this. Clipboard in hand, she strode purposefully up to the doors. 'Started without me, eh?' she asked in a passable accent. 'I'd better not waste any more time,' she added, pushing the door open and going through, finding herself at an entrance to the dock area that she had seen from Froebe's office. 'Oh shit.'

Outside, the guard shook his head at the antics of the scientists, disturbed only by the niggling sensation that he'd overlooked something. A few seconds later, he gasped in realization: hadn't the scientist referred to his tardy colleague as 'he'? It was but a short step from there to the deduction that the woman was the one they had been ordered to look out for, and the guard shouldered the door aside, bounding inwards.

He ran straight into Benny's outstretched foot, which slammed into his stomach. Doubling up, he didn't even see the cable-cutters which smashed into his skull and ended his conscious thoughts in a white flash behind his eyes.

Hastily, Benny shoved the guard outside, not bothering to check whether he was alive or not, and bolted the door.

Benny found herself standing in a smooth-floored entry-way that opened on to the docks about ten feet further on. The two scientists had vanished to their destination. When Benny moved to the end of the vestibule – striding boldly as if she belonged, hoping to attract less attention than a furtive visitor would – she was momentarily stunned at the sheer scale of what lay before her.

The cavern was so huge that Benny thought they must have hollowed out the entire mountain. There was, however, something about the regular yet enormous features of the cavern that suggested that man could never have performed such a feat in this time zone. But nor did it seem natural. She began to have a very bad feeling about the whole thing. She briefly wondered if it was perhaps the work of Earth Reptiles, but swiftly dismissed the idea, since not only did the style not match theirs, but there was no sign of their hibernation hives. The cave was several hundred yards across and just as high, dimly lit by lamps that stretched down from the indistinct ceiling on impossibly long cables. Several other sets of doors were dotted around the floor and, far off to the left, a black maw opened up in the wall, with so little light coming from it that Benny was certain the tunnel beyond turned several times before reaching the outside world.

The two large and rusty freighters that were berthed in the docking area, however, were very definitely of human manufacture, as witnessed by the sweaty crewmen who swarmed all over them, almost as numerous as the dead fish which clogged the oil-choked water. Other men bustled around on the wide dock area, busying themselves with large stacks of metallic drums which were stored in one deeper hollow directly under the window of Froebe's office. All of the drums were marked with a little skull and crossbones symbol. Only then did Benny realize how little was actually visible from that window, for in addition to the thousands of ten-gallon drums directly below, there were also large house-sized tanks like mini-gasometers on the far side of the docks. Hoses snaked across the floor from the freighters to the tanks, while cables stretched out from blocky generators like the arms of octopi. The shouts and calls of maintenance men and sailors echoed noticeably and there was a constant blast of noise from the generators and the ships' engines. In the dim upper reaches of the roof, she could now make out a cylindrical object with a dulled metallic glint. Surely not a rocket, she thought, then spotted the low-slung gondola with its attached propellers and radial engines. This too was connected by lines to a strangely designed gantry which jutted out from the wall.

She took a pen from one pocket of her purloined white

coat, flipped to a new page on the clipboard, and wrote 'BLOODY HELL!' on a report form. Putting the pen away, she considered her options. Trying to find her way back out was obviously a nonstarter but staying here she would probably be spotted fairly quickly. Chewing on her lip in thought, she finally set off towards the ten-gallon drums, reasoning that she might as well try to find out as much as possible while she was here, and run like hell when the time came. This was living history, after all.

Clipboard held tightly under her arm, she strode purposefully over to the area where the thousands of drums were stacked in a sprawled, looming maze. She passed several men, but none gave her a second glance. She wondered wryly whether to be thankful for small mercies, or to feel insulted. Pushing the thought away, she stepped out of sight into an alleyway whose walls were formed of stacked drums. The death's-head symbols leered at her as she moved between them, trying to avoid brushing up against any of them – just in case.

Satisfied that she was safely hidden from view, Benny began swiftly examining the drums for labels that might give her a clue as to what was in them. Most of the drums only showed the edges of labels, however, being turned at such an angle as to have the label obscured. Eventually, however, she found one whose label was visible. Smoothing out the paper, she crouched down. 'Bugger,' she muttered, as she saw that the labels were written in German. She tried to recall what twentieth-century German she knew, but was too rusty, and realized quickly that she would never be able to translate the labels on her own. The only alternative, in her view, was to simply copy the wording verbatim and hope the Doctor could translate it. She knew from her first meeting with him that he couldn't always understand written languages the way he could speech, but if he visited Earth so often it was probably reasonable to assume that he would know languages other than English.

She had just about finished, when she began to make out footsteps approaching from deeper in the maze of drums. Hurriedly, she jotted down the last few words, and started back out, but it was too late. The two scientists whom she had followed came round the corner.

'Ah, there you – ' one of them began, before he took in the fact that it was a stranger standing in front of him, rather than the third scientist. The scientists looked at each other in astonishment, and in that instant, Benny bolted.

The scientists pounded after her as she hurtled out on to the open floor, almost bumping into a pair of guards who were doing their rounds. Without thinking, she elbowed through them, sending them sprawling to the floor as the scientists dashed out shouting. Benny sprinted for the doors she had come in by, but already more guards were arriving from their stations, and the first few shots buzzed past her.

Throughout the cavern, men looked about at the commotion, and those in the vicinity scattered for cover, while the two scientists cast terrified glances at the huge expanse of drums and called in vain for the guards not to shoot.

Fighting down an abrupt rush of fear as she zigzagged across the stone floor to avoid the rifle fire, Benny pulled out one of the small plastic sample bags she always carried, and dropped the paper on to which she had copied the drum's label into it. Some part of her tried to convince her to make for the door, but she knew they would expect that. Realistically, she thought, there's only one way to avoid a diet of non-stop cabbage – or worse. I just hope those fish died from the oil, not some other weird substance they're messing with here, she thought.

Ahead, as she approached the edge of the floor beyond the freighters, several men converged on her. Gritting her teeth, she lowered her head, and barged through them, swinging the cable-cutters with wild abandon. The men fell back, or fell down in some cases, and Benny leapt off the edge of the dock just ahead of a swarm of angrily buzzing bullets. Hitting the water in a blast of spray, she drove herself as far under as she could, trying not to gasp at either the impact of her mistimed dive or the surprisingly low temperature of the water.

Guards seemed to be loosing off shots blindly into the water, perhaps hoping to hit Benny by sheer concentration of fire. Benny forced herself forward, her eyes tightly shut against the sluggish water, hoping that she was still heading towards the dark opening in the wall. She ground her teeth with the effort of keeping her strained lungs in check, using all four limbs for propulsion through water which echoed hollowly with the slap of bullets seeking her. After what seemed like a couple of hours, but was actually about twenty seconds, she began to rise involuntarily, and something bumped her shoulder painfully. Barely managing to hold her breath for the extra few seconds, she hauled herself to the other side of the object first, before surfacing. It turned out to be one of the buoys which marked the safe limits of the channel for the ships entering and leaving the cavern.

The buoy shielded her from the view of the guards, and she used that advantage to get her breath back. The respite was not to last however for, just as she heard the guards wondering aloud if they had hit her, someone on one of the freighters pointed her out with a cry. She didn't know how long it would take for someone with a gun to get into position to fire at her, so she took another deep breath, and threw herself away from the buoy, cutting under the surface as she headed for the opening. The bullets were no longer coming close, however, and by the time she pulled herself into the shadow of the side of the opening, they were chipping the rock several feet away. Though her lungs were aflame with her efforts, she rolled over and set off into the darkness of the tunnel that led outside before anyone could think to send a boat for her – though at least there were hiding places here in case they did.

Soaked in noxious-smelling slimy water, and watched only by the sightless eyes of rotting fish, Benny left the cavern.

Since the university was American funded and run, Colonel Mortimer had considered it prudent to pay it a personal visit as soon as was possible. Captain Glen had recently reported that the university had been retaken with little opposition, and Mortimer had immediately set off.

On his arrival, he had been satisfied to see the defences that had been set up around the hospital, and had every intention of congratulating those responsible. Until, that is, Dr Howard Phillips had pointed out that the defence of the building had been arranged and conducted by a former Haitian militia officer and an Englishwoman.

Mortimer had asked Howard for as much detail about these people as possible, since he was naturally suspicious of the Haitian's motives, and was also rather curious as to the Englishwoman's interest in matters. He knew the British government had their own sugar and sisal companies here, of course, but it irked his militarily trained mind that they wouldn't go through proper channels.

When Ace arrived back at the hospital with Petion and the Doctor, she found Howard talking animatedly, but not entirely cheerfully, to a hawk-faced man in Marine uniform and what she thought of as a Smokey-bear hat. Howard seemed to be making a doomed attempt to explain the Doctor's business on the island without mentioning zombies, the *Necronomicon* or anything similar that the military men might find difficult to accept.

As soon as he noticed them, Howard beckoned the Doctor, Ace and Petion over with a relieved expression, and introduced them to Colonel Mortimer of the USMC.

Ace stood silently as the Doctor doffed his hat, and gave Mortimer a cheery smile. There was something about Mortimer that made her uneasy. His hooded eyes were lifeless, and he had the air of a killer, but there was something in his stance that spoke of a rather different man. Perhaps it was the way his eyes flicked about as if hoping for an attacker to appear, or maybe it was the slight inclination of his head. Whatever it was, Ace found

166

that she couldn't place his style of soldiery, and that made her nervous.

'Pleased to meet you, Brigadier,' the Doctor said.

'Colonel actually, but thank you anyway.'

'Sorry, force of habit. Are you in charge of this force?'

'I've been given the responsibility of securing the capital, if that's what you mean.'

'Excellent. Now, let me guess: you're to arrest rebels and militia alike?'

'How did you know?' Mortimer seemed momentarily puzzled, but let it go.

'Lucky guess. You are also to clamp down on, er, native religions?'

'Damn right. All that black magic foolishness of theirs stops here.'

'That's humans for you,' the Doctor muttered, too quietly for Mortimer to hear. 'How would you like it if I were to let you know where you could stop the *Wete Mo Nan Dlo*, the biggest ceremony this year? I imagine that would fit your duties well?' Ace thought the Doctor sounded as if he were trying to coax a dog to do a trick. Perhaps, she thought, that was what all this was to him.

'I have more important – '

'Do you?' The Doctor fixed Mortimer with a level gaze, catching him with those blue eyes. Or were they grey? 'You want to do important things.' It was no longer a question.

'Yes – '

'You will do important things; you'll save more lives than you can imagine.'

'I'll save lives . . .' Mortimer wondered why he hadn't thought of that before. But whose lives?

'You will stop the ceremony tonight.'

'Stop the ceremony . . .'

'That's right.' The Doctor's voice, which had briefly seemed to come from the air all around, returned to a cheerier norm. He looked relieved, and slightly surprised. 'That way, my young friend won't be turned into a *zombi*, and neither will anyone else for the moment.'

167

Mortimer shook his head to clear the cobwebs, thinking that here was a chance to see some action. 'Very well, Doctor, I'll have a squad readied. Where and when exactly is it?'

'I'm just about to find out.' Taking a surprised Ace and Petion in tow, the Doctor led the way into the TARDIS.

Once inside, he took out the canister with the dust sample from the museum, and headed for the laboratory. 'How do you do that?' Ace asked curiously.

'It's just a knack and a not entirely reliable one,' the Doctor replied, 'but of course I had a very good teacher.' His face took on a faint expression of sad remembrance. 'Or he was, before he took a wrong turning on one of the roads of life that we walked . . .' He shook off the mood with a shrug and grinned back at them. 'Come on, I want to get this analysed before our friendly neighbourhood *houngan* arrives.'

The small village was completely silent as the Marines who had landed at the small fishing jetty moved up into the plateau where the houses were built. They advanced cautiously, wide brims shading their eyes from the climbing sun, constantly on the lookout for signs of life or opposition.

A young buck private saw the first body as they approached the village. It was an uninjured man, lying sprawled in the dust, flies crawling over his smooth eyelids and into his gaping mouth. The skin was unbroken and smooth, as if it were now untroubled by worries in endless sleep. Except that he wasn't breathing. The young private threw up on the spot – somehow that unblemished body was more disturbing than one with an obvious cause of death.

It hinted at the indiscrimination of death, that it was not just confined to the sick or injured. Anyone could be sprawled there.

It was a matter of seconds before another body was found. And another.

And another.

When they began to investigate the tiny houses, they found other bodies: men, women, children . . . The old and the young, the sick and the healthy, all limp and lifeless in the morning heat. Even the goats in the corrals lay in unliving sleep, and the village dogs would never bark again.

Nothing lived in the entire village, and there was no sign of what had caused the deaths.

The men began to wonder if the people whom they had laughed off as superstitious niggers weren't right after all. The lieutenant in charge, a man called Davis, dispatched the private and another man who looked unsteady back to the jetty to guard the launch they had arrived in, while the rest formed into burial details.

Even back at the jetty, the two Marines couldn't help but shake at what they had seen, though neither dared talk about it. So they sat wrapped in their own morbid silences, each harbouring his own private fear about what had happened to the village and how it could happen to them. The monotonous cawing of seabirds was soon to be broken, however, and not by quite such a fearful development.

The Marines were staring morosely out to sea, when a glimmer of unusual movement caught their eyes. They were speedily, if only temporarily, relieved of their worries when a head appeared amidst the gently rolling waves a short distance from the beach, which soon resolved into the – quite pleasing – shape of a woman struggling exhaustedly out of the sea and up the beach beside the jetty. The Marines jogged over to her, not trusting their eyes, while the woman collapsed to her knees in the sand, coughing up water which was viscous with oil. Shaking the water from her matted hair and sodden white lab coat while drawing a series of relieved gulps of air, the woman looked up at the Marines with a weak smile.

'Call the newspapers,' she croaked, 'I've just broken every bloody speed record in swimming. And,' she added, 'if any of you start singing about mango trees and honey, I'll break your kneecaps . . .'

169

Chapter Sixteen

It took only a few minutes for the Doctor to break down and analyse the strangely oily powder, using the lateral molecular rectifier to be absolutely certain. 'A bit of an exotic mixture,' he announced. 'Sphoeroides and bufus venom, extracts from a variety of plants. Some diodon in there as well, by the looks of things. Quite a powerful neurotrope, and certainly topically active, as I suspected.'

'Lethal?' Ace asked.

'Far worse,' Petion put in sourly.

'You could put it that way,' the Doctor agreed. 'It slows the autonomic nervous system to the barest limit of operation, but doesn't affect the higher brain functions. The effect is rather like being in a sensory deprivation tank, in that you can't move or react at all. Unlike a tank, though, you can see and hear as normal, though the nerves that transmit pain and physical feeling are completely dead.'

'How long does it last?'

'It depends. The sphoeroides and bufus venom make all the difference, since they disrupt the nerves by preventing sodium ions from passing into the cells. If swallowed it kills in seconds, if absorbed through the thinner membranes in the mouth without swallowing, it kills in hours. If, however, it's absorbed by osmosis through the skin, it simply paralyses in a death-like state for anything between a few hours and a few days, depending on the dosage. As for this dose – ' he frowned in thought, ' – perhaps enough to keep her out of action for a day.'

Ace's brow puckered, as she considered this. 'Isn't that a bit sophisticated for nineteen fifteen?'

'No. All the ingredients are natural ones which have

been put to use in this way for centuries. Ah!' He thumped the worktop sharply.

'What's wrong?,' Ace snapped, half rising from her stool.

'I should have realized! When Howard and I were attacked on our way back from the hills, two of the men were carrying Lugers – they're unmistakable.'

'So?'

'So, the Luger's a German gun – and who were the first major users of chemical weapons on this planet? Exactly,' he continued, without waiting for any answer other than the look on Ace's face. 'I wonder . . .'

'But the *Necronomicon*, and the Old Ones?'

The Doctor sobered a little. 'After their disappearance, all the records of their influence speak only of effects on the minds of their followers. That's their trademark. Rather than come and conquer physically – which they can't do anyway, since part of their consciousness is trapped – they nudge people's minds in the direction they want them to go in. They plant the seeds of ideas in their followers' minds and harvest from afar the results of putting those ideas into action.'

'And if they put into Mait's mind the idea of crossing German willingness to use biochem weapons with the ancient potion-making skills of his own people . . .'

'Precisely. If that idea proves feasible, they could zombify most of Europe for long enough to walk in unresisted.'

'And,' Petion added, 'if they are also aware of the properties of the plant called the *zombi concombre* – '

'That's a datura-related psychotrope, isn't it?' the Doctor asked rhetorically. 'Yes, if they added that, they could also have their conquered victims become willing slaves, so long as they give regular dosages. I've seen similar situations on company planets run by the Usurians, but I never thought I'd see it on Earth.'

'But wait a minute,' Ace interrupted, 'this could just as easily be the idea of a human as these Old Ones of yours. How do you tell the difference?'

'You're not supposed to, that's how they get away with

it. Or at least, that's how we suppose they get away with it if the legends are true and they really still exist. It's always hard to tell with these things,' he finished gloomily.

'You're telling me,' she said.

'Anyway,' he perked up, 'if it is the Old Ones, it would explain the telepathic pollution, and there'll be more to it that we haven't thought about yet, but we'll find out later.'

'Isn't there always? And if not?'

'Then there isn't much difference. The Old Ones never appear in person, so we don't have to worry about them anyway, but a cultist who only believes he has their powers or blessings and acts accordingly is just as dangerous as one who genuinely has their powers and blessings.'

'Hoo-rah,' she drawled sarcastically.

Benny awoke from a dream of Daleks and childhood memories to find herself rocking gently with the motion of a boat. Sitting up with a groan, she saw that she was in a small motor launch, approaching a wall into which a flight of stone steps had been built. The other occupants of the boat were a Marine sergeant and one of the soldiers who had found her at the village. The sergeant noticed her movement, and came over with a canteen of water, which he offered wordlessly, but with a kind look. She took it gratefully and sipped a small amount, but it was stale and she handed it back.

'Can't say I like it much either,' the sergeant commented, 'but it's all we've got.'

'I'd have preferred a bottle of Chardonnay to be quite honest, but that did the job.' She pinched the leg of her damp coveralls with a grimace. 'Well, these are past their best.' She looked at the sergeant and the private, and realized that these must be two of the Marines the Doctor had talked about. 'Have you secured the city yet?'

'More or less, but these niggers are a feisty bunch.'

'Niggers? Is that an Old Earth slang term?' Benny forgot herself in her curiosity.

'Whaddaya mean? You're no American, but what else do you call these black folks where you come from?'

'Usually we call them by their names like everybody else.' Her tone grew colder as she realized what the sergeant meant.

'But they ain't like everybody else,' the sergeant scoffed. 'You sure got some weird ways.'

Benny glared, and wondered maliciously what this narrow-minded type would make of a Draconian, or a Centauran. 'Well, at least I'll be able to get changed once we get back.'

'Actually, I think the Colonel will want to speak to you first.'

'And where is he?'

'Up at the university.'

'Perfect!' Benny exclaimed. 'That's where I'm going anyway. I have some friends waiting for me there.' If they are still there, she added to herself as a dark afterthought.

The Marines had sent her off in a small wooden-bedded truck that seemed to have no springs or shock-absorbers whatsoever. Sitting between the driver and the sergeant, she gritted her teeth as her bones were pounded by every pothole in Port-au-Prince. They had almost passed the Royale, when a thought suddenly occurred to Benny, and she stamped the driver's foot to the brake pedal.

'What the hell are you doing?' the sergeant snapped.

'At least one of my friends might be waiting for me inside,' Benny said. 'If you can bear to wait here for a couple of minutes, I'll go and see.'

'I don't know . . .' The sergeant looked at her closely, obviously wondering if she planned to run off for some reason. Finally, he seemed to decide she wouldn't risk disappearing into Port-au-Prince, and nodded reluctantly. 'Okay, five minutes only. Any longer and I'll have you arrested.'

Benny realized with a shock that he meant it, and began to have second thoughts. Nevertheless, she decided not to be put off by him, and climbed out of the truck when he slipped out to make way.

The mulatto who had greeted them the previous morning was not in evidence as Benny passed through the lobby, for which she was grateful. She ascended the stairs and entered her own room first, but there was no one there. Shrugging, she moved to the Doctor's door, and pushed it open, stepping lightly inside. She was surprised to find that the room was in darkness, the window shutters closed. As her eyes adjusted, she noticed a figure sitting cross-legged on the bed, leaning right across it to rest against the wall. 'Doctor?' she asked cautiously.

There was no answer. Moving carefully, Benny stepped around the edges of the room, and opened the window shutters. Her momentary horror at seeing the unmistakable form of General Etienne was only slightly dulled by the realization that the stiff posture he was in could only mean he was dead. She examined the body as best she could without touching it, its contorted features being a suitable disincentive to touch it. Strangely, one of the spars from the bed's headboard seemed to be missing.

Benny reached out to turn the body, hoping to see if there was any clue to what had killed him. As the body flopped aside, Benny jumped back, startled by the sight of a small snake, which hissed into wakefulness when the body no longer shaded it. 'Hiss off,' Benny muttered, and was back in the truck well within the five minute limit.

Mait's villa was in a shady cutting on a hillside above Port-au-Prince. The cool halls and rooms, separated from the outside by removable screens rather than walls, were silent and empty, since the few servants Mait employed were busy in the kitchens and the garden outside. The TARDIS materialized under an arched portico, its sound not carrying far enough to attract anyone's attention.

Though the Doctor was first out, looking around in calm appraisal, Clairvius Dubois almost knocked him down in his surprisingly sprightly enthusiasm to see what Mait's home was actually like. Ace had been amazed that

174

Dubois had shown virtually no reaction to the TARDIS, beyond a comment that it was 'almost as strange as the domain of the *zombi astral*.'

Petion, who had already experienced TARDIS travel, simply looked uncomfortable. 'Remember,' the Doctor said sternly, 'don't touch anything unless you're wearing the gloves I gave you.' He held up his own pair of rubber gloves to emphasize the point, then turned and went into the lounge. Petion moved down the sparsely decorated hall to keep an eye out for anyone approaching. Dubois went to investigate a spacious bedroom, while Ace found her way into a study situated off the lounge.

The Doctor found himself in a room bordered by folding screens which opened out on to a wide area which was covered by a light wooden roof supported by thin, widely spaced poles. The roof was perhaps twelve feet above the ground, and stretched to the far end of the open area. For a moment he paused at the threshold, but then turned back inside, taking in the sight of an ivory chess set, a small telescope, a number of small fluted carvings, and the fine hangings adorning the wall, observing everything with a cocked head as if listening for something. From a pocket he drew a small cylindrical probe, and he stalked slowly around the room with it, pointing it at every piece of furniture and ornamentation with a sensitive ear tuned to the probe's faint hum. None of the items he checked affected the probe – though he gave the chess set a suspicious glance – until he moved to the wall hangings. Receiving a faint beeping from the probe, he threw aside one of the hangings to reveal the strange arrangement of wheels, rods and mirrored lenses that was concealed in the alcove behind it.

He put the probe away and studied the device with a frown, searching in vain for recognizable wiring or circuitry. All that was there, however, was a complex mass of brass mechanism, though many of the pieces seemed to be inlaid with solid-state etchings. 'So,' he muttered, 'our friend has a focused neuro-pattern enhancer, eh?'

He sniffed disparagingly. 'Just the sort of trinket that would make his type feel superior.' He paused. 'A bit like digital watches with musical alarms, and about as useful.' He affixed a small jewellers' eyeglass to his eye, and peered in at the device's workings more closely.

With cautiously gloved hands, Ace flicked through papers from a locked cabinet, which she had opened by means of a knife she usually concealed in her boot. The papers were incomprehensible, however, and she soon gave up on them, settling for opening cupboards in search of more obvious evidence. The study was lined with bookshelves, which she investigated first, curious about whether Mait had one of those hoary old secret passages behind a bookcase. There was no sign of one, but Ace did discover a locked section of one case which, upon being broken open, proved to contain the sort of books which one certainly didn't find in the local W H Smiths. Several of them were bound in a strange dry leathery material, which Ace was happy not to know the origin of. The titles were not ones with which she was familiar: *The Book Of Dzyan*, *The Book of Eibon*, *The Golden Bough*, Ludwig Prinn's *De Vermiis Mysteriis*, *The Beginner's Guide to the Necronomicon*, and others whose titles were written in so indecipherable a script that she couldn't read it. Briefly, she wondered if this weren't the sort of thing the Doctor was after, but decided to continue searching.

It was then that she discovered that the balsa-wood screens which formed the walls could be folded open. Outside them, by an open area and a covered section, a small flight of steps led down to a low outbuilding which faced the open area. Curious, Ace stepped out into the sun, and went down to the door. This door, strangely, wasn't locked, but when she removed her hand from the handle, she saw that the thick rubber glistened with some oily substance, and was glad she had put the gloves on as a precaution.

Pushing the door open, she entered a dim chamber similar to the one in which they had first met Dubois.

Above the altar, however, in place of the religious painting in Dubois's house, was a chillingly small human skull. The chamber was also filled with rather more stoppered bottles and clay jars than Dubois had. Ace decided that it was time to fetch the Doctor. Swiftly, closing the door behind her, she exited the building, and returned through the study to the hall. She was surprised, and not a little worried, to find Petion missing. Every sense alert for trouble, she slipped silently over to the lounge door.

The Doctor stepped back from the device as Petion entered, but his welcoming words died on his lips as he saw the liveried servant who followed Petion in, a machete held loosely and comfortably in his hand with the certainty of one who knows how to use it. 'Mait will want to talk to you,' he said, closing the door, 'but he'll understand if I have to cut you.'

'Don't worry.' The Doctor smiled placatingly. 'We won't try to harm you.'

The servant sneered, failing to notice the door opening quietly behind him. 'How many more of you are – ' he broke off with a stifled gasp as a hand clutched the skin exposed at the side of his neck by his wide and unbuttoned collar, and he folded to the ground.

The Doctor looked at Ace in genuine amazement until, with a smile, she raised a hand so he could see the oil glistening on her gloved fingers. She nodded at the limp body. 'There's a building out there with this stuff on the handle. I figured if it was a security precaution it'd probably work fast.'

'It would seem you were right. We'll pay a visit there next, but first . . .' The Doctor returned to the device behind the wall hanging, and began to readjust the mirrors' alignment.

'What is that thing?' Petion asked.

'Well, it's a sort of focused neuro-pattern enhancer. He most likely uses it for private communication with his lackeys, and for controlling his *zombis*.'

'What, you speak into it?'

'No, you think into it. It enables non-telepaths to communicate by thought waves.' He sniffed. 'It's a rather shoddy model though, a lot of psycho-spoor left lying around when it's in operation – that must be what I was picking up.'

'And is it alien technology?' Ace wondered.

'Well, the actual components and manufacturing skills required are accessible to humans of this time period, but the concept and design are much further advanced. I wonder where he got the idea for building it, eh?'

'So, are you buggering it up now?'

'Sort of. It usually works by acting as an external focus for the electric fields generated by the brain, and directs them at a receptive machine or conditioned brain elsewhere. However, if I can just shift these mirrors right – ah, done it! Now I've engendered a feedback loop, so that if Mait, or anyone else, tries to use it, the enhancer will focus his concentration, feed it back, and drain it off again in a continuous loop that should keep him rooted to the spot for the rest of his life – or until someone else separates his gaze from the lenses. You could say he'll bore himself stiff, in fact. Now, about this building you – wait a minute, where's Dubois?'

'The last I saw of him was as he entered the bedroom,' Petion replied.

'We'd better check up on him.' The Doctor let the wall hanging fall back into place, and hurried out, turning down the hall to the bedroom.

Petion and Ace followed him, arriving just as he threw open the door of a spartan room with expensive mahogany flooring, and bumped straight into Dubois, who was backing towards them while scattering something on the floor. Dubois jumped up with a start, and visibly relaxed when he saw who had interrupted him.

The Doctor glanced inside, and saw that Dubois had left several feathers on the bed, and had scrawled a strange symbol on the wall above the headboard. 'What are you doing?' the Doctor demanded.

'Mait has committed crimes against the people of this

178

island, and against the *Bizango* itself. I am simply passing sentence now that the opportunity has arisen.'

'An eye for an eye? Very human.'

Dubois glared at the Doctor with a tinge of anger. How dare this *blanc* try to interfere with the way things have been done for centuries? 'Two wrongs may not make a right, Doctor, but sometimes the second wrong helps the first rest easier.'

'Not while I'm here,' the Doctor said.

'You're perfectly welcome to sweep my *coup poudre* back up, if you like.'

The Doctor looked for a moment as if he might continue to argue the point, but seemed to relax, and turned to Ace. 'Let's have a look at your discovery.'

Together this time, they followed Ace out through the study. Since they were all gloved, the Doctor wasted no time, simply pushing the door open. 'Well done, Ace. This is Mait's *Bagi*.'

'His what?'

'The place where he keeps his altar and spirits – disembodied spirits, that is.' He began examining several of the clay jars and bottles, while Ace stood by, wondering what she was supposed to do in a place like this. Petion stayed nervously by the door, and Ace joined him there, watching suspiciously as Dubois checked everything with a professional eye. Ace wasn't willing to trust Dubois further than she could throw him, since he seemed to use much the same methods as their enemies; perhaps that meant he was no better than them. It was Dubois, however, who called the Doctor's attention to a small antechamber in which several grotesque fish and toads were hung on hooks beside dried roots. A set of bottles and jars sat below them. When the Doctor joined him, Dubois waved a hand in their general direction. 'These are the materials with which Mait will have trapped your friend's *ti bon ange* – her soul.'

'Puffer fish and toad, just as the lab analysis suggested. Good, that means we still have a good chance.' The Doctor returned to the main chamber, and picked up a bottle which he had been examining when Dubois called. 'This explains the rest of it,' he told Ace. 'Mescalin.'

'Never heard of it,' Ace said distractedly, wondering why she had bothered coming along. This just wasn't any fun.

'A solution of processed peyote root. It acts as a so-called mind-expanding drug,' he added with distaste, 'which opens the higher centres of the brain that humans aren't ready to use yet. Users often report experiencing the sort of twisted non-Euclidian dimensions associated with the Old Ones, so it's reasonable to assume that this is how Mait made contact with them, or with whatever race memory remains of them, which amounts to the same thing.' He sighed. 'I've seen enough here. Ace,' he said, gesturing back into the *Bagi* as he exited past her, 'your department, I think.'

Ace grinned, and drew out a pair of thin doughy wedges from the deep pockets of her duster coat.

'What is that girl doing?' Dubois asked slowly as the Doctor ushered him and Petion back out.

'Ending Mait's reprehensible ways, with any luck.'

'She knows that much of the ways of *vodoun*?' Dubois asked incredulously.

'No, she knows the ways of ka-boom would be a more accurate description.'

'How long?' Ace called from the *Bagi*.

'Five minutes,' the Doctor called back.

Inside, Ace folded one piece of plastic explosive round the corner that led into the anteroom, and placed the other above the altar. Into each piece she inserted a small two-pronged cylinder the size and shape of a small capacitor, and twisted each of them. She then rejoined the others outside, and the Doctor led them back to the TARDIS. 'Shall I blow the rest of the house as well?'

'That would be excessive.' The Doctor set the controls on the console. 'There's a small cemetery on the slope below the other side of the house. Bring the Colonel's men there at one in the morning.' Without waiting for an answer, he exited the TARDIS.

Ace moved after him, ready to demand an explanation of where he was going and how he knew there was a cemetery, but before she reached the doors, they closed of their own accord, and the time rotor began its stately rise and fall.

The Doctor looked back from the short flight of steps leading down to the entry hall, and watched the TARDIS dematerialize with a feeling of pain at seeing his ship go without him.

He slipped through the house, silent and insubstantial as a shadow, and left via the front door. A twisting road led down into the bushes, and the Doctor set off down it. When he reached the bottom, where a large gate was permanently rusted open, he walked straight past a dozing guard, who failed to notice him. Stopping outside, he checked his watch, and was rewarded with a sudden sharp blast from upslope, followed by a rain of small pieces of wood and clay brick which had once been a part of the *Bagi*. Ignored by the guard, who was running towards the house after being startled into wakefulness, the Doctor eyed the cloud of grey smoke critically, wondering how much damage would have been done to the villa itself. 'Show-off,' he muttered.

Chapter Seventeen

Henri answered the insistent buzz of the telephone, almost instantly holding it out to Mait, who came in from inspecting the *hounfort*. 'Yes,' he snapped into the mouthpiece. 'What! When? I'll be there immediately.' He turned to the taller man. 'Henri, start that car you have hidden, we must return to my house at once.' Retrieving his hat from where he had left it, he hurried out.

The TARDIS arrived back at the hospital just as two Marines escorted Benny inside. Howard leapt to his feet from the chair he had been sitting in. 'Professor Summerfield! Are you all right? You look like a drowned rat – nothing personal.'

'I feel like a drowned rat as well. It hasn't been a very good day for me.'

'Evidently not.' Howard indicated the hawk-like officer who was with him, and who was examining Benny and the Marines with a bemused expression. 'This is Colonel Mortimer, in charge of this arm of the expeditionary force.'

'Hello,' Benny said without enthusiasm.

'Report, Sergeant,' Mortimer urged.

'Yes, sir. This lady here came ashore at landing point theta, and promptly collapsed. The Lieutenant recommended that we bring her to you, as she was carrying this.' The sergeant handed over the plastic bag with Benny's notes.

'What sort of material is this?' Mortimer asked.

'A plastic bag – new invention,' Benny said hurriedly.

Mortimer removed the papers and examined them closely. 'These notes are written in German. Would you care to tell me how that can be?' Mortimer's voice took on a purring note.

'I saw that written on some drums – a lot of drums. Since I don't remember enough German to translate it, I copied it down until I could find someone who could.'

Mortimer scrutinized her with narrowed eyes, then nodded to himself. 'You're with that British agent, aren't you?'

'The Doctor? Yes. I was – ' She stopped as Ace and Petion came through the office door with a black man she didn't recognize. Ace gave a cry of relief, and even Petion smiled.

'Where the hell have you been?' Ace asked in a tone that betrayed the worry she'd been trying to hide.

'It's a long story. Where's the Doctor?'

'Off somewhere on his own,' Ace answered more soberly. 'Planning something, no doubt.'

The Doctor followed the narrow road down through a small valley, before climbing back up towards a bare hilltop where he could make out a number of tiny wooden crosses, like a forest of lifeless bonsai trees. His features reflected the grim thoughts that filled his mind, eyes flicking only briefly to right or left, secure in the knowledge that the path would be fairly safe until nightfall.

Pacing himself steadily along the dusty track, the Doctor halted when his flickering eyes fell upon an unnatural addition to the landscape. A car was squatting on the roadside, listing heavily to one side as a pair of its wheels were in a low ditch. Approaching cautiously, the Doctor examined the open-topped interior of the car, which was spotted with dust and bird-droppings on the cracked leather. The black paint on the body was already peeling from the heat, though the Doctor guessed from the depth of the dust layer that it hadn't been there more than a couple of days. He quickly checked the tyres, but they were intact, and he wondered to himself why someone would simply stop in the middle of this countryside. Acting on impulse, he slipped into the car, and tried to

183

start it, but the engine simply coughed and died. 'Bone dry, eh?' he said. He left the car again, and saw something else on the other side of it – a pair of legs jutting out from the bushes nearby.

The stench that the Doctor noted as he approached bore witness to the speed with which decay took place in the tropical climate, and he found that he had to clap a handkerchief over his mouth as he knelt to examine the body. It was a white man in middle age, dressed in a light beige suit. The tissues, especially around the torso, looked puffy and bloated as the cells within decayed into methane and other gases. There were already colonies of maggots at work on the body, particularly, the Doctor noticed, on the stump of the right wrist, and on the hand which was severed and lay a couple of feet away. Why cut off one hand? the Doctor wondered, before the reason struck him: the man must have carried a briefcase or similar object cuffed to his wrist, and his assailants hadn't been willing to expend time on subtleties like lockpicking.

Grimacing in distaste, the Doctor lifted the man's jacket aside to reach into the inside pocket, the flesh underneath giving way with the unnatural softness of rotting fruit. As soon as the man's wallet was in his hand, the Doctor retreated hastily back to the car to peruse the contents.

The wallet contained a small amount of money in francs, dollars and local gourdes, but the Doctor was more interested in the identification papers which named the man as one Robert Blake, of the British Consulate. The Doctor nodded to himself as one piece of the puzzle clicked into place, explaining why everyone thought he was looking for a missing British Consul, obviously this man. 'I wonder what was in the briefcase that someone wanted it so badly?' he said aloud. Shrugging, he slipped Blake's identification into his pocket, and tossed the wallet carelessly back into the bushes beside the corpse.

Checking his watch, he set off for the hilltop once more.

Moving quickly in spite of his elderly bulk, Mait went directly up the steps leading to his peristyle, and saw the wreckage where his *Bagi* had once stood. 'Who has done this thing?' he hissed. Behind him, Henri silently peeled off a card. It was the image of the young knight.

Mait entered the house through a shattered French window, and went straight towards the alcove in the study. Flicking the Arawak hanging aside, he set his gaze on the central mirror of the enhancer.

Concentrating his will, he sent it into the mirror. Into the mirror . . . Into the mirror.

After several long moments had passed, it began to occur to Henri that something wasn't working properly. 'Mait?' he asked. There was no reply, Mait simply standing and staring into the mirrored lens. Henri frowned worriedly; Mait was the only one who knew exactly how their plans could be completed, and Henri wasn't about to let his guide to power be zombified himself. Taking a deep breath, he grasped Mait's arm, and pulled him away from the enhancer.

Instantly, Mait came round, clutching his head with a gasp. 'The device has been misaligned – deliberately.'

'But who would have the knowledge to do such a thing?' Henri asked, losing his usual composure at the thought.

'The *blanc* you have been so concerned about, perhaps.'

'The gate guard did say he saw a *blanc* leave shortly before the explosion.'

'Yes . . . Perhaps we can tell. If he looked into the device, he may have left something of himself.' Carefully turning the mirror aside so as not to be trapped again, Mait examined the intricate network of rods. 'There it is.' He smiled grimly. 'It will be a simple matter to reset it.' With a deft motion of surprisingly nimble fingers, he shifted the misaligned parts back into their correct placings. 'Now, let us see.'

Concentrating once again on the central mirror, he focused his will on the device itself, and its past.

Slowly, an image built up in the mirrored lens. An image of a white face under a white fedora. Mait had never seen the man before, but it was obvious that since no one other than himself had used the device since he had built it, this must be the man in question. He concentrated further, trying to drag the man's thoughts which had gone into the device back out again.

Concentrate.

Focus.

Images. Random thoughts. Memories of other similar devices flickered for an instant. Devices on other worlds, in other times. Time. The Time Winds that the Great Ones could travel were briefly remembered, as part of time travel performed by the Doctor. The Doctor, one time traveller among others. Others who called themselves –

'Time Lords!' Mait exclaimed, staggering back from the enhancer with the tiredness of expended effort. 'So, our opponent is the Doctor, a Time Lord.' He scratched his moustache thoughtfully.

'What is a Time Lord?' Henri asked confusedly.

'I'm not quite sure,' Mait replied with lowered brows. 'I received . . . images of what they do, but it was so garbled and confused . . .' He steadied himself on the arm of a chair. 'There was the feeling of great power, and of familiarity. The Great Ones know of these people, and consider them a danger; that much I know.'

'How can anyone be a danger to *them*?'

'This Time Lord is also from beyond the stars, Henri, just like them. He may have known ledge of them. He, or others, may have met them before, and fought against them.'

'Then we just kill him first.'

'A most dull and unimaginative way to proceed, but I fear you may be right. Did the guard say which way he went?'

'Towards the cemetery.'

'What! The cemetery where the ceremony will begin? If we are quick, we may be able to stop him from desecrating the site.' Mait lifted the telephone.

General Froebe slipped on a pair of reading glasses, and

shuffled through the papers on his desk, glancing briefly at the timetables and lists that adorned each one. 'Why didn't you bring this sooner, Mister Richmann?'

'This is how long your clerks took to translate Blake's work. It seems they didn't trust me to do it for you.'

Froebe looked at Richmann, who lounged back in a chair, his feet up on Froebe's polished mahogany desk. 'I wouldn't either,' he growled.

'Is that any way to talk to your officers?' Richmann asked cheekily.

'Subordinates,' Froebe corrected him. 'I can speak to subordinates in any fashion I wish – a privilege of rank, which I surely don't have to tell you about.' He leant back and laid the papers down. 'Besides, as a foreigner, your commission is mainly honorary.' He knocked Richmann's feet from the desktop with a disdainful sweep of his arm.

Richmann's scowl deepened, but he restrained himself from snapping an answer back at the General.

'Still,' Froebe continued, 'these observations of our movements will now never be delivered, and we have the names of his contacts in Cuba and Jamaica. That's something, I suppose.'

'Do you want me to take a trip and get rid of them?'

'No. So long as the Americans are only afraid that we might land on this island, and don't know we're already here, they will pay no attention to our activities. If I let you wander off killing people all over the place – '

'I was born and bred in Philadelphia – '

'Your men weren't, and I'm sure the Americans would find some way to make even you talk. Besides, Mait has decided to perform his ceremony tonight. Only after that will he turn the remaining details of his *zombi* control over to us for the final phase on the island. That means we all lie low in here.'

'Why is he holding out until then?'

'Religious objections, if you can call that superstitious rubbish a religion. I'll let him have his fun tonight.'

'And tomorrow?' Richmann asked eagerly.

'Tomorrow, you make sure that he can't give details of the formula to anyone else – ever.'

Richmann smiled. The silence was broken by the sudden ringing of Froebe's telephone. He answered it instantly. 'Yes? Ah, Mait, we were just talking about you. What?' Froebe looked puzzled. 'The one Richmann failed to kill? Very well, I'll have him seen to.' He hung up the phone.

'Trouble?'

'That interloper who was in the car, calls himself the Doctor apparently – he's on his way to the cemetery. Make sure he gets the maximum use out of it.'

The Doctor walked curiously around the small cemetery, noticing the patterns of footprints in the dusty ground. They seemed centred on one particular grave, so the Doctor stepped over to it for a closer look. On the ground in front of the simple headstone were several dark splashes, which could only have been made by blood.

Straightening, the Doctor looked around, noticing for the first time that the hill he had asked about earlier when he was with Howard, was also visible from here. On impulse, he stepped away from the grave, and put his ear to the ground once more. Sure enough, he could make out the same almost subsonic throbbing as he had heard earlier. Once again, it seemed to be coming from the direction of the hill. Sighting along his umbrella, the Doctor realized that the hill, the cemetery, and Mait's house were all in a straight line. Trying to mentally recall a map of the island, the Doctor didn't think there was anything of importance further along the line inland, but he wondered what there might be out to sea . . .

He walked over to the rickety wooden gateway, drawing from his pocket a small jar he had purloined from Mait's *Bagi* before Ace had blown it up. Since he wanted to delay the ceremony, but didn't want to go to the trouble of desecrating any graves, he only had one option.

Carefully, crouching to hold the jar low against the ground lest the wind whip any of the powder back towards him, he sprinkled the contents of the jar across the end of the dirt road just before the gate. Tossing the empty jar aside, he then pulled out a piece of chalk and drew a complex symbol full of mind-twisting curves on to each gatepost. 'That should give Mait pause for thought,' he muttered, straightening and stepping back into the cemetery to retrieve his umbrella.

'I'm sure it will,' a voice agreed in a cynical tone.

The Doctor spun around to see a German officer leaning against a skeletal tree, his Steyr automatic aimed comfortably at the Doctor. 'Another of Mait's puppets?' he asked.

'Hardly,' the man answered in a quiet yet disparaging tone. 'The Doctor, I presume?'

'So some people say. You haven't introduced yourself.'

'There isn't much point; you're not going to live long enough to have to introduce me at parties.'

'You could always consider it a last request.'

'I suppose.' The man smiled wolfishly. 'I'd have asked for a final orgy myself, but each to his own. I'm Major Paul Richmann, and you seem to have got on the wrong side of General Froebe somehow. You've also got yourself on my bad side; since I hate to fail on any assignment, your survival yesterday was most irritating.'

'So naturally your answer is to shoot me now,' the Doctor said contemptuously.

Richmann seemed to think for a moment, then smiled. 'I think we can arrange a more amusing death for you.' He gestured with his free hand, and several other men appeared from their hiding places, two of them grasping the Doctor tightly by the arms. 'I think we'll send you for what you British might call a long stretch . . .'

Something crashed into the back of the Doctor's head, and everything went black.

Chapter Seventeen

It was clearly evening when the Doctor's eyes blinked open. A momentary disorientation took him when he found that not only could he not move, but that he was staring straight up at the sky, and there appeared to be no ground underneath him. Some deep throbbing vibration seemed to be keeping him in the air, and his limbs ached.

It was only by craning his neck to a painful degree that he saw that he was suspended in mid-air, a foot or so above the sea. Suspension was provided by two thick hawsers, one attached to his ankles and firmly anchored ashore to a boulder the size of a double-decker bus, the other attached to his wrists and fixed to a large steam yacht's anchor fitting.

An approaching wooden wall resolved itself into the form of a small boat, in which Richmann sat, with another man using the oars to hold position. 'Comfortable?' Richmann asked with a smirk.

'Not particularly.'

'Good, I can see this is going to be as amusing as I had hoped.'

'You'll forgive me if I don't die laughing?'

'*Laughter* on your part is purely optional, Doctor, don't worry about that. I believe this situation is self-explanatory, so I won't bother you with details; suffice it to say that the best engineers in Germany have convinced me that the weakest point in this chain is your body. I expect you can figure the rest out for yourself.' Richmann looked over at the steam yacht, and made a circling motion with his hand. As a deep rumbling and a few wisps of smoke were produced by the yacht, he turned back to the Doctor. 'The yacht is a rather slow model of course, so it may take some time for you to die.' He leaned in closer, the false cheeriness leaving his features. 'The pain will be exquisite, Doctor, and I shall savour every nuance of your screams. Nothing personal.'

Leaving Howard to try and persuade Colonel Mortimer to take his men to the cemetery that night – reasoning that one American to another would get a better result – Ace, Benny and Petion returned to the TARDIS, where Ace indicated the remaining pilfered weapons in her shopping trolley. 'Take those and hand them out to the hospital staff and patients – just in case,' she said.

Petion wheeled the trolley out as Benny looked on disapprovingly. 'You can't go about encouraging more violence, Ace,' she said.

'I can try to make sure they can protect themselves, can't I?'

'That's not much of an excuse. They could protect themselves at least as well by simply keeping their heads down.' She sighed, realizing that Ace wouldn't be swayed, and decided to change the subject for the sake of peace. 'Anyway, I suppose I'd better see what translation the TARDIS computer can offer of these papers.' She held up the notes she had copied down from the drums in the German docks.

'Yeah, sure. I'll be in the lab if you need me.'

A steady burning sensation gnawed at the Doctor's joints as the steam yacht slowly churned the water. He was beginning to wish he'd built another K9 to get him out of these spots. 'I wouldn't have thought this was your way, Richmann,' he called through gritted teeth. 'And I'd always seen myself as leaving my body to medical science.'

'You are. The breaking strain of your body will be carefully noted. Never know when the knowledge might come in useful.'

'I'd also have thought that shooting people yourself was more fun for your type.'

'As a matter of fact, it is. This was Mait's idea.'

191

'I've got myself on his bad side as well, eh?'

'So it seems.'

'It's nice to know you're so obedient, Richmann.'

'When it suits me, I am.'

'For the moment,' the Doctor replied scornfully.

'Really?'

'Yes, really. You'd better get used to doing what Mait and Henri tell you.'

'Why do you say that?'

'They don't plan to leave you and Froebe in charge when this is over.'

'I don't doubt it,' Richmann laughed. 'But they're going to be dead by dawn tomorrow, so I don't think the General or I will lose any sleep over it.'

'If your precious General sleeps tonight, he'll never wake up again.' The Doctor began to talk faster as the pain built up.

'Explain!'

'Mait has a plant in your base, you kn – ' The Doctor's jaws clenched shut to bite back a cry. Immediately, Richmann made a slashing motion with his hand, and the strain began to ease.

'I'll tell you what, Doctor. You tell me about this plant, and I'll kill you quick – bullet in the head, no more pain.' Richmann leant back and waited – it was a reasonable offer, after all.

'I tell the General, or no one at all.'

'This sounds like a trick to buy time,' Richmann snarled, raising his hand to signal the yacht.

'I saw Mait's files in his house; that's what put me on his bad side,' the Doctor added hurriedly.

'You were in Mait's house?' Richmann looked at the Doctor doubtfully, trying to read the inscrutable face.

'Yes,' the Doctor answered firmly, fixing Richmann with a penetrating gaze.

Richmann pursed his lips in thought. This could be a trick to save his skin, he thought, but if he *does* know something and he dies without telling it . . . 'We can always kill you later, I suppose,' he said wistfully.

Ace was busy remachining parts from several guns as Benny rushed in, waving the print-out she had got from the computer. 'I've found it, Ace! The stuff in the drums!'

Ace looked up from where she was starting to fit the parts together into what looked like a home-made machine gun. 'What is the stuff then?'

'There are three separate substances. One's a volatilized mixture of puffer venom and umpteen different plants – it slows the metabolic processes of the body to as near to full stop as it's possible to get.'

'That's the same shit they used on you – the Doctor analysed some of it he scraped off the stones you'd been handling.'

'Exactly. The second batch has a datura-based compound that blanks out the will, making the victim a mindless vegetable who'll obey any order at all.'

'Christ! And the third?'

'A less potent version of the first, with just a hint of the second. I can't figure out what that'll do though, or why they want it.'

'Well it's obvious why they want the first two – so they can use it as gas on the Front and turn the whole of Europe into zombies.'

'No doubt.'

'Ace, Benny,' Petion called out as he entered, 'the Colonel has decided to take a force to the cemetery. We leave at twenty-hundred hours. That gives us two hours to get there and two hours to prepare before Mait's people begin to arrive for the ceremony.'

Ace slammed a magazine into her finished gun. 'Right,' she said eagerly.

Von Stein had been checking the wall clock in the laboratory then looking back at his notes for some time. Now, however, he lifted the internal phone, and dialled Froebe's office. 'It's dusk,' he pronounced when the phone was answered. 'Time for the next phase – the use of Compound Two.' He put the phone back.

In Froebe's office, the General rattled the telephone

hook to clear the line and dialled another number. Moving to look out over his command, he gave a series of orders into the phone.

As the sun faded into a blood-red haze, Lieutenant Davis and his men finally sat down around a nest of campfires which a small detail had built earlier. Rather than pile all the bodies into one large mass grave, Davis had had his men dig serried rows of shallow graves and lay the bodies into them as they were, without coffins, which would have taken far too long to make.

Some of the graves were very short.

While the sky above darkened to a deep purple, the Marines below looked about, made nervous by the steadily increasing pace and volume of drumming that floated down eerily from the surrounding countryside. In an attempt to prove they were unaffected by this, they raised their voices as they chatted to each other, and pretended not to glance uneasily at the nearby rectangles of darker, freshly turned earth.

The sudden cessation of the drumming was, peculiarly, more unnerving than its presence.

Above the village, almost invisible against the velvet shroud of the night sky, something huge silently blotted out the stars.

The Marines got to their feet, clutching their rifles for reassurance. Davis himself was the first to notice the mist that rolled towards them. The wavefront of mist rolled over the Marines in a billowing carpet, though once the first rolling wave was past, the mist was much thinner, merely causing a watery distortion in everyone's vision.

While the mist rippled around them, the drumming began all around once more. This time it was louder, closer, and of a more discernible and fervent, regular rhythm.

One or two of the young soldiers fired into the surrounding mist, but the drumming was totally unaffected, and Davis stopped the shooting with a barked order.

'What do they want?' he wondered aloud, drawing the attention of the nearest of his men. They shrugged.

Suddenly alerted by something seen out of the corner of his eye, one of the young Marines felt an icy death-grip on his spine. Turning slightly, and almost against his own will, he looked over at the dark graves. Surely he had imagined . . .

A clod of earth rolled off one long mound.

The Marine tried to tell himself it was something simple like a mole, but then paused to wonder if they had moles in Haiti. Others had noticed by now, however, and were turning to watch the makeshift graves with expressions of alarm. Several more clumps of earth rolled off graves. A couple virtually flew off, landing several feet away.

As if it were a natural follow-on from this behaviour, the earthen surfaces of the graves began to rise and fall like the chests of sleepers. Some began to ripple and undulate as if snakes were spasming below.

The activity began to shake soil loose, still more clods now almost exploding off the surface of the graves. At one of the nearby graves, there was a sudden scattering of earth away from the grave, leaving a pair of arms visible – the normally dark skin was now the grey of the fungal covering of a rotten potato, while the undersides of the arms were almost black with blood that had gathered there since the heart had stopped pumping.

The arms were moving.

The fingers clenched jerkily as the arms flailed at the sides of the grave, tossing dirt aside in an attempt to gain a purchase on the soft earth.

The Marines backed away fearfully, eyes wide.

Arms threw dirt aside, stiffly pulling torsos out of the earth, shoulders shovelling the dirt aside to allow heads to rise and turn uncertainly, glancing about blankly through bulging eyes which looked at everything and saw nothing.

With mouths open in silent pain, their muscles and ligaments cracking like gunshots, figures began pushing their way out of the graves in an obscene parody of birth.

The Marines were supposed to be afraid of nothing,

195

but the sight of the villagers clawing their way back into the world was too much. Some of them broke and ran, while others began shooting into the group of zombie villagers.

The villagers who had broken free of their graves began advancing on the Marines. Their eyes bulged sightlessly from sunken sockets. Their skin was a mouldy grey, while gravity had gathered their uncirculating blood at the lowest points – under the chin, the undersides of the limbs, and around the area of the lower ribs, buttocks and kidneys. Trickles of earth, ridden with worms and insects, fell from their hair and rolled out of slack mouths which formed 'O's of suffering.

Those who advanced under the rifle fire of the Marines who had remained in position did not fall. They didn't even bleed.

Charred-edged holes appeared in their skin, while behind them little dry chunks of flesh fell into the powdery dust that covered the ground.

Slowly constrained by muscles mostly in the grip of rigor mortis, the zombies advanced inexorably on the few remaining Marines.

The Marines began to lower their guns, uncertain of what to do. Davis watched this display in terror and wondered why his men had stopped shooting. The thought occurred to him that he should give them some orders, but he couldn't think of any. He wished someone would tell him what to do . . . His face a mask of puzzlement, Davis sat down to wait for someone to tell him to do something. All around, his men stood or sat, looking at their rifles, and wondering what to do with them. Should they shoot or do something else?

No longer interrupted by shooting, the zombies continued their steady slow pace, completely ignoring the Marines other than to step around any Marine that was in their path. Stiffly, they walked out of the village into the surrounding darkness.

Enveloped by a thin and slightly sweet-smelling mist, the Marines waited for orders.

Chapter Eighteen

Rather than disturb the patients at the hospital any more, Ace and Petion had followed the Marines to their staging area at the customs receivership, which Ace judged to be about the size of an aircraft hangar. There, Mortimer conducted a briefing for some fifty of his men, who had volunteered to go on that night's operation. The briefing, however, mostly consisted of Mortimer's dividing the force into groups and assigning them positions to take up in the scrub around the cemetery, which was illustrated by a simple chalk sketch Petion had done on a blackboard.

Mortimer also generously offered his three guests weapons from Marine stores, but they refused, since they were well-equipped with items Ace had hijacked from the Palace. Petion carried a rifle, a Browning and several grenades. Benny had elected to carry only a revolver, though she had tucked a couple of grenades in the pockets of a second safari jacket she had pilfered from the TARDIS's wardrobe. Ace, on the other hand, still had the Browning and the knife, but had added two packs of C-4 Plus to her pockets. Over her shoulder was slung the home-made sub-machine-gun she had assembled in the TARDIS lab.

When Mortimer had assigned everyone positions for the operation – Ace, Benny and Petion to remain with him – he checked his watch. 'We move out at twenty-two hundred hours – that's two-and-a-half hours from now. Until then, I suggest you all get some rest, because you're going to need it. Dismissed.'

Drifting outside to sit in the cooler evening air, Ace, Benny and Petion chatted together.

'There must be something we're missing,' Benny said,

'or else why would the Doctor think it so necessary for us to stop the ceremony tonight?'

'I dunno,' Ace shrugged. 'What did he call the thing tonight? Wet moan and low something?'

'*Wete Mo Nan Dlo*,' Petion corrected.

'That's it! What is it?'

'It is a ceremony by which the *ti bon ange* can be trapped in a *corps cadavre*.'

'Meaning?' Benny pressed.

'The *ti bon ange* means little good angel – '

'The soul, you mean?' Ace put in.

'No, the soul is in two parts: the *gros bon ange* is the big good angel, the part that deals with instinct and all the functions of life that we do without thinking about.'

A vague suspicion began to tug at Benny's mind, and she frowned in thought.

Ace, meanwhile, continued the conversation. 'The subconscious,' she suggested slowly.

'If you like. The *ti bon ange* is the other part, that makes us individual, like the personality.'

'Of course!' Benny shouted, drawing startled stares from some Marines. 'That's what the Doctor said. These Old Ones of his that Mait's supposed to be working for, the Doctor said their consciousness – their personalities – were trapped outside their bodies, in the Vortex.'

Petion looked at her with a worried frown as he tried to link the two concepts. 'Then Mait may be using tonight's ceremony to reunite the Old One's mind with the rest of it . . .'

'He must be!'

'No, wait.' Petion shook his head. 'The *Wete Mo Nan Dlo* must be performed one year and one day after death. If these Old Ones were around last year, we would have noticed, I think.'

'Time is relative, Petion,' Ace said darkly.

'What?'

'You're thinking in calendar time. But there's also sidereal time, lunar time, galactic time. . . .'

'If all this happened as long ago as the Doctor suggests – ' Benny thought aloud.

'But a year is a year, surely?' Petion said.

'No, a calendar year is the time the Earth takes to orbit the sun. A galactic year, for example, is the time the galaxy takes to rotate once completely – all the outermost stars orbiting the centre. That takes a quarter of a million Earth years, or thereabouts,' Bernice explained.

'The galaxy is also one of a group of galaxies,' Ace added, 'who have an even longer year of their own. These Old Ones probably came from one of the other galaxies in the local group.'

'And that year?'

'Millions of Earth years.'

'The question,' Benny interrupted, 'is how he intends to do it.'

'Well, the *ti bon ange* is usually brought to the *corps cadavre* in a *canari* – a protective clay jar.'

'They couldn't shelter a – the enhancer!' Ace slapped her forehead.

'Of course,' Benny nodded. 'The Doctor said it transmitted mental power . . .'

'So he'll have it at the ceremony,' Ace concluded.

'Assuming he's fixed the Doctor's sabotage.'

'He will have,' Petion predicted gloomily.

'That must be why we have to stop the ceremony – to make sure he can't tap the mental energy of the congregation and use it to supplement the Old One's autonomic functions enough to pull the rest of it out of the Vortex,' Ace finished, and sat back with a cheery grin.

'The simple plans are always the best,' Benny quipped.

The Doctor was thrown into a cell, and left alone. He no longer had to consciously listen out for the psychic interference that pervaded the island. This far underground, not only did Mait's enhancer have no effect, but he could sense a strong source of pure malevolence which was almost tangibly present all around. One of the first things he did was to activate a small probe, with which he scanned his surroundings. 'Psychic wavelength, that's point three-three-eight microbars . . .' he mumbled as he adjusted the probe's sensitivity. When it was pointing at the far corner of the floor, it emitted a stream of high-pitched bleeps. Thoughtfully, the Doctor put the probe away. 'A cellar dweller, eh? No imagination,' he said.

It wasn't long before a guard opened the door to admit a well-built black man with an unreadable face, and an aging, overweight black man whose hair and moustache were going grey.

'Henri, and the infamous Mait, eh?' the Doctor said. Not bothering to rise off the unpadded bunk, he appraised the pair critically, a slightly crestfallen look passing across his features when he considered Mait.

'I'm not used to being so quickly dismissed, Doctor. Perhaps it's sour grapes, since I have plainly avoided the *coup poudre* that was left for me. Richmann, of course, is having the entrance to the cemetery cleared as well. Alternatively, you may be commenting on my handling of the revolution,' Mait said, grinning in exhilaration, 'playing both sides off against the middle to divert attention from the construction of all this.' He waved a hand around.

'Backfired a bit, didn't it? Anyway, it was nothing personal. I was half-expecting someone else, that's all. I'm also rather surprised the General hasn't come to visit,'

'Unfortunately, it appears that the aide sent to inform the General of your arrival somehow forgot the message.'

'How strange,' the Doctor commented with a crooked smile.

'Which is fortunate really, since the idea of your warning him about my plans isn't one I find worthy of consideration, Time Lord.'

The Doctor looked up quickly. 'Time Lord?'

'Your kind are known to us, Doctor, and have been for longer than you can imagine.'

'I can imagine quite a bit. Who exactly are "us"?'

'Myself, and the one I serve. His memories go back a long, long way.'

'I wonder which one it is. Or is it nameless, or unname-able even?' He shrugged. 'And your memories?'

'Mine go back further than most humans'.'

'How far?' the Doctor pressed him.

'How old do you think I am?' Mait asked abruptly.

'Sixty, perhaps.'

'No, Doctor.' Mait shook his head with a smile. 'I was born,' he began slowly, 'in seventeen forty-four. I was the first son of an Efik tribesman in the Kingdom of Dahomey. When my village failed to supply the requisite number of slaves from the Araba tribe of Yaruda to the west, the entire village was cleared by the *blancs*. They felt,' Mait continued bitterly, 'that if we had no one to offer, then we offered ourselves. And they took us. That was in seventeen-fifty. Most of us never arrived here. There was a storm as we passed the southern tip of Cuba, and the ship I was on was smashed on to offshore rocks by the weather. Only two of us survived – myself and, as I discovered later, the *Egbo-Obong* of the village.'

'Leopard Chief?'

'Yes, the head of the leopard society and therefore the supreme tribal authority on matters of the spirit world. It was he who went on to train me to the point where I could begin to set in motion a way to extract revenge from the *blanc* nations, and ensure that no one would so betray us again. It was also he who told me of the Great Ones,' he went on with a faraway look, 'and how they had chosen us to be saved to do this.'

'I see.'

'I thought you might. We are much alike, Doctor – firm in purpose, resourceful, ruthless . . .'

'I see,' the Doctor went on with a harder edge in his voice, 'that you are the sort of hypocritical egomaniac who talks about betrayal when he's condemning thousands of his own people in Haiti and millions in Africa and else-where to living the lives of mere insects!'

'What?' Mait seemed taken aback by this outburst.

'I also see that we're about as alike as chalk and cheese, because I would never sell out a whole species for the wrongs of one group. Have you forgotten that your tribe, the Efik, were among the most notorious slavers on the slave coast? I know, because I was there. In fact, myself and my two human companions were forced to take the calabar test. It's a miracle we all survived. No, you're just a pathetic monomaniac who's lived too long and has become obsessed with the idea of making the entire planet suffer for an ancient wrong that was perpetrated by a mindless minority!'

'Who do you think you are, to talk to me in that manner?'

'Ask him.' The Doctor indicated Henri. 'Pick a card, any card.'

Uncertainly, Henri drew forth his tarot pack and spread the cards in a fan. Angrily, Mait snatched one, and looked at it.

Mait blanched.

'Recognize me now?'

Speechless with rage, Mait hurled the card in the Doctor's face before storming out of the cell. Henri followed and locked the door. The Doctor lifted the card, studying the image of the scythe-wielding skeleton.

He crushed the card to a ball in one hand.

The sky had darkened to violet by the time Mortimer had formed up his troops for the march out of town, and a star-speckled dome was overhead when the column of fifty Marines, plus Benny, Ace and Petion marched out of Port-au-Prince at a slight jog.

Mortimer had ordered that they reach the cemetery by eleven – one hour before the ceremony would start, or so Dubois had told them before he had returned to his own *hounfort*.

Under a moon that hung balefully overhead like a watching skull, they left the city.

By knocking continually on the door of his cell, the Doctor had finally managed to attract the attention of the guard outside. Glowering at having been woken from a satisfying doze, the guard opened the eye-level flap to find the Doctor's eyes only an inch or two from his own.

He tried to tear himself away from them, but they seemed to draw him in, seeming to darken as if they were wells that were dug deep beyond the limit of the sun's rays. Or perhaps it was his imagination.

The guard never even knew that he opened the door and locked himself in once the Doctor had gone.

Mait managed to calm himself after leaving the cell area. 'Has the device been taken to the cemetery?'

Henri nodded. 'Carrefour has taken it there personally.'

'Get Froebe to let us have Richmann. The other *blancs* are still on the loose and may try to interfere.'

The Doctor slipped through the tunnels like a ghost, hiding in the shadows whenever anyone approached. Soon he began coming across doors. Most of them opened on to storerooms, or offices, which he wasn't interested in, but eventually he found one door that opened into a chemical laboratory whose air was tangy with scents that irritated the nasal and throat passages. Slipping inside and closing the door, he switched on the light and examined his surroundings. To his right, stood a large walk-in cupboard marked as chemical storage, its door slightly ajar.

The Doctor tut-tutted. 'Very careless. Fortunately.'

Checking his watch, he stepped into the cupboard inquisitively.

When the Marine column finally reached the hill cemetery, the moonlight made the land look sparse and dead. No one seemed to be around, but nobody was willing to take any chances, and so they left the road and approached cautiously across country.

Benny moved along with a strong sense of adventure, and had to resist whistling a jaunty tune as she crept through the scrubby vegetation that surrounded the cemetery.

Their caution was well-founded, for several pyres stood ready but unlit in the cemetery, and several members of the Secte Rouge, wearing cross-belts of sisal rope, guarded the place with wicked-looking machetes.

Ace was tempted to move in and take out the sentries, but knew that it would be a foolish move, since they would be missed by the congregation when they arrived, who would thus be alerted. Reluctantly, she settled for striving to keep quiet and hoping the sentries wouldn't notice them.

Mortimer was also tempted to go for the sentries, but also recognized the folly of such a move. Ever the professional, he silently directed his men with hand signals, ensuring that they took up the correct positions. In five-man squads, they silently encircled the cemetery, and settled down to wait.

There were forty minutes to go.

The Doctor exited the laboratory with bulging pockets, carefully closing the door behind him. 'Now for those ships that Richmann mentioned, and the gas drums . . .'

Chapter Nineteen

The first sign that something was happening came when the interminable drumming from the countryside began to break up into two distinct and separate cadences, one deep and threatening, the other a nerve-jangling collection of notes that seemed to have no coherent structure, but somehow managed to sound rhythmic.

The sound crept out of the hillside vegetation, and approached the cemetery with an insectile life of its own.

Checking that the straps on her equipment were tight enough to prevent anything moving and making a noise that might alert anyone nearby, Ace slipped through a stand of bushes to get a better view of the road.

Benny noted her movement and thought to intervene, but by then it was too late, and she didn't want to risk causing any noticeable disturbance.

Placing her feet carefully, Ace crept around the perimeter of the low scrub that surrounded the hilltop, finally finding a position overlooking the road, where she could keep an eye on whoever was approaching.

Sure enough, a sparkling line of firelight was twitching its way up the hill, the red gleam of flame shifting constantly in the slight breeze, and disappearing now and again as the marchers tracked up or down slopes in the road.

Below, a mass of people followed the procession, the ragged figures' bare feet pounding the dirt into a smooth surface. In the lead was a grim-faced man with a candle. Following him were four men carrying a coffin. Once again there were a hat and feathers atop the lid. Behind were two women with candles, then four robed priestesses, and finally the main group of worshippers, some carrying candles or torches. In the midst of the crowd was a decaying sedan chair still gilt with polished finery in that strange Haitian mixture of poverty and riches.

As a distant bell in Port-au-Prince tolled out the stroke of midnight, the drums ceased and the candle-holder in the lead halted at the rickety cemetery gates. Lifting his arms high, he called upon Baron Samedi to admit them to the cemetery.

In the darkness outside, Mortimer tapped Glen on the shoulder. 'Pass the word,' he whispered. 'Wait for my signal. We'll let them get on with about half the ceremony – just in case there are any stragglers.'

The drums took up a slower beat now, and the procession wound its way into the cemetery. The pallbearers laid the coffin down in the clear space at the exact centre of the cemetery, and moved to the edges, standing amidst the grave markers like ragged vultures.

The remainder of the followers now spread out around the clear area – a makeshift *poteau mitan* – touching their candle flames to one of the pyres and then laying their candles on the ground at the edge of the clear ground. The sedan chair was set down in a space of its own, and the curtains drawn aside. Within sat Mait, in plain robes, and a black woman whom Ace hadn't seen before, who was dressed in a network of silk strips that left much of her body visible.

'Those who belong!' Mait shouted.

'Come in!' the crowd replied.

'Those who do not belong!'

'Go away!'

The drumming now began to increase in tempo, and several followers began to sway on their feet. The man who had led the procession stepped forward and sprinkled the coffin with spiced rum. He then circled the *poteau mitan*, sprinkling rum into the dust. Next he tossed a small coin on to the coffin. One by one, everyone else, with the exception of Mait and the woman beside him, also stepped forward and tossed a coin. When this was done, the four priestesses lined up opposite four young men, and stood waiting.

As the drumming built to a crescendo, the coffin lid snapped open, scattering coins into the dust. From the coffin leapt a tall and muscular figure; his features obscured by a goatskin devil-mask, he was dressed in almost African fittings of grass and leather, small rodent skulls dangling from his waist. He danced around the area, shaking an *Ascon*, a gourd filled with snake vertebrae.

He stopped as the drums stopped. The drums then took up a regular beat as he stalked back to the coffin. Throwing it open, he lifted out a sinewy and almost reptilian form, holding it aloft and going down the line of young men, offering it briefly to each in turn.

Reaching the end of the line, he danced over to where Mait sat in the sedan chair, and offered him the strange object. The drums ceased in anticipation.

Mait raised a hand as the worshippers waited expectantly. 'Change skins,' he said, quietly yet clearly enough to be heard by Ace and the Marines. A cheer went up from the worshippers, who donned masks of animal heads. Immediately, they began to throng and dance, the accompanying drums thrashing out a fervent beat that spoke of the fulfilment of man's base desires.

Like forms that briefly flicker in and out of existence in the heart of a flame, the worshippers danced to a staccato rhythm, their bodies jerking sharply yet smoothly in the infernal light of the crackling fires.

As the dance continued, some of them began to snap their limbs about with convulsive movements that Ace would have thought would have dislocated those limbs in an instant. They seemed unaffected however, and threw their heads back, howling with unnatural laughter as they twisted their bodies in ever more contorted movements, some of them even brushing into one or other of the fires and continuing their dance as if they hadn't noticed.

It wasn't long before one of the young men dancing opposite the priestesses also began to act in this way. As he thrust his hands into the fire and pulled out a burning branch which he waved around without the slightest sign of discomfort, the goat-headed figure thrust his arms out for silence.

Everything stopped. The four priestesses led the man over to a freshly dug grave, where he lay down as the goat-faced figure produced a black cockerel. The figure halved a calabash, laying one half on the youth's navel, emptying the sacrificed cockerel's blood into it, before bidding the youth to drink from it. Goat-mask turned expectantly to the sedan chair, and stretched out a hand.

Mait nodded to the woman beside him, who rose and made her way towards the youth. Before she got there, however, there was a faint cracking from the surrounding darkness. With a shout, several Secte Rouge members dashed out of the lit area, engendering sudden sounds of struggle from outside. Soon they returned to the *poteau mitan* clutching a struggling figure who was bound with ropes of sisal cord.

It was Ace.

With a hissing intake of breath, Benny grabbed Petion's arm, and pointed to the figure they had seen dragged into the open. 'We've got to go in now!'

'No.' He laid a restraining hand on her shoulder. 'If we do, they'll just kill her before we can reach her. They'll try to incorporate her appearance into the ritual, which should give me time to slip in.'

'Ritual? What?' Benny glanced back at him, to find him laying down his gun and removing his tunic. Finally, slipping off his boots and making a few tears in his trousers with a bayonet, he gave her a quick grin, and melted into the night, just one more peasant among many.

The worshippers dragged Ace before the sedan chair, throwing her to the ground. Despite the bonds around her arms, she managed to pull herself up, determined not to show any sign of how difficult she found it. The demonic goat-faced figure strode over, passing a hand in front of Ace's eyes. In the time it took to flicker across her vision, a card appeared in it, depicting a young knight. With a strange cock of the head that made Ace certain he was grinning, the figure handed the card to the overweight, elderly man in the sedan chair.

Mait took it with a wry expression. 'You have caused me some inconvenience, woman, do you know that?'

'You must be the one they call Mait.'

'Very perceptive of you.'

'Not really. After I saw the furnishings in your house I just knew you'd be a fat bastard.'

'Henri here,' he said, indicating the man in the goat mask, 'told me you might be rather uncouth.' In a flash, Mait backhanded Ace across the jaw, knocking her to the ground. As if it had never happened, he continued in the same tone: 'You are a foolish child, to come here with your toys.' He waved a disdainful hand at her holstered gun, which they hadn't even bothered to remove. 'Any fool can pull a trigger, girl, so it means nothing.' Mait stepped down from the sedan chair and glanced around the worshippers. 'Watch and learn, girl.' Slowly, he raised a finger and pointed at a man in the crowd, beckoning him forward in a friendly manner. Mait kept his eyes fixed on him as he approached – a malnourished skeleton of a man. When he was a few feet away, Mait's features suddenly twisted into a malevolent burning-eyed glare, and he spat a single word at the man: 'Die!'

Instantly, the man dropped in his tracks, and the crowd backed away from him in awe and fear. Mait laughed as he addressed Ace again. 'That is power! You can't fight that with your toys.'

'Assuming he's really dead, of course.'

'Oh, he is, I assure you. As is your friend, the Time Lord.' He smiled.

'Never!' A thought struck her. 'How do you know – '

'We have charted the progress of all who enter the Vortex for aeons. His tampering with my mirrors was sufficient to allow us to glimpse his mind.'

'Us?' Ace didn't like the sound of that.

'My master and I.' He waved a hand in a cutting-off motion and changed the subject. 'I was rather hoping something like this would happen, actually. I'd rather not have to use one of my people for the sacrifice unless it is absolutely necessary.'

Ace stared at him. 'Sacrifice?'

Wordlessly, Mait waved one of the worshippers forward. A man approached, and was handed a machete by Mait, who indicated a chipped gravestone at the head of the newly dug grave. Grabbing her bound hands, he shoved her towards the gravestone. As he did so, Ace felt a brief strain and a sudden freedom as her hands were released from their bonds. She tensed to spring at her escort, but relaxed slightly when she heard the familiar voice: 'I hope I remember the stories correctly.'

'Petion? What the hell are you – '

'Benny and I saw you captured. If we'd just attacked they'd have killed you immediately, so I thought it best to try and get you to a safer distance before anything happened.'

'Right.'

'Turn around.' They had reached the grave, and Ace obediently turned to face the crowd, so that they couldn't see her freed hands, which had previously been hidden by Petion's body. Petion stepped up to the gravestone, and traced a cruciform pattern over it with the machete before tapping the blade to the stone three times. Almost immediately, the sound was answered by a low, liquid chuckle that froze Ace's spine.

Benny and Mortimer, watching from the bushes, started in surprise as a tall, lithe figure coalesced out of the darkness. Even with the whitewash skeleton painted on to him, Benny had no difficulty recognizing the serpentine man who had kidnapped her from the museum.

All the worshippers in the area dropped to their knees, crossing themselves with a moan half of fear and half of expectation, as Carrefour slipped around the gravestone with a stately grace. On his chair, Mait watched with a building sense of joy as Carrefour came round to face Ace.

Extending one finger to trace a line down Ace's jaw to her jugular, Carrefour felt a trembling of excitement at the prospect of ending this one's life.

Carrefour laughed.

All hell broke loose.

Even Mortimer felt a tingle of horror as he saw the figure approach Ace and laugh, but he was momentarily taken aback when Ace's hands suddenly whipped round and grabbed the man's shoulders, and she kneed him swiftly in the groin. At the same instant, Petion hurled the machete at the nearest Secte Rouge guard who also carried a machete.

Benny and Mortimer immediately launched themselves from the bushes, the rest of the Marines following, firing at any worshipper who had a weapon.

Ace drew her Browning and fired at Mait, but he had ducked behind the wall of the sedan chair and the bullets ricocheted off what could only be metal.

The Mambo who had sat beside Mait joined the priestesses in running for the cemetery gates, while the rest of the congregation scattered to the winds, fleeing the hail of bullets that crisscrossed the *poteau mitan*.

Leaping over fallen worshippers, Ace made for the sedan chair, but was forced to dive for cover when Richmann appeared from behind it with the Winchester drawn. The shot he fired missed her by inches and killed a Marine a short distance behind. Sheltering behind a gravestone Ace returned fire without success.

The Secte Rouge guards had been charging the Marines with their machetes, to little effect, though a couple of Marines had gone down. Their weapons were promptly snatched up by the Secte Rouge, who added their own shooting to the confusion.

Giving up with the Browning, Ace lobbed a grenade at the sedan chair, and was rewarded by the sight of Mait leaping out with surprising agility instants before the chair was blown apart.

Petion dropped to the ground beside her, struggling to catch his breath, and cursed as he saw Mait vanish into the night. Ace poked her head around the stone with the idea of following, but covering fire from Richmann blasted chunks from the stone and forced her to duck back again.

Mortimer had emptied his Browning by now, and couldn't risk the time to reload. With a rush of glee, he lifted a fallen machete and swung at the nearest Secte Rouge, biting deep into his side. Kicking the body off his machete, Mortimer made for Carrefour, who was frantically scraping at the grave.

Ace glanced back and saw him, instantly realizing what was going on. 'The enhancer! Don't let him get to it!' she shouted. Another Secte Rouge blocked Mortimer's path, however, and no one else was in position to attack Carrefour, so Ace slammed a magazine into her Browning and fired a couple of shots. It was too late, however, and Carrefour ducked, zigzagging off into the darkness with the enhancer clutched in his arms.

As the fighting died down, and the Marines began to drag away bodies and herd prisoners together, Mortimer came over to where Benny had joined Ace and Petion. 'We've certainly put a stop to this disgusting display,' Mortimer said.

'Not really,' Ace corrected him. 'The main men got away.'

'Well, it'll be a while before they – '

'Colonel, if we don't get them tonight, we won't get another chance. Besides, we know where they're going.'

'Where?'

'A German naval base under the mountain.'

'What!' The disbelief Mortimer felt vied with rage at the thought that they had known this and hadn't divulged it earlier.

'That's why we brought so many of you,' Benny put in.

212

'In the hope of following them to the base, since we don't know where the land entrance is – I only saw the inlet that allows ships in.'

'We're going to find that rather difficult in the dark,' Mortimer pointed out.

Ace waved a finger in a 'wait a minute' gesture, and slipped her hand into an inside pocket of her duster. Grinning, she pulled a pair of infrared night goggles from it. 'Just follow my lead.'

Chapter Twenty

The Doctor ducked back behind a stairwell as two sailors walked by, talking loudly and animatedly in blissful ignorance of the intruder. His face shadowed by the dim light, he crept out and slipped through a door behind the bridge. The corridor inside was a grey conduit for numerous pipes and fittings, lit by plain white bulbs. Pausing a moment to work out the best route, the Doctor set off to find a stair leading down.

He found one in moments, and silently went down into the hold. Below, a tightly-packed steel chamber, dark but for a few naked bulbs, was filled with squat metal ten-gallon drums. Listening for any sound of activity from the crew, the Doctor threaded his way through the drums, eyeing the occasional label with a scowl of revulsion. Judging himself to be deep enough within the maze of gas drums, he drew a small waxy brick from inside his jacket. The surface of the brick was still gelid and adhesive, so that he was able to stick it to the side of a drum near the hull, separated from the fuel tanks only by a steel bulkhead.

Next he took from his pocket a small circuit board, which had hastily soldered connections jumbled across it, linked to a small cube. Extending a short prong from the board, he rammed it into the upper surface of the brick. A small LED began pulsing, and the Doctor quickly took out his pocket watch and pressed a stud on it. It began counting down from a starting position of *30:00*.

Moving with the sureness of a cat on the prowl, he flitted back through the hold and outside.

Twisting the knob to magnify the image of four ghostly

white shapes amidst a field of darkly glowing emerald, Ace recognized the bulky figure of Mait and the whip-like form of Carrefour as they hurried along the edge of a sisal field. In front of them was the black mass of the mountain, but just above the ground level was a slightly brighter irregular ovoid, whose barely perceptible light seemed to drift slightly upwards. Pistol in hand, she paused just long enough for the others to catch up, and handed the goggles to Benny, deciding she'd probably better play it safe and not risk letting any of the inhabitants of 1915 get an idea of how they worked. 'What do you make of that?' she said.

Benny made a minute adjustment to configure the goggles to her own eyesight, and frowned invisibly in the darkness. She was acutely aware of the presence of Petion and the Marines around her, and felt somewhat guilty about using the advanced technology. 'Don't think rubbish,' she muttered to herself, and made a mental note to castigate Ace for bringing the anachronistic device along. It was bloody useful, though, she thought. 'They've got three ships in there, and God knows what other generators and so on, all of which generates quite a bit of heat. I'd say what we can see is some of that heat surviving long enough to escape through a cave mouth,' she said to Ace.

Ace nodded. 'That's what I thought as well.' She held out a hand for the goggles, but when Benny returned them, she simply tucked them away. 'Colonel?'

'We're ready,' Mortimer answered firmly.

'Time to earn your keep.'

Henri reached the cave mouth first, shortly followed by Mait, Carrefour, and finally Richmann, who had been keeping a rear guard.

Two sentries stepped to intercept them, drawing back when they saw who it was. Constantly looking back, Richmann hurried inside and waved at the sentries. 'Seal the doors!' he ordered.

'Sir? The General's permission is nee – ' The Steyr

boomed like a cannon when fired in the cave, and the sentry dropped with a bloodied chest.

The other sentry's trouser-leg darkened as he shakily but hurriedly turned the locking wheel set into the wall. With a rusty squeak, a pair of steel doors slid inward, locking in the middle with a solid clang.

When he turned to seek approval, the four newcomers had already disappeared, leaving him alone at the doors with the corpse.

The Marines approached the cave in their usual leapfrog manoeuvre, and found themselves facing not an enemy, but the steel doors.

Benny, Ace and Petion arrived to find them milling around the door, testing it for electrification with a bayonet whose handle was securely wrapped with oilcloth. 'Never know till you try,' Mortimer commented, putting the bayonet away.

'You're not going to make it to retirement taking risks like that,' Benny chastised him.

'Who wants to retire?' His face took on a mask of blankness. 'To wither away like my father? No . . . I won't be dying bedridden.'

'Who says you would? Benny said.

'The doctors do.' His mouth crooked wryly. 'Since Coombs' Syndrome is hereditary.' He turned back to the door with a movement that stated the conversation was over.

Benny couldn't blame him. 'I'm sorry,' she murmured, too low for anyone but Ace to hear.

Ace also felt a twinge of sadness for the Colonel, but felt it best to get on with the job in hand. She suspected that he would prefer that as well. 'All right, nanocephs, stand well back, and I'll open this door for you,' she said.

'We haven't enough explosives to get through that,' Petion protested.

'As a matter of fact, I have, but I'd rather keep them for more important things. Besides, if I blow this open, they just might notice,' she finished dryly. As the Marines and Petion backed away, Ace knelt and looked up at Benny. 'Stand just behind and to the left of me, to block their view,' she whispered.

Benny was about to ask why, but before she could, Ace had produced her blaster and was busily setting it for a narrow beam to cut through the door. Ask a silly question, Benny thought, and rolled her eyes.

Once she was satisfied that Petion and the Marines were far enough away, Ace triggered the energy beam at the base of the door, and slowly drew it upwards, describing an arch wide enough for two people to pass through.

On the other side of the door, the sentry watched in mounting alarm as a fiercely glowing spot of light hurled sparks into the cave, cutting a gap into the door. He wasn't sure what sort of threat this presented, but was certain it definitely was a threat. With trembling hands he thumped an alarm button set into the wall beside the door wheel, and turned and ran.

Outside, the sudden clamour of the hooting siren was clearly audible. 'Shit,' Ace muttered, 'there must be a sentry.' Flicking the blaster setting back to normal, she stepped back and loosed a couple of shots at the right-hand side of the metal, which hadn't yet been cut.

A pair of incandescent explosions ripped the metal apart, and the door was knocked spinning into the cave.

The Doctor looked around from under the stairwell when the alarm began hooting, but saw nothing. A slow smile spread across his face as he realized that it must be Ace with the Marines. Men appeared from every corner of the docks, some in uniform, others in civilian garb. They bustled to and fro across the dock and swarmed on and off the ships. Taking a chance, the Doctor stepped out of hiding and descended the gangplank of the *Raubvogel* quickly, but with the confident air of one who has a job to do and is doing it. Crossing his fingers mentally, he

217

hoped that everyone would assume he was just someone else answering the call to action.

His 'act as if you own the place' approach seemed to work, and he made it to the double doors that opened into the main tunnel complex, not even pausing as he attached a circuit board to a second brick and casually tossed it into the heart of the pile of drums on the dock nearby.

No one noticed, and he walked calmly out.

The Marines swarmed into the tunnel like bubbles disappearing down a plughole, Mortimer at their head, eyes bright, looking for the first sign of the opposition. Ace, Benny and Petion had to struggle to keep their places in the line, and the young soldiers all looked both eager and scared.

Ace glanced about at the peculiar angles that joined the walls to the floor and ceiling. 'Those carvings in the museum must have been tossed out with the rubble when they dug this place,' she suggested to Benny.

'Not this tunnel, it's much older. When constructing the docks or Froebe's office I'd say.'

Slowing to a crawl, Mortimer looked back, searching for Benny. 'Which way?' he said.

'Downhill until you feel a breeze, then follow it to its source.'

'Right. Stay here!'

'Drop dead molecule-mind!' Ace called back.

Mortimer didn't answer, however, and he and the Marines trotted off down the tunnel, bayonets fixed and rounds in the chambers.

'Mait won't have been heading for the dock,' Ace reasoned.

'No. The General's office, maybe,' Benny said.

'You know where that is?'

'More or less.'

'Good enough. Lead on, MacDuff.'

Large caverns had been fitted out as barracks and guardroom, and these were a hive of activity as the base personnel stumbled from their beds to snatch weapons, rushing into the tunnels half-dressed.

The officers' quarters in the guardroom contained a large board labelled with the names of different areas. A bulb under the label marked 'Main Door' was flashing redly. Officers joined their men, directing them to take up positions in the main access tunnels, while the main group was despatched to keep an eye on the dock area.

Soon the tunnels echoed to the rumble of many booted feet.

Froebe rushed into his office from his private quarters, which were behind a door concealed by the filing cabinet. Lifting the phone from the desk, he demanded to know what was going on. When appraised of the situation, he turned white, and slumped into his chair. 'Instruct the freighters to make revolutions immediately and head for the open seas as fast as possible,' he said.

Moving to the windows overlooking the dock, he watched his men work, a look of dismay on his face. The image of a home in the country vanished from his mind. His grand plans for a hero's welcome disintegrated into a mass of fears over how the High Command would view this night.

A solitary tear escaped his eye, and he cursed himself for it.

Katze dashed on to the bridge of the *Raubvogel*, gasping for breath. Somehow, Kapitan Weber had got there first.

'Urgent orders, Herr Kapitan. We are to leave immediately – the base has been penetrated by a force of United States Marines.'

'Make revolutions for five knots and issue the crew with side arms,' Weber ordered unflappably.

Mortimer almost ran headlong into a patrol of Germans as he traversed a long gallery, but the Germans were hampered by uncocked weapons, and Mortimer downed two of them with his Browning before ducking behind a turn in the wall, his men loosing a volley of rifle fire into the surviving guards. Covering the sprawled guards constantly, Mortimer hopped over the bodies and continued downwards, his men jabbing the bodies with bayonets to make sure.

Mait drew to a halt, Henri, Carrefour and Richmann pulling up beside him. 'Give me the device,' Mait commanded. Silently, Carrefour handed over the enhancer. 'Even though the ceremony was disturbed, there should be enough power stored within the mirror to open the gateway,'

'There are only a few minutes left,' Henri warned.

'I know, but I will succeed. Then we will serve the power that guides us, and Haiti will never be exploited by the *blancs* again. Carrefour, go and stay with Froebe. Make certain the *coup l'aire* is safely moved away on the ships.' He shuddered as he pronounced the last word. 'Henri, you assist in the defence of this place.'

'Yes, Mait' they chorused.

Mait turned and left, taking an unlit and unused side tunnel. Carrefour also departed, back the way they had come.

Henri looked at Richmann – who watched him in turn – with a calculating expression. 'You, Richmann, will – '

'I will return to my employer as contracted,' Richmann growled. He had been thinking about the Doctor's earlier words, that he should get used to obeying Henri, and had come to the conclusion that doing as he said no longer suited him.

'You will obey – '

'Froebe, Henri. I will obey Froebe.' He smiled thinly as his personal dislike of the arrogant black overcame his veneer of polite obedience. 'Tell me, did you foresee this in your cards?' In the blink of an eye, Richmann drew the Steyr and shot Henri between the eyes.

Henri swayed on his feet for a moment, though he was already dead, then toppled over.

'Evidently not. That's why I stick to poker.' Chuckling to himself, Richmann followed after Carrefour.

Benny waved Ace and Petion to a halt as the sound of footsteps approached. Ace and Petion slipped off the safety catches on their automatics and pressed themselves in close to the walls, ready to spring. When the footsteps reached them, they leapt out, guns levelled – directly at the Doctor's head.

Snatching her gun back to point into the air, Ace drew a startled breath. 'Frag, I nearly killed you!' she said.

'Think things through next time, then,' he snapped. 'Nice to see you, Benny. Have you seen Mait?'

'He came in here somewhere, but we don't know where.'

'I know where he's going. Did he have the enhancer?'

'Carrefour had it,' Petion answered.

'We figured that if this was all about focusing the mind's energy, he'd have it at the ceremony,' Benny added.

'Perfectly correct, but the thing stores energy as well as transmitting it, so if he gets it to where he's going, we're in serious trouble.' He shifted impatiently as if annoyed at himself for having to stop to think. 'Right. Are Colonel Mortimer's men here?'

'Making for the dock,' Ace told him.

'Excellent. Petion, follow them and lend a helping hand. I don't want any of the German personnel searching the dock or the ships.'

Petion nodded and set off at a trot.

'Why not?' Benny asked.

'Because if they do, it's possible they might discover that they've only got their *zombi* gas for about another twenty minutes. After that, it goes up with the biggest bang this side of the Manhattan Project.'

'Excellent!' Ace said.

'Indeed. You come with me, Ace. Benny, keep an eye on Petion and Mortimer.'

'I don't think I have anything else planned for tonight.'

Petion caught up with Mortimer just as the Marines reached the wider tunnel, into one side of which was set a pair of doors which Benny's description indicated led to the dock. They immediately had to dive for cover, however, as the Germans had set up a pair of machine guns in front of the doors behind hastily piled crates.

Everyone pressed themselves flat to the floor as the heavier-calibre bullets smashed a spray of rock chips and dust across the floor.

Undaunted, one of the Marines took it upon himself to pop out from hiding just long enough to hurl a grenade at the gun position.

The bomb detonated with a sharp crack, sending tiny but razor-sharp pieces of metal into the backs of the gun crews. One flew forward, obviously dead, and the others were disoriented long enough for several shots to send them sprawling across the tunnel.

As the acrid smoke cleared, the Marines advanced, keeping to the edges of the doorway, which was not locked, the mechanism apparently having jammed.

Mortimer paused to savour the moment – this was what soldiery was all about, he thought. Heart pounding with excitement, he barged through the door and into the dock, where Germans both on the dockside and aboard the ships ran for cover, beginning to open fire at the intruders.

Soon the Marines were pouring through, blazing at the enemy as they split into groups to head for the fuel tanks, the gas drums and other targets.

The Doctor and Ace sprinted downwards through tunnels of increasingly obviously artificial, but increasingly bizarre and twisted architecture, the Doctor having taken from his pocket some kind of homing device, though he didn't say what it was homing in on. Sure enough, they soon saw Mait, as he rushed out of the other side of a grotto they were just entering.

'Got you,' the Doctor muttered.

Benny ran through the tunnels, making for the dock, but soon she passed a familiar doorway. Smiling to herself, she glanced into the room, and saw General Froebe staring out at the dock with a melancholy gaze.

It occurred to her that she really should go to the dock, but she decided that here was a chance to do something more useful. Checking the magazine of the Luger she had tucked in her waistband, she threw open the door and leapt in, the gun aimed unwaveringly at Froebe.

His eyes widened in surprise. 'I thought my guards had killed you,' he commented.

'Perhaps this is my second life,' she quipped.

'There's no answer to that,' he shrugged.

'No, I suppose not. But, it does seem that I have you – '

'Right where we want you,' a quiet voice completed her sentence from behind her. Slowly, she turned around.

Richmann stepped out from behind the door with a gun trained on her. Off to the side, Carrefour watched mockingly from a comfortable chair.

'More than six feet under,' Richmann continued, and slipped off the safety catch.

Chapter Twenty-one

Benny met Richmann's cold gaze levelly. Inside, she was crying out that it wasn't fair for her to survive the worst technological terrors that twenty-fifth-century man could devise, only to have her short life ended by the crude but effective mechanism of an old Steyr. 'Get your jollies from killing unarmed women, do you?' she said.

'Not usually, but as a special favour to you I'll make an exception this once.' A vein pulsed in Richmann's temple, giving silent voice to his irritation. He aimed for Benny's stomach – it would be a slower, more painful death that way. He smiled.

Benny hawked and spat into his face.

Carrefour started, looking round from the door, the sound echoing in his mind. He felt a peculiar sense of dislocation, and the sounds of those in the room seemed to be coming from a great distance away. He saw Richmann wipe his face, the hand holding the gun shaking almost imperceptibly with suppressed rage.

Benny straightened. 'Get on with it then,' she jeered. She was determined not to give Richmann the satisfaction of seeing her cry, beg or show fear.

To Carrefour, her face seemed to darken, perhaps in shadow. He saw Richmann's clubbing motion with the gun almost before it happened, and a voice from the past called for him to run. He no longer saw Benny standing before him, but a dark-skinned woman, whom he barely recognized after such a long time. There was a sure sense of kinship, however, and he knew that this was his mother. But she was dead . . . as was her killer, who had taken weeks to die of Carrefour's poison.

Richmann brought the gun round again, his mouth

twisting, and Carrefour recognized the look of murderous anger from the scenes being simultaneously played and replayed in front of his eyes. He could almost see Richmann's anger – that of the other man who had killed his mother in a similar fit of rage all those years ago. This was the emotion he had tried to purge himself of by identifying with the snakes that had taken up residence in the ashes of his family's land.

He hadn't purged himself as completely as he had thought.

Richmann never noticed the sudden widening of Benny's eyes, or if he did he must have assumed it was fear at her imminent death. As a result, he was taken completely by surprise when twelve stone of lean muscle powered into him at snake-like speed and wrenched the gun aside, the shot slamming into a very surprised Froebe, who staggered back, the impact of his body cracking one of the windows.

Richmann tumbled to the ground, warding off blows from Carrefour's flailing arms. With a sharp pang of defeat, he noticed Benny dive headlong through the weakened window, ending up in the water below with a huge splash. In fury, Richmann threw Carrefour aside, and snatched up the gun which had skittered across the floor. Carrefour was on his feet again. Whipping out a dagger that glistened wetly with venom, he lunged for Richmann with a speed as close to that of a striking cobra as is humanly possible. There was just too much distance between him and Richmann, however, and Richmann needed only to move his hand a few inches before firing.

Carrefour faltered, doubling over as the bullet caught him just below the sternum. Strangely, he felt more pain from crashing to the floor than from the shot. Eyes wide with surprise, he found that he couldn't draw another breath, though the growing pain forced him to try. He couldn't move as Richmann passed out of his field of vision, not caring enough to even notice Carrefour any longer. Carrefour smelled the burning flesh of his memory once more, but was no longer sure whether it was truly his memory or was a result of the hole in his chest. The shadows took on forms and approached him, wreathed in the phantom smoke that matched that which had taken them from his life.

Mait had trained him to be the personification of Death, his own private Baron Samedi. Carrefour was surprised that he could die. As his fading vision blanked out all but the shadowy wraiths which welcomed him, Carrefour's last thought was that his family would be whole again.

The Doctor and Ace pounded breathlessly through the grotto and down the tunnel after Mait. In short sharp breaths, Ace asked him how such an old man could run so fast.

'Because,' the Doctor answered, a little hoarse himself, 'the enhancer works both ways, and the Old One's survival instinct is letting him draw on its excess life-force to try and bring it back into the world. At this point in time, he could win every gold medal in the book.'

'Can a human body take that much?' Ace asked incredulously.

'Not for long. He must be both desperate and close to the end to take such an enormous risk. How much explosive have you got?'

'Two packs of C-Four Plus.'

'Give me them both,' he demanded urgently, halting at a junction. Ace handed him a pair of canisters. 'What are they set for?'

'Instant, fitted with motion sensors. Will they be enough to kill this whatever it is?'

'No, they can't be killed at all, or at least not in this dimension. I just hope this is enough to bring down enough of the tunnel to stop Mait getting to that full-sized enhancer. Now give me that blaster you didn't bring with you.'

Wordlessly, she drew the twenty-sixth-century weapon from behind her back, and handed it over.

'Good. Projectile weapons will kill anyone you want, but I'd find it rather difficult to drill through the tunnel floor with an old Browning.' He held up a hand to silence the protest she was about to make. 'I want you to get back to the docks and get everybody out as fast as you can. Got that? And I mean including the Germans, if you can drive them out. I don't want to be responsible for needless deaths.' His tone indicated that he didn't hold out much hope, and that his conscience had already grown that little bit heavier in anticipation.

'And if I have to defend myself?'

'Well, any Germans who don't get out are dead anyway . . . But think twice before doing anything rash.'

'Right. But the Marines won't have taken the base yet.'

'Doesn't matter, I only brought them as a diversion anyway. Here, take this.' He handed her his watch. It read *11:14*, and counted down continuously. 'That's how long you've got to get everyone away from here. Now go!' He waved her away, and set off further down the tunnel.

Ingrid Karnstein swept a row of glass beakers to the floor with one gloved hand, the crashing sound muffling the noise of the door. Next, she tossed a lit match into the lowermost drawer of the nearest filing cabinet, and slammed it shut.

'What the hell are you doing?' It was von Stein. He rushed at her, knocking the remaining matches from her grip. His eyes bulged in fury at the destruction that had been wreaked on his lab. Everything was smashed, over-turned or burnt.

Making sure those Americans don't piece all this together.' She fixed him with a stare, defying him to think otherwise.

'Just an excuse. I know you've thought about this for a long time,' he hissed, gripping her shoulders tightly to prevent movement.

'You know something? You're absolutely right.' Without any warning signs, she kneed him in the groin, and dashed for the door, one flailing arm smashing a gas tap from the bench. A low hissing filled the room as she bolted out and slammed the door.

Von Stein had fallen to his knees, and stared dazedly about him at the ruined lab. He was frozen there with an appalled sense of waste, that his cohort had denied him his greatest discovery. He looked around in alarm when he began to smell the escaping gas, and quickly noticed the smashed tap. Stumbling to his feet, he fumbled with the broken pieces, trying to staunch the gas flow.

He failed to notice the flames licking around the drawers of the filing cabinet.

A wave of hot air rushed around the fleeing Karnstein and down the tunnel. She barely noticed.

Everyone on the bridge of the *Raubvogel* ducked as a pane of glass was blown apart. Weber scurried to the ship's blower, and shouted down it in fury, while Katze knelt below the shattered windowpane and took potshots at the dock with his Luger.

Weber slammed the blower shut angrily, obviously disappointed at something. 'Katze!' he shouted above the din. 'Get down on deck and have the machine guns uncovered and lay down support fire.'

'Wouldn't the cannons – '

'No! Shellfire might bring the roof down on us. Go now!'

'Yes, Kapitan.' Katze ducked out of the door, keeping his head down.

Weber looked thoughtfully out at the battle-torn cavern, and slowly reached out to the ship's telegraph, ringing up the order to start engines.

Mortimer crouched at the corner of the short tunnel through which Benny had entered the previous day. Bullets bounced off the rock with alarming frequency as he tried to get a look at the situation. Several other men crouched beside him, a couple leaning out to give covering fire. 'Lieutenant,' he began, 'wouldn't that ship – ' he indicated the *Raubvogel* ' – give us an excellent field of fire across the cavern?'

'If we could take her,' the lieutenant said doubtfully, 'which I don't think – '

'It's only a merchantman at port, young man. There are probably only a few crewmen on board, not combat trained. That gangplank is still there, so we should take the opportunity, I say.'

'Er, yes, sir . . .'

'Excellent. Let's go.' Without further ado, he slipped around the corner, and rushed towards the gangplank, ignoring the shots that zipped past. His men followed, shooting up at the ship's railings, and elsewhere at the other Germans in scattered positions. Halfway across the dock, however, there was a metallic scraping, and the sheet metal forming the outer skin of the oddly shaped bulges in the hull at deck level fell away. Behind each of the two was a two-inch naval gun, and a pair of Schwarlose model 07 machine guns.

Realizing there was nowhere to run in time, the Marines concentrated their fire on the crouching figures behind the guns, but they were too well protected. A hail of gunfire responded, ripping through the Marine ranks, and bloodily smashing men to the ground.

Mortimer hurled a grenade upwards, blasting one gun and tossing its crew aside, but the others were unharmed. Mortimer continued to shoot upwards with his automatic, a manic grin on his face as he realized he was finally being granted his quick and glorious death.

His body virtually disintegrated under the sheer concentration of machine-gun fire.

The Doctor hurried along the tunnel, Ace's blaster held loosely in one hand, a little black box in the other. The box gave out a constant stream of beeps as the Doctor walked, occasionally doubling back on himself. Eventually, satisfied that he had found what he wanted, the Doctor halted, waving the box around for final confirmation. After another series of beeps, he put it in his pocket beside the explosives, and made some adjustments to the blaster's power setting.

Carefully measuring out distances and angle of fire, the Doctor triggered the blaster on its constant wide-beam setting, directing it at a spot on the tunnel floor a few feet ahead, where there was a sharp corner.

Slowly, like melting toffee, the rock began to soften and bubble while clouds of acrid smoke streamed out.

Mait limped painfully down a connecting gallery, desperately clinging on to the enhancer, which was getting heavier with every passing moment. The mere fact that he was still alive was surely a sign that he was destined to succeed – wasn't it? He grinned to himself, certain that soon, with the power of the Great Old One behind him, all the *blancs* would be at his mercy.

Kicking aside a shattered bone, he hurried on.

Moments after he had passed around the corner, a section of the wall near the roof glowed a fierce red and burst with a scattering of sparks and molten droplets. The glow faded in mere moments, during which time the Doctor dropped into the corridor, snatching his hands back from the sides of his newly created tunnel with sharp gasps. Pausing to get his bearings, he blew furiously on his fingers to cool them down. From the corner of his eye he noticed Mait's footprints in the dust. Listening carefully, he could just make out sounds of movement from somewhere down below. 'Less than a minute ahead,' he muttered. 'With any luck, I should overtake him this time.' Sweeping the black box around this new tunnel, he picked a spot, and began firing again.

Returning to the main cavern at a dead run, Ace threw herself to the side as a cluster of boxes not far off exploded with a sharp blast, hurling several of the defenders into the oily waters. She found herself next to Petion, who was trying to pick off men on the nearest freighter. 'Bloody hell,' she muttered, 'it's all go around here.'

'A group of them are concentrated around the gas drums.'

'Forget them, then. They'll be dead in ten minutes – and so are we if we don't get out by then.' Ace glanced cautiously over the rock barricade, taking in the positions of the defending Germans, and several groups of Marines. 'How many frags have you got?'

'Frags?'

'Grenades.'

'About half a dozen.'

'Excellent! Give me a couple.' She held out her hand for the Mills bombs.

'What are you going to do with those?'

'Most of the er, dastardly Huns, I think you call them in this time period, seem to be up by the door to the General's office which, according to Benny, is also a quicker route out. These should be effective against such a tight group.'

'If you can get there alive,' Petion said pointedly.

'That's the one slight problem with this plan,' she said cheerily, 'which is why I brought this.' She held up an extremely odd-looking weapon that looked like a cross between a Sten gun and a stick insect. 'The local shooters are too slow, so I cannibalized some from the palace armoury to build this in the TARDIS. Fully automatic, fairly rapid fire, and my own special recipe in the hollow tips.'

'Astounding,' he said admiringly. Then, his smile turning sour, 'More efficient death.'

'No shit. Listen,' she said seriously. 'I don't like doing this, but nowadays it's about the only thing I'm much good at.' She looked slightly wistful. 'Perhaps when I was younger, I should have – ' She broke off, clamping down hard on the thought. She didn't need any what if's. 'Anyway, it needs to be done.' She started to rise, but froze when his hand clamped on her arm.

'Ace, be very sure about that sort of need. If you don't

231

you'll start to enjoy it, and see that need everywhere. I've seen it happen.'

She looked at his imploring face, and felt a stab of guilt, that he was right, that she'd better take care . . . But she was Ace; she knew the score, and could keep an eye on herself. 'Hey, it's me, right?' She slid back the bolt on her home-made gun. 'Keep the ones on the ship busy.'

With a troubled look in his eyes, Petion nodded, and turned his attention to his targets. With a deep breath, Ace slipped out from behind the rocks, and ran in a crouch down the length of the wall, keeping up a steady rate of fire from her gun. Small blooms of fire exploded all around the sandbagged post and the steel door, the defenders huddling down for cover.

Petion saw her go from the corner of his eye, and fired at the crouching figures on the freighter's deck with grim determination. The thought that Ace could go bad rankled him for some reason, and he mouthed a silent prayer that her judgment would remain sound.

Stray shots buzzing all around, Ace threw herself behind a large fallen stalactite a few yards from the sandbags, just as her ammunition ran out. Shouldering the gun in the sure knowledge that the Doctor would be seriously pissed off if she let it fall into local hands in this time zone, she drew the grenade from her pockets, and poked her head up just long enough to check the distance. Myriad chips of shattered stalactite flew in her face as the Germans opened fire on her position. With clenched teeth, Ace pulled the pins on the grenades, paused for a couple of heartbeats, and hurled them over at the German position. From the enemy there came a sudden clamour of shouts. They tried to leap over the sandbags, but were too slow. The grenades exploded sharply, the heated fragments of their steel casings ripping through the fleeing bodies, sending them sprawling in pools of blood.

Swiftly, Ace clambered over the red-stained sandbags, and checked the door. It had been blasted loose from the lock. 'Petion!' she called. 'The door's open, get everybody out!'

Petion waved in reply, and called the message down the line towards the Marines at the far end of the docks. They began to fall back towards Ace and Petion, pausing where there was cover to shoot back at the Germans on the freighters or on the other side of the docks. Someone threw a stick grenade into the middle of the Marine column, which exploded to put half a dozen men out of action, though Ace was too far away to tell whether they were dead or wounded. Petion returned fire, and the grenade thrower pitched into the water with another grenade at the ready. It exploded as he hit the water, sending a geyser of water and blood into the air.

Resetting a fallen Maxim machine gun to lay down covering fire, Ace stepped out to meet Petion and the first of the arriving Marines. Most of the Marines were experiencing their first combat, and the strain of combating the fear as much as their enemies was telling on their pale faces. Petion's jawline was set as he forced his emotions under control, and Ace envied him that, for if anyone had asked she would have had to admit she was terrified. This didn't stop her, however, from loosing a stream of automatic fire across the water to the other side of the docks, where men were smashed backwards by the force of the impacts.

She was so busy with the Maxim, however, that she failed to notice the door opening fully behind her, and Richmann stepping through like some black-cloaked angel of death, his shortened Winchester being raised into position.

'Ace!' The warning cry came from Petion, who got off a single shot at Richmann before the mercenary major swung the Winchester around and fired it with a roar.

Ace spun round in time to see Petion drop his rifle and spin to the ground in a spray of blood, while Richmann swung his gun back to her, working the lever action.

Ace was faster, however, and had her Browning out of the holster in time to fire before Richmann.

The bullet took Richmann in the shoulder, shocking the shotgun from his grip. Seeing only the spray of Petion's blood, Ace fired again and again, the shots punching continually into Richmann's body and causing him to jerk like a marionette before toppling backwards into the steel door. The look frozen on Richmann's dead face mirrored his shock that a mere woman could out-shoot *him*. Ace's finger remained clamped down on the trigger even after all seven bullets had gone and the slide had locked back in the 'empty' position.

A blast of superheated rock fragments heralded the Doctor's arrival into a huge circular chamber. Several supports broke up the smooth appearance of the walls, and joined the floor and ceiling at angles that didn't seem really workable. A number of squat triangular doors opened on to other rooms and tunnels. A quick glance through the nearest showed it to be an empty chamber built of oddly fitted blocks of Cyclopean size. A larger block, perhaps an altar or sarcophagus, crouched in the centre with a strangely organic air of menace.

Turning back, the Doctor examined his surroundings with a growing feeling of horrified awe. The chamber was almost as large as the cavern above in which the Germans had built their base. A number of thick pillars, shrouded in a miasmic fuzz of mould, were placed around as roof supports while, in the centre of the chamber, was a circle of more squared-off pillars, as if someone had decided to use a megalithic circle as a set of buttresses. Set into the floor were several open pits, which exuded a dank stench even as they pulsed with the chill luminescence of putre-faction.

Cautiously, the Doctor approached the central circle of pillars, slipping between them as quietly as possible, despite the fact that there was no one around.

Inside the circle was a huge altar stone, about thirty-feet across, upon a raised dais. Carved into the stone was more of the same type of repulsive alien art that had become so familiar over the past couple of days. Most impressive, though, was what was hanging from the ceiling directly above the altar stone.

Slowly rotating, like an old gibbet, was an enormous concave mirror, surrounded by satellite mirrors and infinitely complex arrangements of rods and cogs. It was a gigantic version of the same type of enhancer that Mait had.

Set in the centre of the altar stone's upper surface was a small depression that was just the right size for a normal-sized version of the device. The Doctor let out a long slow breath, and considered his options, since even if he succeeded in stopping Mait, there was always the risk of someone else finding this place the next time the stars were in the correct alignment. Briefly, he raised the blaster, but swiftly lowered it again. 'If I blast an enhancer that size,' he muttered, 'I could blow the whole Caribbean off the map. I can't reach it to perform the same trick as on Mait's . . .' Suddenly, he grinned, and clambered up atop the altar stone. Setting the blaster to low power, he directed it at the indentation, melting the rock slowly and gently. In a few moments, he shut the beam off, and admired his handiwork.

The top of the stone was now all at the same level. Shifting slightly, he drilled a new indentation a few inches from the original. 'That should do it, just in case,' he murmured. He jumped down off the stone. A faint vibration briefly throbbed through the floor, and the Doctor looked around in alarm. He stepped from the dais and glanced back, only now noticing that the altar stone wasn't quite set in place, and that there was a thin gap beneath one end, which seemed to indicate that there was another pit beneath the stone.

He told himself that he should go right now and plant the explosives to bring the tunnel down, but the Doctor's curiosity was one of his strongest features. Almost against his own will, he knelt by the gap, and peered in.

The space underneath was filled with a harsh light of burnished gold. There wasn't a wide enough field of vision to make much out, beyond the slime-laden walls of the pit, but, just for an instant, the Doctor could have sworn that something moved in the reflexive way of an uncomfortable sleeper.

The Doctor couldn't quite make out what it was that had moved, but going by the gelid fluidity of the apparent movement, he didn't really want to.

Jerking back from the dais, the Doctor slipped back through the circle of megaliths. Stiffly, he walked towards the entrance tunnel. 'Time Lords are supposed to remain calm,' he told himself, 'but then again, I don't want to risk being late to meet Mait, do I?' Glad of the excuse, he ran from the chamber.

He didn't run far, however, because all too soon he heard Mait's dragging footsteps.

He removed Ace's explosives from his pockets, and fixed the first pack to the ceiling directly above him, flicking the arming switch with the sensor positioned ahead. Moving a few yards along the tunnel, he found a crevice into which to wedge the second pack, with the sensor directed behind. When that too was armed, he moved further forward, and waited for Mait to appear.

It wasn't a long wait. In a matter of seconds, the aged *bocor* limped around the corner, and approached warily.

'What kept you?' the Doctor asked.

'How did you get ahead of me?'

'I took a more direct route.'

'There isn't one.'

The Doctor drew the blaster and drilled a shallow hole in the wall by way of demonstration. 'There *wasn't* one.'

'And now you're going to kill me with that? Ruthless, as I said.'

'I'm not going to shoot you with this or anything else. I'm just going to ask you to see sense and leave.'

'And if I refuse?'

'Then I'll step aside and let you pass.'

'Really?' Mait laughed, feeling that the Doctor must have lost his mind.

'Yes really, because I know that if you go down that tunnel, you'll be dead.'

Mait faltered slightly, then perked up. 'Nonsense. If there was such danger, you'd be dead, wouldn't you? I heard you come out of the Hall. I suppose it's possible you've set tripwires,' he went on, 'but I have excellent night vision.' He stepped towards the Doctor.

The Doctor frowned as if having second thoughts, then stepped aside as promised. Mait hesitated again, instantly suspicious. Much to his surprise, the Doctor simply turned and left, heading back the way Mait had come.

Mait had gone only a short distance when he heard the faint beep from above. Looking up, he saw the explosive wedged into a crevice, and thought it fitting that the *blancs*' devices should fail them now.

He didn't realize that Ace's motion sensors were set only to be triggered by an approaching movement source. It took only another few steps for Mait to come within range of the other bomb.

It detonated with enough force to bring down huge chunks of rock from the ceiling. Fragments of rock, and of Mait, flung backwards by the blast, also set off the other bomb and in moments, several tens of yards of ceiling had collapsed in.

The Doctor retraced Mait's footsteps in the dust. Each time he passed an opening into a tunnel he had drilled, he loosed a couple of shots at its roof to collapse it.

A hand falling on Ace's shoulder startled her back to reality, and she found herself facing a dripping Benny. 'That's the second time in twenty-four hours I've had a swim in that damned water. Are you all right?' Benny said.

'Yes!' Ace snapped savagely, causing Benny to step back from the unexpectedly vicious tone in her voice. Ace looked down at Petion, who had taken the blast meant for her, and the gaping hole in his chest. 'I'm always all

237

right,' she snarled derisively, 'because I'm Ace.' And it seems, she added in silent self-reproach, that I stay all right at the expense of everybody else.

'I didn't mean it that way,' Benny apologized. She hadn't missed the way Ace's hands shook, and the slight guilty lowering of her head as she glanced at Petion. 'You didn't have a choice.' She knelt beside the young mulatto, and checked for a pulse. There was one, but it was weak. 'He's still alive, just.'

Ace's head snapped up. 'Stretcher party!' she yelled. 'How is he?'

'I wouldn't like to say. His heart's still beating, but going by that gurgling I'd guess he's got a collapsed lung. I wouldn't give any odds on him keeping that right arm, either.'

Ace didn't speak, but instead picked up Richmann's fallen Winchester, and checked it. It was empty. Dropping it on the red-pooled floor, Ace stared back at Richmann's body and the sticky smear it had left on the grey metal of the door.

'What are you thinking about?' Benny asked quietly.

Ace remained silent for a moment, unable to tear her eyes away from Richmann. 'Maybe my future,' she finally answered with a shudder. With a sudden flash of rage, she hurled the Browning far out across the dock, where it splashed into the water and disappeared.

Benny reached forward and twitched the hem of Richmann's jacket aside, so that Ace could see the Steyr in its shoulder holster. 'No choice, Ace, not this time.' She pulled Ace upright. 'Come on, time to get out of here, there can't be long until your bombs go off.'

'What?' Ace shook herself to clear her mind. 'Oh yeah, right.' She glanced at her watch. 'About four minutes.' She turned to wave to the approaching Marines. 'Hoi, you lot! Drop everything and get over here now, the whole place blows in four minutes!'

The Marines didn't wait to be told twice, but simply began running for the door, firing as they went. Either someone on the German side understood English or the

TARDIS's telepathic circuits were at work again, because the Germans also began dashing for the exits on their side of the cavern.

As the gunfire ceased, Ace and Benny ushered the Marines through the door, the group including a pair of medical orderlies who added Petion to their own collection of wounded, and followed after them through the tunnels that led upward more steeply than the others. About twenty Marines accompanied Ace and Benny out through the tunnels. The lights flickered on and off, illuminating others bustling back and forth, too busy in their own rush for the exits to bother with the intruders. As they ran, mentally counting down the seconds, both Benny and Ace's thoughts were of what had happened to the Doctor.

The Doctor passed the door to the main cavern with approximately a minute and a half to go before Ace's explosives detonated. Rubble and bloodstained corpses were scattered across the dockside, and acrid smoke from burning oil filled the air.

The *Raubvogel* had just entered the short tunnel that led out of the cavern, when Katze finally found what he'd been looking for. Attached to the bulkhead between the hold full of gas drums and the fuel pumps, there was a large brick of strange pliable material with a wired board and cube set into it. Katze had never seen this type of explosive, but it didn't take a scientific genius to work out what the thing was. Having no idea of the detonation mechanism, he mentally called up the shortest route to the deck, while grasping the device and pulling it off the wall.

The explosion lifted the ship a few feet clear out of the water, smashing the superstructure against the low tunnel roof even as the hull burst open with a blaze of fire. As the freighter slammed back down, the solid rock above began to loosen, huge boulders crashing into the decks.

Soon, the whole tunnel roof was collapsing on top of the ship.

The shock wave deafened the Doctor, and caused him to stumble on his way. The lights died altogether, and he was forced to use precious seconds to dig a small torch from his pocket, even as he wondered why that explosion had come early.

Benny and Ace also had torches, with which to help lead the Marines out. 'Somebody must have tried to move or defuse one of the bombs,' Ace shouted above the noise.

'How long till the rest go?'

'Thirty seconds.'

They hurried on.

Froebe's eyes opened weakly, and he coughed in a huge racking spasm. Spitting out a gobbet of blood, he dragged himself over to the window, to look down on the devastation below. 'You may have won the battle, Doctor, but not the war,' he hissed. The other explosives went off.

Within seconds of each other, the two remaining freighters were ripped apart in great swathes of flame, sending white hot metal and sprays of burning oil through the cavern. The remaining gas drums were torn apart in a huge blast, and a series of titanic explosions ripped through the fuel tanks in their area, the shock wave breaking loose enormous chunks of rock from the roof. Those, in concert with fiery remains of the ships and tanks, consumed the airship in a sun-like conflagration.

The cavern began to fill with falling rock, even Froebe's entire office overhang splitting from the living rock and falling into the inferno below.

The Doctor pounded along the tunnel as hard as he dared, when he was suddenly pitched to the ground by a huge invisible hand. A blast of heated air rushed past, and poisonous smoke belched towards him. Abandoning all cares and concerns, he dashed headlong for the surface, dodging rocks that were jarred from the ceiling.

Benny and Ace also staggered as the main explosions hit, dust pouring on to them from above. A white opening was visible, however, and they redoubled their efforts, tumbling out on to the gentle open slopes within seconds. The Marines, gasping for breath as much as they were, followed, virtually racing, charging headlong away from the mountain.

They stopped at the edge of the sisal fields, turning to look back. The mountain shook for several long seconds, after which time they were delighted to see the Doctor hurtle out of the cave mouth and hurl himself down towards them.

The barest instant after he was free, a tongue of flame blasted out of the cave at his heels, and pieces of the higher slopes disappeared inwards as flames and gouts of smoke exploded out of the weaker points of the mountain.

The Doctor flung himself down beside them just as a final blast scattered small chips and stone fragments over them.

The deep rumbling of the explosions dying down to a hissing of falling dust, everything grew quiet, and the twenty or so survivors collapsed against a low wall to get their breath back.

The Doctor grinned up at Ace and Benny's grime-streaked faces. 'You know, I think we're going to need another holiday to recover from this one,' he said.

'Not yet,' Benny said slowly. 'Look.'

They followed her pointing arm with their eyes, and were chilled to see a group of thin figures form out of the darkness all around, shambling towards the group of tired combatants.

Remnants of rags hanging from their stiff and unresponsive bodies, the population of the nameless village shuffled mindlessly towards them . . .

Chapter Twenty-two

'They'll be well looked after, I assure you,' Howard was saying. 'The poor devils should recover in a while, since they've had no more doses of the datura-based stuff that makes them willing slaves.'

'It'll probably take me a while to recover as well,' Benny said dryly. 'I nearly had a coronary when they all shuffled out at us like that.'

'Just obeying the last instructions they were given,' the Doctor pointed out.

'Yeah,' Ace added, 'you had to feel sorry for them just milling around like sheep, because Froebe and his buddies had done that to them.'

'So this creature, this Old One, will have been killed in the explosions?' Howard said.

'No no no.' The Doctor shook his head, and pulled a bunch of grapes from his upturned hat, depositing them at Petion's bedside. 'As I told Ace, they can't be killed in this universe. They originally came from some other universe, other dimension – one of the outer planes, most likely – and part of their being still resides there. Another part exists in their physical form, but that can't do anything without the third ingredient.'

'Their consciousness?' Benny suggested.

'It's as good a word as any. Their consciousness can travel on its own, riding the Time Winds, even. But it's reliant on the natural forces of the universe to open gateways for it.'

'When the stars are right, you mean,' Howard said.

'Exactly, the tidal forces of stellar masses in conjunction are sometimes enough to rip a hole through the fabric of space-time and give them the path they need. So long as their consciousness is out there, it can't physically do anything, but the body's automatic instincts can still be powerful enough on the telepathic wavelengths to attune themselves to receptive minds and influence them into providing assistance when the stars *are* right.'

'Why do they need assistance? Can't they just slip back into their bodies like a *zombi astral*?' Petion asked from where he was propped up on his bed.

'No, because the universe is constantly expanding and evolving, which means the stars will never quite return to *exactly* the same formation they were in when that consciousness left. Therefore they need followers to perform rituals that attract the attention of the autonomic instincts, which can then generate that extra bit of focus necessary to bridge the difference between the positions of stars then and now.'

'So when will the stars be right next?' Howard asked worriedly.

'There are some things even I don't know, unfortunately. And that's one of them. Anyway, we'd better be going, I suppose. Now that the island is secure, you can join your wife, Petion, and at least you'll have some interesting tales for your grandchildren.'

'But Doctor, you can't go now,' Petion said in surprise. 'We'll have to celebrate – '

'You and Howard can celebrate. Now that the Americans are firmly in charge, people might start asking too many questions about who we really are. Anyway, maybe we'll come and visit you sometime, eh? Come on Ace, Benny.'

Murmuring goodbyes, Benny followed the Doctor from the private ward. Ace wordlessly gripped Petion's remaining hand for a moment, and silently followed, wrapped in her own thoughts.

The TARDIS was still parked in the mortuary, and the Doctor ushered Ace and Benny inside, then set the controls.

With its familiar mechanical groaning, the TARDIS faded from the room.

Ace had gone straight through the console room and off to her own quarters, while Benny sat in the armchair to watch the Doctor manipulate the controls. 'Will she be all right?'

'Probably, but the conscience can be capricious, which makes it difficult to tell, particularly with you humans.'

'Oh, thank you.'

'No offence.'

'I'd say she needs time to get over it.'

'Would you?'

'We all do. Even you. You came out of that cave running like a startled rabbit.'

'What! Me? Never! What are you trying to suggest?'

'I think we could all do with a relaxing tranquil break.'

'That's what we were supposed to have just had,' he said pointedly.

'Well, it's your own fault for choosing Earth; there's always something nasty going on there.'

'Well,' he began uncertainly, 'I don't know, I rather like the place actually.' He smiled. 'Or have you got a better idea?'

'Have you ever been to the Eye of Orion?'

'Well, actually . . .'

Ace lay back and tried to relax, letting her eyes fall shut. Soon, she saw herself gunning down Richmann, again and again, emptying the gun into his flesh. Blasting the life from him with an outpouring of anger.

She had got angry, so she had killed, brutally.

Her eyes snapped open. What was she becoming? Like Richmann?

Her hands began to shake again.

Dreams fade after the briefest of lives, slinking back into the mire of the subconscious as smoothly as they arise from it. Something huge had dreamed, and so the dream lasted for days, but even those dreams must fade and dissipate.

Until the next time the connections in the huge multi-lobed brains take sufficient form for a new dream.

Whenever the stars are right . . .

Already published:

TIMEWYRM: GENESYS
John Peel
The Doctor and Ace are drawn to Ancient Mesopotamia in search of an evil sentience that has tumbled from the stars – the dreaded Timewyrm of ancient Gallifreyan legend.

ISBN 0 426 20355 0

TIMEWYRM: EXODUS
Terrance Dicks
Pursuit of the Timewyrm brings the Doctor and Ace to the Festival of Britain. But the London they find is strangely subdued, and patrolling the streets are the uniformed thugs of the Britischer Freikorps.

ISBN 0 426 20357 7

TIMEWYRM: APOCALYPSE
Nigel Robinson
Kirith seems an ideal planet – a world of peace and plenty, ruled by the kindly hand of the Great Matriarch. But it's here that the end of the universe – of everything – will be precipitated. Only the Doctor can stop the tragedy.

ISBN 0 426 20359 3

TIMEWYRM: REVELATION
Paul Cornell
Ace has died of oxygen starvation on the moon, having thought the place to be Norfolk. 'I do believe that's unique,' says the afterlife's receptionist.

ISBN 0 426 20360 7

CAT'S CRADLE: TIME'S CRUCIBLE
Marc Platt
The TARDIS is invaded by an alien presence and is then destroyed. The Doctor disappears. Ace, lost and alone, finds herself in a bizarre city where nothing is to be trusted – even time itself.

ISBN 0 426 20365 8

CAT'S CRADLE: WARHEAD
Andrew Cartmel
The place is Earth. The time is the near future – all too near. As environmental destruction reaches the point of no return, multinational corporations scheme to but immortality in a poisoned wood. If Earth is to survive, somebody has to stop them.

ISBN 0 426 20367 4

CAT'S CRADLE: WITCH MARK
Andrew Hunt
A small village in Wales is visited by creatures of myth. Nearby, a coach crashes on the M40, killing all its passengers. Police can find no record of their existence. The Doctor and Ace arrive, searching for a cure for the TARDIS, and uncover a gateway to another world.

ISBN 0 426 20368 2

NIGHTSHADE
Mark Gatiss
When the Doctor brings Ace to the village of Crook Marsham in 1968, he seems unwilling to recognize that something sinister is going on. But the villagers are being killed, one by one, and everyone's past is coming back to haunt them – including the Doctor's.

ISBN 0 426 20376 3

LOVE AND WAR
Paul Cornell

Heaven: a planet rich in history where the Doctor comes to meet a new friend, and betray an old one; a place where people come to die, but where the dead don't always rest in peace. On Heaven, the Doctor finally loses Ace, but finds archeologist Bernice Summerfield, a new companion whose destiny is inextricably linked with his.

ISBN 0 426 20385 2

TRANSIT
Ben Aaronovitch

It's the ultimate mass transit system, binding the planets of the solar system together. But something is living in the network, chewing its way to the very heart of the system and leaving a trail of death and mutation behind. Once again, the Doctor is all that stands between humanity and its own mistakes.

ISBN 0 426 20384 4

THE HIGHEST SCIENCE
Gareth Roberts

The Highest Science – a technology so dangerous it destroyed its creators. Many people have searched for it, but now Sheldukher, the most wanted criminal in the galaxy, believes he has found it. The Doctor and Bernice must battle to stop him on a planet where chance and coincidence have become far too powerful.

ISBN 0 426 20377 1

THE PIT
Neil Penswick

One of the Seven Planets is a nameless giant, quarantined against all intruders. But when the TARDIS materializes, it becomes clear that the planet is far from empty – and the Doctor begins to realize that the planet hides a terrible secret from the Time Lords' past.

ISBN 0 426 20378 X

DECEIT
Peter Darvill-Evans

Ace – three years older, wiser and tougher – is back. She is part of a group of Irregular Auxilliaries on an expedition to the planet Arcadia. They think they are hunting Daleks, but the Doctor knows better. He knows that the paradise planet hides a being far more powerful than the Daleks – and much more dangerous.

ISBN 0 426 20362 3

LUCIFER RISING
Jim Mortimore & Andy Lane

Reunited, the Doctor, Ace and Bernice travel to Lucifer, the site of a scientific expedition that they know will shortly cease to exist. Discovering why involves them in sabotage, murder and the resurrection of eons-old alien powers. Are there Angels on Lucifer? And what does it all have to do with Ace?

ISBN 0 426 20338 7